# GAFF

## Wisdom from the Sea

By Lorena R. Peter, PhD

ISBN     145053953X

EAN-13     9781450539531

I dedicate this book to Aurore, Jonathan, Bru.

And to Seamus, who can look forward to all of life.

# chapter 1

Gaff opened his chair and set it on the beach, in his spot. The chair was ratty and old, the way he felt today. This had been his spot for years and even when the beach was crowded, somehow it was always empty, waiting for him. The cooler went beside the chair, ready. He turned to gaze at the waves breaking on the sand.

He said to the surf and to the wind, "Good morning. I'm always happy to see you, my friends. Thank you for inspiring me — letting me breath in your energy." Gaff inhaled deeply.

He took off the baseball cap to run fingers through his hair. It was silver now, only peppered with the light brown it used to be. At least there was still lots of it. He studied the cloth in his hands, a faded green the color of the sea. Words decorated the front: "Kure Beach, North Carolina," it said. Although old, the thread was still bright enough, embroidered with a fish arched against the hook. He ran fingers through silver hair again before he replaced the cap. Of all his hats, this was his favorite.

Of all the places in the world, Kure Beach was his favorite and he loved caps that proclaimed his loyalty. Shaded by the bill, brown eyes hid behind dark sunglasses. The dark lenses protected his eyes from the sun. They were also a screen that allowed him to watch his world unobserved. This camouflage didn't prevent his eyes from seeing into the very heart of people he met. And he met a lot of people.

It was his goal to live life to the fullest, to learn from all that life had to offer, and this morning he was feeling the strain of it. No matter. He'd sit on his chair to gather strength from the blessings of nature. The beauty, and the wisdom, placed there by the creator of this ocean and the sand it watered. He brushed sand from his arms. His skin was tanned from the days, months, and years in the sun.

Finish your work first, Gaff, he thought. He hammered rod holders into the sand halfway to the water. He baited hooks and cast them into the surf on the far side of the sandbar. He flipped the bails of the reels and placed rods into holders. The gear was good, expensive for a man who seemed to live on the beach, and he took good care of it.

The last thing he took from his wagon was the flag: a huge pirate flag that he planted in the sand to the left of his chair. That flag set him apart. He stood looking at it for a moment, remembering encounters it brought to him. Black background with white skull and cross bones and a red scarf at a jaunty angle on the skull. So big that it was visible from the next public beach accesses, and that was a quarter mile down the beach. It might even be visible from the pier. All over Pleasure Island he was known by that flag.

He stood by the flag and looked toward the brightly colored houses behind his wagon, on the other side of the dunes from the beach. They were relatively new, built in the style made popular in Wrightsville Beach. They were raised up on sturdy columns so the living quarters were above the water that might flood the area when a tropical storm hit the island. Some of them looked like three story buildings, but he knew that the ground level was storage only or garage or an apartment used to pull in extra money during the summer. It was a disguise, a good one. Building codes today required the ground level to have walls that could break away when water hit them. The idea was it was better to lose the basement than to lose the entire house. He had seen houses left a pile of rubble by the storms.

Ordinances also forbad people from walking through the dunes that separated the beach from the village. They were carefully planted to anchor the sand against the force of the waves. As Gaff looked up and down the beach, he saw dozens of walkways to carry people from the parking areas or from houses to the beach. A great deal of effort had resulted in a good growth of grasses on those dunes and no one wanted them trampled. They were there to protect the beach… and the houses that lined it.

The original houses were small fishing shacks, uninsulated and not really suitable for year-round living. That didn't stop people from living in them full time. They wanted to live right on the beach as long as they could... until the wind blew them away. Now that he thought of it, this was the third row of houses—the other two had been swept away by high winds and storm surges. So had the original road. Now we do more to protect the island, he thought. We're getting smarter.

Storms had stolen a lot of those houses, but the developers had taken more. He had to admit, these houses were prettier. At least, that's what his wife Julia was always saying. They were painted bright colors: pink, blue, green, yellow, orange. Bright cheerful colors. Still, he did sort of miss the small houses that were painted the colors of the sand and blended into the background.

Truth to tell, he really missed the view they used to have from their house, built farther away from the beach. He also missed some of the friends that lived in those old shacks. Most of them gone to the great fishing beach in the sky. He shook his head as he remembered some of his old friends.

And then he thought of his neighbors, Sam and Joe at the Pier, Harry and Doris, and Bubba and Ethel. There were a lot of families still here after all this time. Old friends like the old clothes he wore to the beach, comfortable. New friends had moved into the new houses: Sally and Sue and her husband. Some of the houses right on the beach were rented out, a week at a time.

Sally was a widow and new to the beach. Gaff didn't know much about her except her name and that she seemed friendly. She was a pleasant looking woman, with no outstanding trait, except the ready smile and her kind face. She walked on the beach every nice day and stayed in good shape that way. From what he saw, she was obsessed with collecting shark teeth. Could be worse. Harmless as addictions go.

Sue had lived at the beach longer and was married, although Gaff didn't remember ever seeing her with her husband. A curiosity. Even men who didn't like the beach allowed their wives to drag them onto the sand once in a while. That was tradition for people living in a village like this. But then he remembered that his own wife only came to the water's edge when the grandkids were going in the water.

So many people had recently moved to the village that he couldn't list them all. It was good to have all those friends, new and old. They had taught him so much about life. His friends and Julia and his family. He was feeling nostalgic... must be because he was tired today, unusual for him.

His attention was pulled by the waves crashing on the shore. There were fish in that water just waiting for him to snag them. It was time to get to it. His hooks were baited and he was ready. He sat in his chair to enjoy the day.

## chapter 2

It was a beautiful day in late August. The sun was hot, the wind was blowing, and the waves were crashing on the sand. Fluffy clouds skittered across blue sky. No sign of rain. Perfect weather for fishing.

He was in his chair and the hooks were in the water, baited and ready to catch the big one. He watched the sky, the water, the woman coming up the beach.

She followed the edge of the water, as she had every day for the past week. New to the area, a renter. Tall, blond, attractive, but something sad in her expression, in her posture, ruined all that. He had watched her move quickly along the strand as the sun came up over the water. She strolled in the afternoon. Distracted in the morning, into herself, keeping a fast, steady pace. In the afternoon, she talked with people along the way. The afternoon walker was a different person from the morning walker: more social. A woman of two faces.

Gaff was in this spot most days and between tending the rods and watching for signs, he watched people. Through observation, he had learned. He knew she was curious about his flag. She looked at it every time she passed. He knew she would talk to him eventually.

This afternoon she returned later than usual. Maybe she talked to more people. Maybe she walked farther. His thoughts meandered, considering the possibilities. Instead of passing by, she walked straight up to his spot and plopped down on the cooler. Although they had only waved or nodded in greeting before today, she seemed to feel familiar with him.

Two sets of eyes watched the waves and the clouds. They said nothing. Comfortable in the silence. Gaff waited.

Suddenly she seemed to remember her manners. "Do you mind if I sit here for a while? I walked farther than usual and I'm tired."

He looked at the top of his rods. "Sit as long as you like."

They sat in silence for another bit of time. Neither looked at the other. Both used to solitude. He was used to having strangers sit with him, happened all the time. All the time.

Finally she began, "My name's Priscilla. What's yours?"

"They call me Gaff." His eyes searched the waters for the signs. Fishing was art and science and he knew both. He waited, that was the biggest part of it, the waiting. Taught you to be patient.

She glanced past him toward the flag whipped by the wind. "All the people fishing on the beach and you're the only one with a flag."

His face hardly moved. "Yeah. The flag."

"You're here every day. Do you catch a lot?"

" Yep."

"What do you do during the winter?"

"Fish."

"Every day?"

"Every day. Some nights, too." Slight exaggeration here, he knew, but she wouldn't.

The sounds of nature flooded in to take the place of words, soothing. Then she asked, "Why do you have the flag?"

Was there a smile edging toward his face? "The Jolly Roger. Used to be a lot of pirates around here. Sir Walter Raleigh was one that stole for the crown. Most of them started like that, by working for one king to steal from another."

She turned to look at him, interested. "I didn't know that."

"Yep. After a while they got smart and kept the loot instead of giving it to the king for some paltry payment. Must have seen the inequity. Maybe they became better businessmen with age."

Her brows scrunched together. "Did I study that in history?"

"Probably. Don't remember because it wasn't important to you. Could be because you're a girl."

He saw her body tense up, her back straightened. Must have reacted to the "because you're a girl" part.

Her voice was tinged with indignation, a sharp edge to cut the insult. "What does that have to do with it?"

He did smile now. "Don't get your knickers in a twist. Boys are more interested in pirates. Girls are usually more interested in the beautiful princess kidnapped by pirates."

Priscilla relaxed. She must have judged this to be a reasonable explanation. "Probably." She watched the water before she repeated her question, "Why do you have the flag?"

His answer was simple, "I like it."

He could see she was disappointed there wasn't more.

Again, the silence surrounded them while they watched birds diving into swells beyond the foaming surf over the sandbar. Finally, he stood and walked over to check his lines. He reeled in the line on each of the rods to clean the hook, replace the bait, and cast them out into the surf.

"Have you caught much today? You're casting your lines way out."

"Not yet."

"What're you trying to catch?"

He returned to his chair and his imitation of a statue with only his eyes moving. "Like to catch some drum."

Her expression told him she didn't know these fish. "Why?"

"Good sport. Better eating." He could see her drawing back, did she expect something else?

She stared out into the water and started without preamble. "I'm a writer. I'm staying here for a month to finish reworking a manuscript."

"You write books?"

She got into her subject, but forced an upbeat inflection into her voice, an energy conflicting with the message of her drooped shoulders. He could tell it took conscious effort.

"Not books yet. I have an agent trying to sell two manuscripts to publishers. That makes me a writer with manuscripts. When I publish, I'll be an author with books."

A smile played at the corners of his mouth. "Makes a difference. Your distinction?"

More energy drained as her back slumped and her voice softened. "Read it in a book about writing. It does make a difference because I'd like to have books and I get frustrated by all the refusals and revisions and more refusals."

"Is it so tough to get published? Don't know much about this." He glanced at her, but quickly returned his gaze to the water.

"It is for a new writer. Everyone wants a proven winner and that means someone who's already in print with loyal readers standing in line waiting for the next one."

As he waited for her to go on, he felt strong emotions wash over her, almost as though they were his. He almost heard the snap of a barrier coming down: her determination to ignore them. She's hiding a lot of pain, he thought. Not just from the refusals, something deeper. He watched pelicans flying low over the water, searching for food. He felt the comfort of the warm sun. In these things he looked for a way to help this woman sitting on his cooler.

She started up a different path. "I walk in the morning for inspiration from the water and the sunrise and the shells left by the night tides. I work all day. And in the afternoon, I walk again, for exercise. I just can't sit all the time."

He said nothing.

She paused. "I walk in the afternoon more to see people than for exercise, if I'm really honest with myself. To see people and the ocean. Writing is a solitary activity." Her voice disappeared into her private place, swallowed up by the thinking.

They watched the waves, enjoyed the warmth of the sun, the pressure of wind on skin.

She asked, but her voice was flat, without interest. "What do you look for? When you look out at the water, I mean."

He waved to a place in front of them. "See that choppy water over there? A school of baitfish."

She squinted, looking for signs of fish. "I see it. Was that a fish jumping over there?" She pointed, now, interest building on her face. She sat up straighter, leaning forward.

"Good observation. When a fish jumps out of the water, there's probably a bigger fish down there chasing it. A game of chase and catch, but the chaser eats what he catches."

She smiled. "Like you... The little fish jumps out of the water and hopes to grow wings to escape his pursuer. And you're hoping the big fish bites the bait on your hook instead of the little fish."

"Little fish probably does, too. A good out for him."

They smiled to think that the minnow was on the fisherman's side in this contest. When the minnow got bigger and it was his time to bite the hook, he would change his mind. Life's like that.

Priscilla looked up and down the beach. "So many fishermen. I didn't realize so many people fished. It must be a lot of fun."

He followed her gaze. "Don't know if I'd call it fun."

She looked at him. "If it's not fun why do they do it? Why do you do it? And for hours like this."

He was thoughtful and then pointed to a man sitting in a chair on a ledge of sand jutting out closer to the water. There were rods in holders in front of him, but the hooks were still secured for travel.

"Harry. His wife's sick. Cancer. Doctors said she'll be dead in six months."

"I'm so sorry…"

Gaff interrupted her. "That was a year ago. He takes care of her at home and their children come to spell him whenever they can. Home care nurses, too."

"That's good of them."

Again he interrupted, "Not good. Just what family does." He stared into the distance.

She was quiet. He could see sadness pull the corners of her mouth into a frown.

Gaff checked the top of his rod to see if a fish was on the line. "I can't tell you what kind of marriage they had through the long years they've been together. Three grown children."

"Do you ever talk with him?"

Gaff nodded his answer. "He's said that her getting sick made him realize what's important. And it's different from what he used to think."

"His marriage?"

He nodded again. "But more than that, his wife, this woman he's taken for granted all these years, and his children, his relationships with them. Didn't spend much time when they were little. Does a better job now."

Priscilla glanced at Gaff before she followed his eyes to the sea. "I'm sure they appreciate that."

"Sometimes it's hard to make up for things you missed. He tells me they haven't forgiven him yet. He still works on it. Has hope."

Priscilla looked at Harry and then returned her eyes to the water and the clouds. "This is a good place for serious thinking. And you're right about the family stuff. I can think of things my dad missed with me. And the time is past. He can't make up for any of it."

"You can't go back, but you can forgive and start fresh today. Every story has a couple of sides. Each side is truth to that person."

"He's dead now, my dad. No making up for anything. Not now. Not ever. I can't even find out why he did what he did."

"What about the forgiving part?"

She shrugged. "It's over and I've moved on."

Gaff frowned his concentration on the place where his line entered the water. "Have you?"

Priscilla snatched up a shell and threw it at a gull perched on some nearby driftwood. "Of course I have. That was long ago. It's all over."

Gaff's features smoothed, so did his voice. "Doesn't sound like it."

The muscles of her face worked to hide the anger. "Well, I thought I did."

"You wouldn't react like that if you had." A simple truth simply spoken.

She looked at him hard: eyes in a slit making creases at the corners. She said nothing, only turning to look toward the water. He knew she was thinking, could almost read her thoughts.

The silence was heavy between them now.

Gaff broke into her thoughts like a wave on the shore. "As I said, don't know what kind of marriage Harry and Doris had, but I do know that whenever she's had a bad day he's here for a while. Just stares out into the water. Sometimes he fishes, but lots of times he casts the bait out and leaves it for hours. Just that one bait. Don't even know if he watches to see if he got a bite. Routine is comforting. Staring into the water and watching the waves and the fish and the birds. Breaking waves lull, like music. Warm sun's comforting. Water's healing."

She came back to now. "I guess a few fish don't matter when you're dealing with sickness and the death of someone you love."

"I reckon she'll die once he learns all he needs to know. And fixes it with the kids."

Gaff watched the clouds rolling in from the southeast, but he felt her looking into his face, fighting to understand. She struggled to forgive. He'd seen it before.

She said suddenly, "I have to go." Just as suddenly, she got up and started down the beach.

He watched her walk. Her step had more energy and her back was straighter, but there was more pulling down at her shoulders. It's tough to forgive, but sometimes you just have to remember the dad did the best he could. He may have believed it was the best for you, too. Not easy to see straight at the moment, sometimes it takes years to understand. He remembered how tough it was to forgive his own dad. Real tough. Sometimes he wondered if he had.

## chapter 3

It was a quarter of a mile to the next public beach access and Gaff watched Priscilla walk beyond that to a private walkway across the dunes. Although they may have touched on some things that bothered her, they had only scratched the surface and he knew she'd be back to go deeper. It might take her some time to figure that out.

Sometimes fish took the bait a little at a time. Gaff got up to check his lines, clean the hook, and thread a piece of cut bait onto it. Still holding the rod, he glanced at Harry who was putting his gear into a wagon, getting ready to go home. Gaff cast a long one. Nodded his approval.

He walked down to the water to get his feet and legs wet, to touch Mother Water, to thank the Creator for this bounty, to strengthen his connection to the earth. There was comfort in this feeling of belonging to something bigger.

As Gaff got settled into his chair, he heard a woman's voice ask, "Why do you have that pirate flag? And so big?"

He looked up to see a young woman in her twenties wearing a bathing suit under a large t-shirt. Even covered by all that cloth, she looked very thin. A hat with a large brim covered her head and under it Gaff could see a scarf. The way she wore that scarf told him tons.

Gaff smiled, he thought about telling her the first flag he got as a gift from Julia, his wife, a kind of joke. Instead, he said, "I'm a fish pirate! I steal fish from the bowels of the sea like pirates stole gold from the bowels of the king's ships."

She smiled. "You're the only one with a flag."

"I'm one-of-a-kind." Humor in his voice, hoping to see her smile widen. His eyes moved from her face to the tip of his rod to see if he had one on the line. It jumped a little. Maybe.

She started to leave, but turned back to him. "My name's Debra. Mind if I sit for a while?"

Gaff gestured toward the cooler: an invitation.

"Maybe you could teach me something about fishing. My husband wants to rent equipment to fish from the pier tomorrow. I don't know anything about fishing."

"What do you want to know?"

Debra sat gingerly on the cooler, shifting her weight to check its stability. "What's your name?"

"They call me Gaff. That lesson was easy!"

She smiled, but didn't laugh at his joke. "Oh, a fishing nickname."

He didn't answer. Returned his gaze to the water, ready for the questions—and the answers.

"How long have you been fishing?"

He thought for a while. "It's been so long I don't rightly know. I'd have to count back. Probably run out of fingers and toes."

Debra smiled broader, but still no laugh. "Guess I came to the right person. With so much experience, you'll definitely be able to teach me."

"Hope I know something after these many years."

"The clouds seem to be blowing in from over the water. Does that mean a storm's coming?"

She didn't wait for an answer. "They're beautiful, all different shades of gray and blue. And if you look closely, there's even purple. I love it when dark clouds are hit by the bright sunlight. It adds a bright white that brings out all the other colors. If I ever learned to paint, I'd paint clouds and sky and sunsets."

"What about sunrise?"

Now, she giggled, "I'd have to get up too early to see that."

"Too early." He remembered when he was young and the sun rose too early in the day for him.

"This is a special trip for us, my husband and me. We're from Ohio and we don't have wide beaches like this and the Great Lakes don't have waves like these either. Although when the wind blows, it does whip the lake up. I've been to the towns around

Lake Erie and they are wonderful, but not like this." She looked up and down the shore to make her point.

Then she opened her hand to reveal an assortment of shells. "The beaches in Ohio don't have shells like these either. There's not much room in my suitcase so I have to be selective. It's hard to choose from so many. I'm afraid of finding too many beautiful shells, but yesterday there weren't many on the beach no matter what time I looked. Must be something about the tides or the waves or the wind. If I stayed for long, I'd have to learn some of these things. I do like hunting for the shells."

He listened to the chatter she used to fill the silence, to avoid her thoughts. He glanced at the shells she held out to him. Patient, waiting for her questions. His eyes returned to the water, concentrating for a moment on the sun warming his face.

She turned her eyes to follow his. "What do you look for?"

"Kinds of waves. Patterns in the foam. Helps me figure out where to put my hook."

She sat up, energized by interest, leaning toward the water. "How?"

He pointed to a swath of foam being pulled toward open water. "That foam going out shows there's a cut through the sandbar right here."

"Oh."

He knew she didn't really understand and her interest was drifting away. He pointed to the left. "See that rough water over there?"

She nodded, looking in the direction he indicated, but he wasn't certain she saw it.

"A school of baitfish. I'm hoping the predators feeding on them will get confused and go after my bait and let me hook them." He wondered whether she'd seen any of the shows on television about sea life.

"You have four fishing poles, all different lengths. Why?"

Gaff jabbed his thumb toward the equipment on his wagon. "The taller ones are for fishing farther out. With the short one there, I can fish for whiting when they swim in the channel between the sandbar and the beach."

She looked at the rod he was using. "So today you're fishing on the far side of the sandbar? In the deeper water."

"Today I am. Fish're there."

She looked out toward the place where his line entered the water. "And you can tell that by watching the water?"

"And watching where the birds dive."

She inspected the rods from top to bottom and then turned toward the water. Gaff could practically feel her mind doing a subject search for another topic to fill the quiet. He was glad she hadn't, but hadn't yet come upon a way to start.

Gaff watched the water. Quietly he asked, "Why do you wear that scarf?" That was one way to start.

She looked at him with frightened eyes. He noted her fear, but continued to contemplate the ocean. His smooth features hid his thoughts, his feelings.

In a small voice, she said, "I don't have any hair."

His answer was more a grunt. "Oh." No more. Wait for her to go on.

She seemed to realize there would be no more and added in that same small voice, "I have cancer."

Again, the grunt. "Hmm." More patient waiting.

Debra seemed nervous, desperate to fill the silence with words. "I have breast cancer, but they only took out the lump. It was pretty small and localized."

"Uh-hunh."

"That's what the doctor said. They found it early enough. I had chemo before surgery to shrink the tumor and after to make sure it was all gone. I lost my hair because of the chemo." She inhaled deeply, like she had said all that on one whole breath of air, her chest constricted by fear.

Gaff scanned the beach and noticed a man to their right, looking anxiously in their direction. He nodded toward him. "Your husband?"

She followed Gaff's eyes and her face was transformed by deep emotion. "Yes, that's Frank."

Gaff nodded, still watching Frank. "Nice looking young man."

Her smile broadened, her whole being spoke of the love she felt for her husband. "He is. Frank's very handsome and I really love him. We've only been married for a couple of years." She seemed embarrassed by her own candid admission, the expression of such strong feelings to this stranger. She looked down and the hat hid a blush.

Gaff looked at Debra. "You make a handsome couple."

She lowered her eyes further and Gaff could feel rather than see her sadness. "We did," she said quietly.

His voice was strong, positive. "You do."

Debra looked into Gaff's eyes. "I don't have any hair. I had long, dark, beautiful hair and now I'm bald. How can you say we make a beautiful couple?" The anguish in her voice was so thick you could almost cut it with a bait knife.

Gaff said nothing at first. He leaned over and opened her hand to reveal the shells there. He poked around to separate them, taking time to look at each one.

Finally, he said, "Beautiful collection of shells you have there."

She watched his every move, visibly relieved by this distraction from her sadness.

She smiled again as she looked at her collection of shells. "They are beautiful, aren't they? I really love these red ones and then there are the ones with stripes and the pure white ones." Her excitement grew.

"All different colors, I see." He stopped to pick up a perfectly shaped black shell. "Black and stunning... except... it has a hole. Did you notice that? Surely you could find a black shell without a hole?" He held it out for her to inspect.

She studied the shell, then took it from him. "But it's different from the others I saw on the beach and the little hole doesn't bother me. To me it's beautiful. I can only take home a few shells."

Gaff looked into her eyes and then returned his attention to her hand. He pointed out specific shells. "This red one is broken on the edge and this is only a part of a conch shell."

Indignation was beginning to show on her delicate face as lines around her mouth. "I picked them from all the hundreds of shells I saw. Each one has some special beauty of its own. Each is unique. I love them even if they're not perfect. They're perfect for me."

Gaff nodded in understanding as he continued to inspect the shells, but he wouldn't let it go. "I don't see one perfect shell here, but they appeal to you. You think they're beautiful. And as you said, you can only take a few home anyway."

She was getting the idea of a moral here. "Yes-s-s?"

Gaff bobbed his head toward Frank. "I'll bet Frank there thinks his wife is the most beautiful woman on the beach."

Debra gazed intently at her husband and he returned her gaze.

"You may have a little hole, but to him you're the best… the one he wants to take home."

She turned to look at Gaff and saw him for the first time with eyes only beginning to see beneath the surface. "He does?" She said this as though it was a new thought for her. The lines between her eyebrows spoke of serious contemplation.

Gaff chuckled. "Of course he does, but he probably misses something."

Her brow furrowed. "What's that?" Instinctively, her hand went to the back of her neck, fingers reaching just under the scarf.

"I'll bet he misses that smile and the laugh and the confidence his wife had… that she lost with her hair."

Debra turned toward Frank, but said nothing. Her hand moved slowly from her neck to touch the shells in her other hand.

Gaff could almost hear her thoughts, could almost feel the love she had for her husband. It radiated in waves between the two young people. Patience. Fishing always took time. Fishing and teaching someone to see the blessings in their lives. Time and patience.

She bowed her head, hidden again beneath the brim of her hat. Her hand dabbed at her eyes and Gaff heard a little sniffle.

They sat together for some time. He watched the world of fishing. The warmth of the sun made him smile.

Debra soon emerged from the shelter of her hat to turn toward the distant horizon. The peaceful sound of breaking waves was punctuated by the call of the gulls. Sandpipers looked for food in sand left wet by the retreating water. The sunlight played on the ocean like dancing jewels. Gaff felt her gathering strength. She no longer needed to fill the quiet with empty chatter. She seemed at peace with her thoughts.

The moment ended when the reel sang the news of a fish taking the bait. The fish was swimming off with the hook, taking yards of line with him. Gaff moved quickly and smoothly to lift the rod from the holder. He flipped the bail to stop the line. He reduced the drag. Then, he started reeling it in.

An excited Debra moved closer to watch. With every yard of line pulled in, she became more energized.

"This one's putting up a fight. Must be big." After he did some convincing: pulling and reeling, Gaff pulled a twenty-four inch drumfish onto the beach. He protected his hands with gloves to remove the hook and put his catch into the cooler. He smiled all the time, grinned. This is why he waited-- to reel in the ones that fought the hook.

Debra giggled and bounced around on the sand near Gaff. "Oh my God, you caught a big fish while I'm here! I love it! You make it look so easy."

Gaff laughed, "It does look easy, doesn't it? But the fish do fight to the very end no matter how long that takes. Some of them get off the line and they get smart. They learn from their near death experience. They change the decisions they make and decide against the easy food. Helps them live longer."

It looked as though Debra had ears to hear even through her child-like excitement. Frank joined them by this time. Gaff couldn't tell whether Frank was more excited by Debra's enjoyment or by his catching the fish.

She gave Frank a hug. "I do want to fish on the pier tomorrow. That would be so much fun. Gaff said we can learn to do this. No problem." She giggled her joy and said goodbye to Gaff.

As they walked away together, Frank turned a grateful face toward Gaff and nodded his "Thank you." Debra and Frank went down the beach, hand in hand. Gaff could see her animated gesturing toward the ocean and the sky and the world. Alive again, a little smarter because of her near death experience, a little more appreciative of her world.

He said to Mother Water, "Thank you for the fish. It's a good one." And then he whispered, "And thank you for helping that little girl."

# chapter 4

Several days later, Gaff was casting his hook when he felt Priscilla walk up to stand next to him. He was thinking about yesterday and the rainy day he spent in his home on the high ground toward the middle of the island. He never tired of watching storms from that big window on the top floor. It was the home built decades ago to raise three children with a view of the ocean, to encourage a love of nature. It nurtured a lot of love, that house.

And then there was his wife Julia and the tasty treats she cooked for their day with the kids and the grands. He loved those family days even more than he loved his time on the beach in the presence of the wisdom he always found here.

He adjusted the line and settled the rod into the holder. He stood watching the spot where the line entered the water, but he was remembering years spent in the job he didn't like, longing for these days on the beach. He regretted the time that job had stolen from his family and from his fishing. Life is good now—so good. That's why he didn't waste time thinking about the past.

Priscilla's voice broke into his thoughts. "You're fishing closer to shore today. And your holder is angled much more. Why? Because you're using the small rod?" She said this without moving her eyes from the water.

"Nope, but you're observant."

He thought again and changed his answer, "You are right in a way because that rod is set up for whiting." He punctuated this by pointing toward the water. "See the rough water in the channel?"

"Between the sandbar and the shore?"

He nodded his answer.

"Is that a school of fish?"

Another nod. "Whiting are skittish. The line going into the water makes a singing sound that scares them off. With the holder angled like this, the line goes in at a different angle. Doesn't seem to scare them so much. Maybe they like this song better."

Priscilla almost laughed. "There's so much to this fishing thing."

Gaff looked at her, more closely this time. "You're happier."

She nodded, still smiling from her heart. "I saw a rainbow yesterday, a double rainbow. It was beautiful. Don't the double ones bring good luck?"

A smile played at the corners of his mouth, ready to stake it's claim. "Think so."

She waved toward the horizon beyond the pier. "They were in the clouds over the ocean after the rain yesterday. Did you see them?"

The joy of remembering the rainbow animated Gaff's face, as he looked in the direction she indicated. "I did. Beautiful." He had pointed them out to the grands… and had them make a wish.

Priscilla gestured broadly. "I'm lucky just because I saw the rainbow in the clouds over the water. Luckier still because I'm on the beach in North Carolina in September and if that's not lucky, I don't know what is."

"Being on this beach any time of year is lucky, if you ask me."

Priscilla turned to face Gaff. "And I feel better than I did when we met. Maybe a part of my luck was meeting you. You helped my mood."

He said nothing, smiling his pleasure. Silently thanking Mother Water for help in the wisdom department. Thanking her for using nature to deliver her messages. Thanking her for the rainbow.

"The rainbow was the proof that being here is good for me. I came to the beach to sort things out, to search for my self, and to write. I scheduled a month to give myself time. I was beginning to think a month wouldn't be enough until I talked with you. You helped me get off zero."

He nodded an acknowledgement.

They settled themselves. He sat in his old chair and put a folded towel on the cooler to soften the seat and protect her from the slime and scales left from cutting bait.

Rather than disturb the silence, Gaff waited, looking out at the cloudless sky over the ocean. He knew that she, too, watched the waves and the birds diving into the water to get the fish swimming there. Did Priscilla see the patch of rough water?

She finally said, "I thought I saw a school of baitfish, but that area of rough water is so big, it stretches for yards. Must be something else."

Gaff didn't need to look, but he did. "Menhaden."

He felt her glance at him and then back to the water. "Menhaden?"

"Type of baitfish. Their schools run for miles. Not good eating," Then he pointed toward a spot on the water. "See that dark patch? It's oil from the menhaden. In deeper water, the fishing boats net them. They're squeezed for that oil."

"Squeezed?"

"They're so oily that it just oozes out naturally. Like the slick over there. Used in cosmetics."

"Instead of whale oil?"

His voice spoke of amusement. "That was a long time ago, but yes."

Priscilla was quiet for a moment, looking toward the waves and the school of fish in them. "Why're they so close to shore?"

"Waves stir up stuff on the sandbar. Fish come to feed."

"A Hoover with fins."

He grinned. "One way of putting it." He did enjoy someone with a sense of humor.

"I came to thank you... really. I felt better after we talked."

"Didn't say much." He glanced at his companion and then at the tip of his rod to see if someone was taking the bait.

"You nudged me in the right direction to find my self and that was one of the reasons I came to the beach."

"Hunh."

"I've been having a hard time focusing and yesterday I was able to get back to writing. Yesterday was very productive for me."

Gaff looked at her, a furrow between his brows. "Was it that easy to find your inner being? One issue and boom! you're done? Your self isn't very complicated. Usually takes more than that." He worried: was that too harsh?

Oops. He could see her back straighten and her tone took on an edge. "I wouldn't say my self was totally revealed. But that discussion, and thinking about it later, was enough to pull me out of the doldrums."

"Is it time to think of your father?"

Priscilla was quiet for some time before she answered. "I guess it is." He could feel her holding back, putting up the barriers.

Gaff waited, watching the seagulls dive into the water.

"You were right about all that. I've spent the last couple of days forgiving my father for abandoning me. He did the best he could, but that wasn't very good."

"You've forgiven him?"

"I think I have now. I really have."

"And have you forgiven yourself?"

A frown replaced Priscilla's smile. "Forgive myself? I need to do more work on it, but I've made a start."

Gaff smiled. "Um-hunh." He glanced at his visitor and then returned his gaze to the ocean. "But about the situation with your father?"

He could feel her tense up, straighten her back, scrunch her eyebrows together. Getting ready to argue, to defend herself.

"Are you saying I need to forgive myself about that? What's there to forgive me? He's the one." She stopped short as if she realized where she was emotionally and was fighting to regain control.

"You think of it and you blame him." Pushing harder.

Her voice lowered and she slowed her words. Gaff could almost see her struggle to keep thoughts and feelings in check. "He's the one who left us. He left long before Mom filed for divorce."

"He's the one to blame?"

"My father never was a family man. Worked all the time. He was never there for school things or birthdays. Then he started drinking and stayed out all night, too. We didn't know where he was."

"Did this on his own, did he?"

"It was his decision."

Gaff could see waves of anger crash around her. Where was that forgiveness now?

"Your mom explain all this to you?"

"She didn't have to. We could see when he wasn't there for dinner. We could see when he wasn't home in the morning when we left for school."

"Your mom told you why."

Priscilla shifted-- uncomfortable in her seat, uncomfortable in her heart. Had he hit a sore spot?

He didn't let it go. "You learned to see the world from her point of view. You ever ask for his?"

She shifted more. Was she going to bolt?

Priscilla snapped, "I came to thank you and here you're talking nonsense, attacking my mom."

"Just sweep it under then. Ignore the storm clouds and later you get wet. Maybe your writer's block's all about your dad and the anger you're holding onto?"

A bristling silence, loud enough to herald a hurricane, but still she sat. He could see from her face that thoughts were charging around behind her eyes. Feelings, too, in her heart. He looked out at the horizon to give her time, to give her space. He wanted to shout at her that he was a father and knew that marriage, any relationship, took both people to succeed. Instead, he stayed in the silence, seeking guidance from Mother Water.

She took a deep breath to energize her words, put an edge to her voice. "You're telling me that Mom told me lies and that I should have asked Dad about it before he died."

"Nope. Try again." Patience, now. Give her room to swim.

She sighed a big one. "He ruined my life and Mom's. She was never the same after the divorce."

"He stayed around to bug your mom for all those years?"

"No, he moved away with his job. We didn't see him much for a while. Then he got married and his new wife tried to bring us together, us kids and him. That didn't go so well."

"How did he ruin Mom's life if he wasn't around?"

"He, ah, he... Mom never got over the divorce."

Gaff interrupted her. "One thing at a time. Your mother's not getting over the divorce is something different. That's what your mom did. Let's focus on what your dad did first. What did he do to hurt your mom after the marriage was over?"

The pause before she answered told Gaff she was thinking about it. Thanks for that.

"Nothing, really."

"So he didn't stay around to make her life miserable. You said he made some choices that you didn't like. That was while he was married to your mom. Is your mother exempt from making choices?"

"Well, no."

"Unless she was passive and let other people run her life, she had some responsibility in all that. Seems to me that she decided to be miserable and to blame him for it. He was a convenient excuse."

Priscilla snapped, "I don't want to talk about this any more."

"Your choice."

Gaff got up to replace the bait on his line and send it back out into the water. Walked down to get his feet wet. Give her time to calm.

He settled into the chair. He knew he should let it go, but couldn't resist adding, "So your mom spent years telling everyone that your dad ruined her life. Does that make sense? Did you see him do anything to her?"

Priscilla suddenly got up and stomped to the water. The air around her felt like the air during a thunderstorm. Gaff could almost see lightning as she moved.

He watched her stand in the waves, pushing against the advancing water as it moved toward the land and the tug as it returned to its home. Like the ebb and flow of life itself. Like the ebb and flow of her emotions.

Gaff thought about his father and the arguments they'd had, his fights for independence. He remembered the years he held that anger in his heart, the years he wasted on regretting not living the life he longed for. He was angry at being forced to go into their business rather than going to school to become the therapist and teacher he was in his heart. Someone had told him long ago that he should be a preacher. He didn't know about that, but he had blamed his dad for not letting him become that something more he could have been. Something more than just, just a businessman.

Once he let go of that anger, he felt much more joy. Once he focused on getting the most out of the life he had, the better that life became. How could he make Priscilla see that there was so much happiness in the sun?

Then he asked for divine guidance and knew he would be answered. Reassured, his attention returned to the now as Priscilla plopped down on the cooler beside him. Priscilla who still could not see. All was well in his world and would be in hers.

He settled in his seat and pointed to the pelicans diving into the water. "The pelicans are my friends. Distresses me when they get hurt by fishing lines and hooks lost in the water. I'm a member of the pelican rescue squad."

Priscilla waited for the rest, thankful for the change of topic.

"When a bird's hurt, people call the office in Southport and the woman there calls me. We capture the injured bird here and put it in a crate. The crate goes by ferry to Southport and she meets it there. She takes the bird and returns the crate to me. She cares for the patient until he's well enough for release into the wild."

The story was to distract her, calm her. But Gaff thought how much Priscilla was like one of those birds, not yet ready for release.

"What else is there then? What else to find your self?"

She looked at her hands and then out to the waves. He sensed her relief at the new direction.

"I'm beginning to wonder if I shouldn't stop writing and just get a real job."

"You like writing?"

"I love writing."

"So?"

"I used to write for pleasure. It was my hobby and I didn't think about getting into print. When I divorced my husband I decided to see if I could support myself that way. You know, getting paid for my hobby."

"So you like writing."

The answer was in her smile.

"Let me get this straight. If I told you to do anything you wanted, you would write?"

"The frustrating part is trying to get published."

Gaff shrugged. "Don't think of that. Write for enjoyment. Why do you want to be published anyway?"

"It's not for great gobs of money, I've heard there isn't much of that. It's being affirmed. Professionals would be saying that I'm good."

"Recognition and achievement. A place on the bestseller list would mean a lot of people like what you do. More recognition…"

She nodded. "Don't get me wrong, I could use the money, too."

"But your passion is the writing. If you focus on that you'd be happier, less stressed?"

"My friends think I should rejoin the world of the living instead of being so solitary. My husband thought I was crazy for spending so much time at the computer. Maybe they do, too. Maybe I am."

Gaff pulled his hand through the sand while he waited for more.

She continued, low as though thinking out loud, "All that time alone can make you a little nuts. That's what my ex said as he walked out the door. Solitude is comfortable to me."

Her voice got louder and she turned toward Gaff for emphasis. "You don't feel crazy from the inside. That's something people on the outside think about you, and say, sometimes. You might say crazy is in the eye of the beholder."

She returned her gaze to the water. The space around them was orchestrated by nature. The sound of crashing waves was background music with melody supplied by birds. He gave her time to process, and enjoy the music of nature.

She looked at Gaff again, to stress her point, "Sometimes I do feel crazy, if I'm honest about it. But who doesn't from time to time?" Again she sank into her own thoughts.

Gaff scanned the horizon and said quietly, "Follow your dream. Don't mind what other people say."

She looked at him, her eyebrows raised in surprise.

Gaff nodded, sad thoughts from his past pulling on him like the undertow. "They may think they know what's best for you, but the truth is in your heart. Only you can see your path."

"Me?"

"A lot of people don't even know their own paths. They're afraid of following their hearts even when they do know. And if you do, they see where they fall short. Makes them regret their own decisions."

"So instead of screwing up the courage to follow their dream, they tell me to stop following mine."

He thought back through his own life to the times when he let other people determine his future. Not all happy and not all the right decisions. He didn't always follow his dream. She should, he decided. It worked out better that way. But it was her decision to make.

**chapter 5**

The beach was dark, lit by a half moon and Jupiter. Not a cloud and the black sky was filled with pinpoints of light in spectacular array. The stars, as plentiful as they were, provided more decoration and entertainment than useful light. Gaff was sitting in his chair, tending his line, watching the display above. Searching the heavens for his favorite constellations, thankful that Julia's bridge party pushed him out of the house to the beach tonight. Wouldn't want to miss this show.

His lines were in the water. Patient, waiting for the big one. He remembered back to the night he caught the big shark. Fourteen feet long and he put up a fight, didn't give up easily. Exciting. Exhilarating, but hard work and at times frightening. He'd do it again any time. Any time. He smiled... maybe tonight.

Suddenly a hand against his forehead pulled his head back, an arm rested on his right shoulder and upper chest, and something sharp and metallic imprinted a line on his throat. Gaff's immediate reaction was a shot of adrenaline that quickly morphed into mental readiness. His body told him to kill his attacker, but his heart said there was no danger. Confusion of impulses. He forced himself to relax into the situation. Trust the Universe. He could always change his mind later.

A gruff voice came from behind his right ear. "What ya got worth anything, old man?"

Gaff had trouble answering with his throat angled back as it was. "My heart," he choked out.

A grumbled chortle. "Good answer. What's to keep me from killing you? Kill you and cut out that heart?"

The hand on his forehead reduced the backward pressure. "To stay out of prison... and save your soul."

Gruff spat out, "You're a fool, old man. They'd never catch me and it's too late for my soul. Who'd miss you anyway? A crazy old fisherman flying a pirate flag."

Gaff responded slowly, buying time. "You may be right." He thought of his wife and family. He'd be missed, but he locked that away in his heart.

"Why the flag anyway? You advertising? I'm the one should have it. I'm a modern-day pirate."

"You want to advertise?" Gaff asked.

A deep chuckle. "I do and will more when I get back home."

Gaff relaxed. Just a scare. A bully's tactic. "How's that?" he asked.

"I do the deed and get patched by my club in California. Everybody can see I'm a full member. Taking my time enjoying the beach. Never been here before."

The hands released Gaff and came to sit on the cooler. A young man, thirties, maybe. All male and tattoos in a Harley tee shirt with a blond ponytail braided down to the middle of his back. Gaff imagined him in a leather jacket in colder weather. Muscles rippled under the shirt: a man who used his body. A pack of cigarettes was rolled up in his sleeve. Did he see that in an old movie? No room in the tight jeans anyway. But which movie? Funny associations. Like this was a caricature of a bad guy.

Gaff relaxed more, allowed himself to smile.

He focused on the moon reflected on the water. Miles of shimmering liquid silver. Then Gaff asked, "You from California?"

"Nah. Oklahoma. Live in California now, though." Did he want to say more or was that Gaff's imagination?

"What's your name?"

"What's it to you? Somethin' for the cops? Didn't do nothin' anyway but play with you a little."

"My name's Gaff. It's easier to talk with someone you know."

"Who says I wanna talk?"

"I was watching the sky so it's no never mind to me. I know the names of some constellations, but I can still talk to the ones I don't know," Gaff said smoothly and looked up again. His heart rate slowed almost to its normal rhythm. A deep breath helped him settle more. "That's Jupiter close to the moon."

"So?" The voice was flat, uninterested.

"Lot of folks think it's Venus, but it's Jupiter this time of year."

Silence.

"Look at that. Shooting star, ain't it?"

"Yep. See a lot of those out here." He didn't bother to explain about the meteors. Save that for later.

The voice softened some, "Ain't looked at the stars much since I was a kid in Oklahoma. Too much light where I live in California."

"You lived on a farm?"

He didn't answer. "Name's Dan. Named after my uncle, so I'm the second. Mama loved that man."

"Your uncle?"

"Yeah. My dad was a son-of-a-bitch. Not much to love there."

Gaff inspected his line and the little glow light at the tip of his rod and the water. He returned his eyes to the sky. "Loved him enough to marry him."

"Looks like. Bastard beat her. Us, too. Should never of married him."

Gaff didn't express his feelings about the inhumanity of man. "Hm-m-m."

"I'm youngest of five and all of us got the belt or the hand or the fist. Someone every night. Six targets."

"And a day of rest?"

Dan chuckled, but it was an unhappy sound. "Six of us wished."

Gaff listened, thinking and watching. And waiting for Dan to go on. It would come out soon enough, Gaff knew.

"Summer I was sixteen, I left. Packed up everything I could fit into my backpack and walked."

"Where'd you go?"

"Wandered around for a couple of days. Ended up at my uncle's house the next town over. The one I was named after. He likely called Mama to ease her mind."

"You talk to her?"

"Nah. Not then. Took some time to talk me into that. Made her happy to know I was OK. Cried on the phone. Begged me to finish school."

"So you went back home?"

Dan shook his head in the dark. "No, got me a job. Did things for my uncle. Had a real good time. Good folks, my aunt and uncle, loving. Not like my dad. Hard to believe they're brothers, come from the same parents and so different. So different, like night and day. Uncle Dan got all the good, I guess. Dad got the bad."

"Not everything is visible from the surface."

Dan blew out a silent whistle. "Could be, but what I did see was nice. Both my aunt and uncle treated me good. First I ever saw that. Felt good to not be afraid whenever I walked through the door. Said I could live with them to finish school."

"Nice change from home. You stay?"

Dan's voice lowered, "Nah. When Dad found out where I was, he was harder on Mom. I couldn't let him hammer her while I stayed at Uncle Dan's. Went back home to take my licks. But after graduation, my bags were packed and I was out of there. All of us did. Graduate and go!"

"What about your mom?"

"She stayed. I promised myself I'd make a home for her. Get her to leave that son of a bitch. Wasn't fast enough."

Gaff looked at Dan now, aware of the sadness in his voice. "How so?"

Dan coughed, but didn't manage to hide the catch in his voice. "Mama's heart couldn't take it. Man beat her all the time, day after day, year after year. More after we left and she was the only one. One time he put her in the hospital. She had a heart attack and died while she was there."

"You miss her."

"Damn straight, I miss her."

"Drink a lot, do you?"

Dan snorted a mirthless laugh. "Me and the guys. We do. And drug. Sometimes we're out of this world for days."

"Nice to take the trip, feeling no pain, but the pain waits for you."

Dan nodded. "Yeah, it does. The going up is good, if only you could stay there and not come down. Sometimes it takes a week to get straight. Makes staying up look better."

"But that's not real life."

"Nah. Can't get nothin' done from that place. Some of the guys stay high, but we hate taking care of them. Soon we just put them out."

Gaff said softly, "You're not to blame for your mom's death."

"You're wrong there. I should've killed the motha before I left. Only I wasn't the man I am today. My brother and me talked about it. Asshole deserved to die. Son of a bitch had the nerve to cry at her funeral. Said he loved her. Said he missed her. Jerk was screwing someone else right away. Started punching on her, too."

"He didn't learn anything."

"Nah, he didn't learn nothin'. She wouldn't take it like mama did. She killed the son of a bitch with a fire poker."

"She got angry."

"Poetic justice, you ask me. Story was, he got her pregnant and said he wouldn't take care of her and her baby. Said he'd throw her out when she got fat. So next time he hit her, she brought out a bottle of booze and drank him into a stupor. Then she hit him a couple of licks with the poker, enough to make sure he'd never get up again. Her bruises were enough to prove self-defense. Said she was defending her baby. Wouldn't let no one hurt that baby."

Gaff closed his eyes. "You and your brothers didn't get mad and want to get back at her?"

"Nope. We all got together after the trial to do shots. Told her she did what we didn't have the courage to do."

"Did you, now?"

"Funny though, she said she loved him and missed him. That he was a good man underneath."

"Your dad said that about your mom."

"Yeah, but she loved her baby and herself more than she loved him. Wasn't gonna let any man do that to her baby."

"Your mama didn't protect you like that."

Dan was quiet, thinking. "Nah, me and my brother talked about that, too. Mama wasn't strong enough. She said Dad started the beatings a little at a time. At first he treated her nice and then he yelled. Years later he started hammering her."

"Sort of snuck up on her?"

"Yeah, snuck up on her. Snuck up. You said somethin' smart, old man. She didn't protect us. She could've stopped having babies or let us live with Uncle Dan when Dad was on a rage."

"Your dad get drunk and then beat you?"

Silence. No answer.

Gaff said almost to himself, "Must've been in a lot of pain."

Dan spat out, "Pain? What're you saying, old man? We were the ones in pain."

"Sometimes when a person hurts inside for any reason, they try to share that pain with people around them. Could be by yelling at them, telling them they're worthless, or by hitting them. Both are abuse."

"Mama did say granddad was mean."

"And you get high to get away from your pain."

Dan didn't say anything.

"Bet you beat up on strangers, too."

"I can brawl with the best of them." Dan's bravado faded quickly.

Gaff was patient.

"You're saying it's due to pain in me?"

"You just told me you blame yourself for not saving your mama. Doesn't that make you sad? You sometimes feel bad about yourself?"

Dan's voice got louder, belligerent. "What're you talking about, old man? I'm just showing how tough I am. Having fun. I'm strong. Want some respect and I know how to get it." He leaned over and flexed his arm for Gaff.

Gaff changed direction, "You ever feel like you want to hit a woman?"

"Like my dad? I do get that mad sometimes, but I remember seeing mama all bloody and crying. Instead, I fight guys. More even odds."

"You win?"

"Mostly. I play like I'm hitting my dad to add power to my punches." He paused a beat. "Never told anyone that."

"You ever feel like it's your dad beating you? You know, does the feeling of being hit remind you of being a kid at home?"

The answer came slowly, "Now I think of it, it does. Like I'm at home with Dad pounding me. I can beat the shit out of him now. I usually win."

"No matter how many fights you win, or people you kill, you won't fix the past that way."

"Fix the past? Shit. It's gone. Can't be fixed."

"Can't it?" Gaff changed direction again to give Dan time to think. "So you graduated and went to California."

Dan's voice was smiling. "Not right away. I moved around. Got odd jobs to buy food. You know, when you're young, you think that high school diploma is worth something. That's all Mama had in her mind, for us to get through high school. She was pregnant at fourteen and that's all she wrote. It's not worth shit, that lousy piece of paper."

Gaff agreed. "Can't do much with just high school. Need a real skill, from a technical school or working with someone who'll train you… or college."

"There are jobs, but low-paying. When you're young, you don't want to buy into one of those dead end jobs."

"You don't see those jobs as a beginning with the chance to work your way up."

"Nah. I drifted. Guess I had a chip on my shoulder that warned people off. Wasn't smart like my brothers to learn a trade. One brother went to college." His voice showed the pride he felt for this brother.

"Never too late."

Dan snorted. "Is for me. I ended up in California, broke. Didn't know nobody. Made friends with some guys always had a good time. Rode motorcycles. Always partying." He chuckled. "All I could afford was a scooter."

He shook his head and smiled. "They put me up. When I owed them, they had me do 'odd jobs.' Gave me a chance to tattoo my anger on someone's face. Worked fine for me." He seemed reluctant to say more, as though he'd already said too much.

Gaff nodded, waiting for the rest. Patiently waiting for fish to take the bait.

Dan hesitated, shrugged, and added, the bravado back in his voice. "Like I said, I'm here to do a 'deed' to earn my patch. I'll be a full member then. A full member."

Gaff thought the "deed" didn't sound good. "And they told you what to do?"

Dan blew out a breath noisily. "Yeah. 'Who' to do is more like it."

Gaff realized his shoulders were tense when they suddenly let go. Relax. No random killing here. "You're enjoying yourself before you get to it."

"Yeah." Dan pitched something toward the water. A shell?

"How'd you get here? To this part of the beach?" He almost said "to my beach," but changed mid-sentence. He looked to the sky and mouthed a prayer of gratitude to Father Sky and Mother Earth, thanking them for protecting him. And asking how to help this young man.

Dan's voice was happier, almost laughing. "Walked on the pier earlier. They were really catching the fish there! This bald girl in a baseball cap was yapping. All about this old guy on the beach that was some sort of magician. Made her feel OK about having no hair and all. Talked about the pirate flag. Decided to check it out."

"You come to kill me?" Gaff hoped the answer was no.

"Nah. Just to see if she was lying." Dan really laughed this time. "My entrance was... an afterthought. You know, thought I'd make a splash that you'd remember."

"You did." Gaff asked, "And was she?"

"You're here. And you didn't scare none. Most people would have messed their pants with a knife at their throats. Would have run, leaving everything."

"I'm still here."

"You're either a fool or know people. I guess I was hoping you weren't the fool."

"You needed to tell your story to someone with no agenda."

"Not a preacher trying to save my soul."

"Something like that."

Dan was thoughtful. "Some old guy with no dog in this fight."

"A listener."

"Someone sees shooting stars."

Gaff waved toward a bright light moving in the sky. "That's the space station. See how it's moving? Slow. An airplane would have flashing lights and a celestial body wouldn't be moving that fast, so fast you could see the movement."

Dan pointed toward the moving light. "That one there?"

"Yep."

"The space station?"

"Yep."

"Imagine that. You can see the space station from the beach in North Carolina." He was transfixed.

Gaff's eyes scanned the sky. "There's a website that tells exactly when and where all the satellites are every night. I have it set on my computer to check whenever I head to the beach for night fishing."

Dan nodded, his voice still smiling. "No shit."

"With good strong binoculars, you can see all sorts of things."

Dan's eyes searched the sky for more. His feet were digging a hole in the sand. Planning to stay?

In a voice slowed to emphasize the words, Gaff added, "Constantly amazes me that some of those stars are so far away that for a long time after they explode into nothingness, we can still see them. People can use them to navigate, even hundreds of years after they die."

"No shit."

"Yep. They don't actually have to do anything much, just be there and be good signposts to help people find their way. In return, people give them names and study them and are glad they're there. Interesting, isn't it?" Fishing takes patience.

Gaff could hear Dan shifting his feet in the sand, digging deeper.

"Kind of like human beings, you know."

"How's that?" The confusion in his voice said that Dan was not following now.

"If you're kind and helpful, and loving helps, too. If you're all these good things, then you don't really have to do much before people are talking about you on the pier."

"Just happens like that?"

"Yep. People don't admire black holes that gobble up other planets and stars. The black holes don't light the path like the stars do. People love stars."

"They don't love black holes?"

"Nope. Not black holes. Don't sit on the beach and watch black holes and remember their names and miss them after they explode into nothingness."

"Nothingness."

"There's a difference, big difference, between stars and people. We don't explode into nothingness. When this physical body dies, our souls and spirits live on."

"You're not giving me that Heaven shit, are you? All about how to save my soul."

"Nope. Don't believe in heaven." Gaff pointed to the sky. "All except that one. I believe in that heaven. No, I don't believe in death really, just transformation."

"Transformation? Mama's dead and there ain't no bringing her back. She ain't transformed to shit."

Gaff allowed the spirit of the night to bring the next words to him. "We go from living in this physical shell to living as a body of light, like those stars almost."

"That hot?"

"We'll have the warmth of love radiating from us, but not hot. More comforting than scorching."

"Now you're going to preach about judgment by God... and fire and brimstone in hell for eternity."

"Nope. Don't believe in hell either. We're our own worst critics, we judge ourselves more harshly than anyone else would, both in life and after death. God's a loving father, not like your father waiting to beat us up. No hell, no court trial."

"What happens then? After you die, I mean."

Gaff could feel Dan looking at him. "We get a chance to see how well we did during this life. We feel the feelings we caused in others while we were here. That's the worst punishment I can think of."

"You're saying my dad's feeling the pain he laid on mama? He's feeling the fists he put in my stomach, in my face? In all of us? Damn. That's heavy."

"Probably is. Think back in your life. Which caused you the most suffering: losing a fight and getting beaten up or disappointing yourself and someone you love?"

Dan's answer came quickly, "That's what bugs me about Mama. I let her down by not keeping him from killing her. He killed her just the same as if he stuck her with a knife. I shoulda helped her." His bitter words drifted out to the ocean.

Gaff's voice softened, "You did the best you could. You're older now and could do more. It's frustrating that she's not here for you to help."

"Frustrating ain't the half of it."

"There're plenty of women in the same position today who need to escape. Have you thought about helping them? You could pretend they're your mom. Protect them for her, in her memory."

Dan coughed and wiped his face on his sleeve. "Don't need a patch for that."

"Earning a patch would probably hurt your chances of helping those battered women... and their children."

"I forgot about the kids... They need help, too, don't they?"

"Lots. You did, didn't you?"

The bravado was back. "You trying to reform me, old man? Won't work."

Gaff could see past that. "I was just thinking that you could help other women get away from the guy that's beating them. You couldn't rescue your mother, but there are plenty of other women out there in violent relationships. Still getting the bruises and black eyes and broken bones from some man who says he loves her."

Dan muttered his anger. "Sons of bitches."

"Maybe you can turn your unhappy childhood into something good."

Dan's words cut the air like a knife. "I could kill a couple of them, I could."

"Would that help as much as protecting the women and their kids? Getting them on their feet and showing them that there're some kind men out there."

Give Dan time to think. Gaff got up to work his line, bringing it in to check the bait. Someone had taken it.

# chapter 6

No news of a killing in the area that sounded like Dan's work. Gaff didn't really expect it. He had a feeling that Dan would be back, but he could wait for that. This was hurricane season and he was always thankful when his beach was saved from the fury of nature… and of man.

This morning, he watched the clouds rolling in from the southeast, black and ominous. A tropical depression was on its way up the coast. Hope it misses us, he thought, but it is the season. His lines were out in the angry waves that announced the coming of a storm.

Gaff said to the waves, "I may need the rain gear today, if those clouds don't cooperate." He glanced at the black clouds storming up the beach.

He said to the cloud, "Are you going up the river so I don't get wet?"

He was watching and listening for the answer when he heard a man's voice. "You're the guy with the pirate flag. My buddy at the pier told me you know everything there is about fishing."

Gaff turned to look in the direction of the voice. A man trudged through the sand toward him. He was pudgy and white, not well acquainted with the sun or with physical labor. Shaved head and trimmed beard, the style with older men these days. These are sure signs of life in the white collar world.

Gaff asked, "Where you from?"

The answer didn't come until the man stood next to him, huffing. "Ohio. I do a lot of fishing in the Great Lakes, but never fished here. It's beautiful."

He put his fists on his hips and looked toward the waves and the sea birds feeding in them. "Looks like there might be fish out there. Will our friends leave us some?" He chuckled at his own joke.

Gaff liked him.

He turned to Gaff, hand outstretched. "Name's Bradley James. Friends call me BJ, but at work they call me Brad. You can call me anything." His handshake was firm and energetic.

"'Anything's' a strange name." Gaff joked.

BJ guffawed. "I like a man who can laugh."

Gaff laughed at BJ's happiness. He, too, liked a man who could laugh.

BJ waved toward the pier, "They told me where to find you. You seem to be some sort of fixture on this beach."

"Been here a long while."

BJ looked around. "On this exact spot? Man on the pier told me right where to find you. How long have you been fishing here?"

Gaff thought a moment. "Don't rightly remember, but may even be decades by now. Don't like to think of it because it'd make me old."

His new friend said, "It doesn't matter anyway. Wait here and I'll get the gear I bought at the pier. The guy sold me everything including the kitchen sink, but he promised you'd tell me what to do with it."

He moved quickly toward the parking area and Gaff heard the sounds of a car door opening.

Gaff turned his attention to the ocean, and said softly, "Mother Water, our conversation will have to wait because I have a visitor today. I'm relying on your help, though. I'm thankful as always and we'll talk more about that later."

The sound of a car door slamming was soon followed by footsteps on the walkway. Gaff turned to watch him.

BJ was carrying two rods, one long and one shorter. Gaff noticed that BJ bought the good stuff, not the cheap rods in the back of the display. He also bought sand fleas for bait.

He started talking the minute his feet touched the sand. "To his credit, I tried to buy some other stuff, but the man at the pier wouldn't sell it to me. Said I didn't need it for the kind of fishing I'd be doing."

"You can use my flea catcher instead of buying from Joe. Save you the trouble of going to the pier. You want to start with whiting? They're the ones eat the sand fleas."

BJ looked toward the water. "Tide's pretty low. Don't they run when the tide's low?"

Gaff nodded his answer as he inspected the rod and reel. "Joe set you up right."

BJ laughed. "That's just what he said you'd say. Like you'd be testing him."

"Keeps him on his toes. Holder?"

BJ reached into a canvas bag and held up the rod holder.

Gaff moved a little away from his area to hammer the holder into the sand with the side of a pair of pliers. Satisfied with the results of his efforts, he placed the rod in it, ready to go.

"Where's your wife? Doesn't she like to fish?"

BJ laughed. "You pegged her right. She'd be on a chair reading, if she were here. We both love the beach, but not for the same reasons. We work well together, Brenda and me. We do work well together." For a moment, he was lost in thoughts that Gaff didn't want to disturb.

Gaff tended his own line, tugging on it, feeling the tension, reeling it in, replacing the bait, casting it into the surf. "Damn fish think I'm here to feed them." He shouted toward the waves, "Bite, damn you. Bite."

He showed BJ how to put a sand flea on his hook. For a while, BJ stood contemplating the direction for his cast. "Now where do I want this hook to be?"

Gaff pointed. "There's a channel between sandbar and shore where the whiting feed."

BJ watched closely and then cast exactly into the channel. He nodded proudly toward Gaff, still holding his gear. He set the bail, pulled the line taut, and put the rod into the holder. He stood looking toward the water with his hands on his hips.

Gaff smiled appreciatively. "Good shot. Now you wait. Want to sit on my cooler while you do?"

BJ laughed. "I have a chair in the car. Guess I should have brought it down before I put the hook in the water. Brenda's always telling me I get ahead of myself."

Gaff watched the waves. "I can watch your line while you get it."

Once BJ was settled in a chair next to Gaff, he said, "I don't usually vacation without my wife, but we've been through a lot this year. I needed to get away and someone has to look after things at home. Brenda volunteered."

Gaff nodded, waiting for the rest. Patient from so many years of fishing.

When he was ready, BJ continued, "Our daughter Debra's been sick this year. The wedding was two years ago and cancer this year. Things are hard at work, too. You know about when it rains… All that stress takes a toll on you."

"It does that."

"Surprises are a part of life, but so many came all together." He blew a puff of air. "Since Debra's doing so well, Brenda wanted me to get away for a change of scenery while I could. She took a few days last week with some of her friends, a girls' trip. Now it's my turn." He looked toward the darkening clouds. "Things are better now."

Gaff remembered Debra. Here last week, he thought. He shook his head as he mused about how the days blurred one into the other.

The silence was filled with the sound of water birds and waves, a comforting symphony.

BJ reeled in his line to find that something had taken his bait. He put another flea on it and cast into the trough.

They talked about the differences between fishing in fresh water and salt water. They talked about types of tackle and live bait compared to lures and where to buy what and all manner of shoptalk. BJ acted like a man given a drink of good fresh water after being adrift in a lifeboat, surrounded by nothing but salt water.

During a break in the conversation, BJ got quiet for a long while. Then he looked at Gaff. "My girl changed after her trip to Kure Beach. Frank told me that she grew stronger everyday, but the biggest improvement was after she met you. I came to thank you for helping her. And I thought I'd get some of that kind of peace to take home with me." BJ's voice cracked with emotion he held in check.

Gaff didn't know how to handle this loving comment, this father's strong feelings. Men are funny about the emotion thing. He didn't respond because he didn't know what to say.

As an afterthought, he muttered, "I'm a dad, too." That was about right.

BJ was easy, comfortable being with himself. Gaff could tell that his thoughts weren't always happy ones. His emotions ebbed and flowed like the waves. Gaff silently asked that BJ feel the healing from being near big water.

BJ reemerged from his thoughts. "There's nothing worse than being told your child has cancer and might die. My heart goes out to the parents whose children do die... from anything. We've been lucky. It changes the way you think about life. Brenda always complained that I spent too much time at work. Not that I neglected my family, but I didn't spend a lot of time with them either."

"Could be worse." Gaff's memory flashed back to his own working days and the struggle to juggle everything.

"I've started taking more days off, more vacations. I realize that my family is more important than the money. Brenda was right all along."

"Some men don't see that until they're on their last leg. Then they want to play ball with a grown kid who hasn't learned to play, who doesn't even know his dad. It's a shame to miss all that, for both dad and kid."

"I'm not all that smart because the kids are all just about out of the house. The big bills have come and are almost gone. Still have a few years of college and a couple of weddings to go. I think we've got enough socked away. Time to relax and spend time with Brenda and with the kids when they come around."

BJ went on, "I played with my children on the weekends. Don't play golf. I got the kids interested in fishing as much as I could and we spent quality time together on the lake."

"I don't remember that Debra knew how to fish."

"Debra and her mom lay out in the sun or sat under the canvas and read. Still, we were all together. In fact, when she got home from this trip, she asked if we could go fishing on the lake--just the two of us. My little girl and me. I love it."

BJ turned to look at the far end of the beach and Gaff knew his eyes weren't dry. BJ continued, "Whenever I have to make a choice now, I use different criteria. I think more about spending time with my family."

Gaff smiled to think that BJ had also learned from Debra's near death experience.

# chapter 7

She approached wearing street clothes, shoes in her hands. Gaff shook his head: she wasn't dressed for a walk on the beach. Her expression wasn't right for the beach either. Edgy, with anger peeking out from behind those edges. Didn't fit with the blue sky and warm sun. Should have come a couple of days ago, during the storm. Then she wouldn't clash with the background.

Gaff groaned when he saw her coming, steeling himself for a tirade against the injustices of the world. He built up his immunity by concentrating on the sun warming his arms, his body. His strength grew as the warmth traveled through the outer layers of muscle and skin to the core protected within, to his heart, and deeper.

The wind off the water brought smells of salt, of fish, of the world beneath the smooth surface. Wasn't there an old song with a line about the ocean having a perfect disguise: smooth above and full of life below the surface? His connection with the planet, with the water, helped him feel grounded in the comfort of knowing, of trusting that the Universe had answers. He trusted in the plan and didn't believe it was arbitrary and capricious. That trust brought him peace. He reminded himself that all questions contain answers if you only listen closely. Once he felt that anchor to the planet, he turned to watch as she trudged toward him. He was ready.

She started talking while still yards away, "I see you here all the time, you and your flag. I can watch you from my window." She turned to gesture toward a yellow house on the other side of the dunes, just a bit down the beach.

"Sometimes you're alone, but mostly you have company. Just wondered who you are that you have so many friends."

Gaff didn't see a question in all those words so he just nodded in her direction and said, "Morning." He watched, waited.

She continued to walk in his direction. Her gait was more lumbering than walking. Although not fat, she was overweight and her movement screamed of a poor physical condition. With hair tied in a bun, he couldn't tell how long it was. Her skin was pasty white: odd, considering that she lived on the beach, right on the sand. Her make-up failed to hide the sadness.

He mused to himself that there are so many sad people in this world. He shook his head in reaction to that thought, but she misunderstood the gesture. There was that anger, welling up into her eyes, overflowing into her words.

Gaff got the feeling that she wasn't comfortable in her own body. Looked almost like she wasn't always in her own body, but flying somewhere else. Was she searching for something to be mad at?

She shot out angrily, "Do I need an engraved invitation to talk to you? Don't I fit into your guest list?"

Gaff shook his head at her response: ready to see negative in anything. Readier still, to lash out against anyone seen as an attacker, and that was anybody. Sad to be so unhappy that you can't see the gifts there for the taking. Gifts all around. He glanced at the top of his rod and then out toward the horizon for another gift of happiness. He felt the sun warming his heart and the breeze kissing his skin. Happiness—always there for the taking.

This time she took the shake of Gaff's head as an invitation to join him. Her nose turned up when she saw the top of the cooler. "Don't you have something to put over this thing so I don't get dirty. I'm working."

The "dirt" was slime left from cutting bait and there was the distinct odor of fish. But what do you expect from a fisherman on the beach? He shrugged it off. These sights and smells were part of his life.

Gaff folded his towel for her to sit on. He breathed in the patience, felt the air caress his body.

She sat, almost dropping onto the cool, expelling a breath in an unladylike grunt. And then, even though she'd been in such a hurry to meet him, she said nothing. She sat looking at the sky and the water and the birds feeding in the waves in front of them.

Watching the ocean is healing, Gaff thought. She needs that. Did she distinguish the calls of the different birds? Could she really see, really take it in? It was glorious when you did.

He looked at the tip of his rod to see that someone was nibbling on his bait.

"My name's Mae," she said without preamble or proffering of hand to shake.

He returned without looking. "Name's Gaff." Scanning the water's surface with his eyes, looking for signs, waiting. Fishing requires patience, takes time.

Mae's voice was harsh. "I'm a nurse. I have a private duty charge down here on the beach. I thought when I took the job that I'd have more time to myself, but I'm 'on call' all the time, 24/7. It's a shame, isn't it, that I live right there on the other side of the dunes and can't even walk down to the water for more than ten minutes at a time. I barely get to the edge of the water before my beeper goes off. Dawn needs me for something. She always needs something." Her statement was punctuated with a snort of disgust.

"Dawn's your charge?" Gaff watched the water and his rod and the cloudless sky and listened.

Mae turned to look at him. "Yep, Dawn, my eleven-year-old charge… You don't say much, do you? A man of few words. Do most of the people visiting you do all the talking? Maybe that's why you're so popular. You just listen." She returned her gaze to the water, but was she seeing it?

"Maybe."

"When I took this job, I thought I'd have time for walking down the beach to Fort Fisher." She gestured toward his rods. "For fishing even, but all I do is work."

Gaff thought about the patience required for fishing and wondered if Mae would live long enough to develop that kind of patience. He laughed inside but didn't dare laugh out loud for fear of overheating the tide pool of anger. He was curious about her job.

The anger in her next words pricked like the sand pushed along the beach by a gale, "I was married for 23 years and left the bastard last year. For all that time, we moved with his jobs and I got whatever work I could. I entertained his customers and his friends. All he thought about was himself and his own needs. In the end, he didn't like anything I did. He didn't even like the way I used cotton swabs to dry my ears!"

She shook her head as she went into that past, a past she held too close to now. "He didn't like the college I attended. Said it was too intellectual, not well-rounded. Said my reasons for nursing weren't right. He accused me of spending too much time on things that didn't mean anything, that were just social."

She took a deep breath to power the next words. "Said I should develop my spirit, something deep inside me. He didn't act that way himself, if you ask me. I did the social stuff to help him with his job. He didn't appreciate that help. He said I made it harder for him, that I didn't support him enough."

She was on a roll now, like a wave crashing in on those things that caused her pain from the past. A tidal wave. "Maybe I should have told him he was wonderful when he told me something I already knew. Maybe I didn't make him feel like he was a king or brilliant. Maybe I should have told him how wonderful he was because he made a lot of money and was respected in his job. I thought I did that, but maybe not enough. Recently, I read a description of him in a book. Said he was narcissistic. That was it, narcissistic."

Gaff gave her time by watching the waves, but did she see herself reflected in the water?

She nodded to herself and was swimming in quiet thought, thoughts of her husband's many transgressions. Finally she said, "I guess after that amount of time together he could no longer see the good in me. Maybe he never did. It was all about him. I got tired of not having a vote, of living according to his plans and not my own. Now that I'm on my own, I live the way I want to." Another swim in the sea of past hurts, or her interpretation of them.

Gaff glanced at Mae. "So you have the job you want, the one you chose. No more being pushed around. You've taken charge of your life. You can focus on being the professional you are."

She didn't say anything. Gaff hoped that she was thinking about what he had said.

Mae was on a different tangent now, still ventilating the anger. "I'm a nurse, but I don't want to work in a hospital. Too much stress. I don't need that any more." She looked down at the shoes in her lap as she held them sole to sole and then side by side and back again.

Gaff waited, sure she would continue. She needed to get it all out.

She nodded, probably agreeing with something in her own head, something she might say later. "I tried living in town, working as a clerk in one of the gift shops on the river front there. In Wilmington, you know. Didn't like it. I lived in Alabama right on the water for years. Gulf Shores, you know. I loved that. Whenever we had to move more inland I missed the shore, looking out my window at the water." More thoughts of the past? Sad memories against the comforting sounds of waves.

Gaff smiled. "I wouldn't want to move away from the beach. We agree on that."

Mae shook her head. "What good does it do me to be so close? Took this private duty job so I'd be down here, but I didn't realize that I wouldn't have time to get out on the beach. Never, ever, not at all." Anger was rising in her voice.

"You see it through the windows." Pointing out the positive.

A pelican dove for food in front of them.

"Yeah." She didn't sound convinced.

"You can walk at night, can't you?"

"Work so hard all day that after Dawn goes to sleep, I just veg out in front of the television."

"Must be hard, pushed and pulled by a child all day and then too tired to even take a walk at night. And no way to change the job, or your feelings about it. Hard way to go."

Her voice got louder. "Not one thing really. I can't change one thing."

"Or the way you feel about it."

"Makes me upset that I have no life."

"Not the life you imagined you'd have on the beach. I can see that."

"That's right." Her voice was strong with anger hardening the edges.

Gaff lowered his voice as if he were speaking to himself, "A professional nurse with all that experience and not able to take charge of her job. Hm-mm-mm."

Was she considering his words, if only to refute them? "I do have some say."

She paused again. "My charge was paralyzed in an accident. Jane Harper, her mother, carries a heavy load of guilt because she was driving. She wants someone with the girl all the time. She's willing to pay a lot to make up for her mistake, short of giving up her own life, that is. I've been there for six months now and to my way of thinking, Mrs. Harper should spend more time with her daughter." She underscored her conviction by tapping the shoes together.

Mae paused to take a breath, but Gaff knew there was more. He became aware of the water and of his line cutting through the waves into the space where schools of fish were swimming. Would one of them bite his hook? Let him pull it in for a short stay in the cooler and then an invite to dinner? He breathed in the peace.

"Yeah. Mrs. Harper feels enough guilt to pay me plenty to be with Dawn, but not enough to cancel one of her bridge games."

She tapped her shoes again for emphasis. "Mr. Harper takes the family for a drive on the weekend when he can, but that's all he does. He has asked what else he can do. I think he feels helpless. He works every day and some weekends. Put an office in the house so he can work there instead of going into town on Saturdays." Mae picked up a shell and brushed it clean before she put it into her pocket.

"They fight at night, in their room. Probably need counseling, but it's not my job to tell them. My job is to care for the girl. Still, I can see Dawn's bothered by the tension."

Gaff thought he saw the tip of his rod dance with fish movements, but it calmed too soon. "Probably is. You are, too."

He could see Mae getting ready to argue to the contrary.

He continued, to cut off the argument. "I saw a snake when I got home a couple of days ago. He was at my stoop, slithering from the grass right up to my front door. I can deal with sharks and all manner of ocean creatures, but snakes… don't like them at all. It was only a garden snake, but to me they're all bad. Since then, I'm nervous when I walk through my front yard, afraid I'll run into him. He may only be a garden snake, but he could bite if I surprise him."

Mae was somewhere else, looking out at the sea. Gaff wasn't sure what she was seeing. Or hearing.

Gaff watched fish jumping just beyond the sandbar, just beyond the foam of waves breaking in the shallows. He knew there were fish to be caught, fish just waiting to grab his bait. But they weren't biting today so far. Maybe in a while. He was patient.

Finally, she nodded. "You're right. I am bothered. It's sort of like a smell in the house that you can't quite put your finger on. It's always there… in the air. Always. Stronger when they're both home. Sort of like the thickness in the air before a storm."

Gaff waited, looking out toward the horizon.

Mae's voice became more insistent, "I am bothered by all the unhappiness. Dawn is, too. She's intelligent. Her mind's OK. It's her body that doesn't work."

"And she's your charge, your responsibility."

Mae found another shell to put into her pocket. She nodded, a new understanding perhaps. "Maybe it is my job to tell them to work it out. They need to get to the place where they can be positive. If not for themselves, for their daughter. Maybe if she saw them as a team on her side, she would improve… grow those nerves back. I've seen that before, where a patient has healed from injuries doctors say are permanent."

"Love heals and unconditional love heals unconditionally." Gaff wondered where that came from.

Mae said slowly. "Yes. You're right. This discord is keeping her from getting better. And I need to forget my disappointment about not being able to enjoy the beach and focus on getting her to the point where she can enjoy it with me. She's probably a lot sadder than I am when she looks out that window."

"You think she may call you back when she sees you by the water because it reminds her that she can't be there?"

"I've never thought of it that way. I've always been unhappy because I couldn't spend time on the beach. I didn't think of her sadness, of her longing to do what other kids can, laughing and playing in the surf. She looks out the window all the time. She watches the beach, probably watching kids throwing Frisbees, flying kites, searching for shells. If I want to do those things and see her as keeping me from it, what must she be thinking?"

"You may have something there."

Mae's body filled with energy and her jaw set with determination. Her voice expressed a growing enthusiasm for her new understanding, her new purpose. "I can work with her to get her to go on the beach with me. Her muscles are not that atrophied. It hasn't been too long since the accident that she can't heal."

"You might ask for some help, too."

Mae's head snapped around to look at him. "From whom?"

Gaff waved his hand toward the ocean. "From the Great Mother Water. From Spirit. From the Universe that heals with unconditional love. From those things with power beyond our understanding."

Mae turned again to look at the water. "There is healing in water, even just sitting next to it like we are now. People used to 'take the healing baths' all the time. Salt water is good for you... But I get the idea that you're talking about God, God in these waters."

"Mother Water is good for you. She heals the soul as well as the body. Seems like that little girl needs some soul healing along with the body healing."

"Her parents do, too. Only they need someone to point out how the solutions are right there in front of them. Right here in front of them."

Gaff repeated, "A lot of times the solutions are here in front of you and you only have to open your eyes to see them."

Mae almost popped up from her seat. "I'd better get back. Can't imagine why the pager hasn't gone off already. They don't usually give me this much time." She stood and took several steps in the direction of the yellow house, but stopped. Mae stood there in thought for a few minutes and then turned back to Gaff.

Gaff smiled. "Maybe they can tell you need some healing with Mother Water."

"I was ready to quit this morning. I figured if they paged me while I was here, I'd just ignore them. I'd ignore the page and then I'd pack my bags when I got back to the house. Just like that. I'd quit, walk out. Of course, if they needed time to find a replacement, I'd stay on for a while. Just long enough for them to find someone else. Life is too short to be this close to the beach and not enjoy it. But now I see things different. I see that it's up to me."

# chapter 8

Gaff didn't remember the snake until Mae reminded him of it weeks later. She walked from the yellow house with confidence and energy in her step, dressed in shorts and sneakers.

As she neared him, she called out, "Seen that snake lately?"

He answered, confused, "Nope."

She laughed, genuine this time. "Me neither. No more snakes."

He folded the towel for her to sit on the cooler. "You're tanned."

Mae laughed again. "And happy. I realized that I never did take charge of my life. Not even after I left my husband so I could. After we talked, I did a lot of thinking. Then I talked with Dawn and started all over with her."

"You did?"

"Her name's Dawn and being with her is the dawn of a whole new life for me."

"Prophetic, hunh?"

"Prophetic. I told her that I was in poor physical condition and wanted to change that. Getting into shape would take work and determination on my part...and help from her."

"Looks like she did help. You look good."

"I told her that I was going to show her it was possible to heal and to change a body, starting with mine. She didn't stop me so I went over my plan. She'd give me time to walk on the beach every day and watch to make sure I did more every time."

"Reasonable. And she had a part to play."

"Then I told her we were going to work her body so that she would be able to go out onto the beach if only just to sit. Told her some of the times I saw people heal injuries like hers. Guess I exaggerated there, but no matter. The plan was to make it a surprise for her parents and so we wouldn't let them in on it. Like a secret pact."

Gaff enjoyed the glow of her energy. The anger was gone, replaced with an excitement, a determination, and the energy to get it done. "That would appeal to a kid."

"I got her parents to hire a good physical therapist. Then I studied some complementary healing modalities through the Holistic Nurses Association. I'm studying Healing Touch and Dawn is my practice patient."

Mae waved her hands around making patterns in the air. "I'm even teaching her to work on herself. You should see the difference."

Gaff was fascinated. "She's a part of the process. Everyone likes to feel they have control over their own destiny."

Mae almost laughed as she warmed to her subject. "And attitude is at least half the medicine she needs. Dawn is better and improving everyday. Now when she sits at the window watching kids on the beach, I sit with her. We talk about how many more exercises we'll do that day to get her on her way down there. We don't let ourselves get the least bit sad-- about anything."

Gaff marveled at the strength in her voice.

"My body's in better condition. Dawn's is, too. Her parents have also changed. I don't understand how it worked."

Mae shook her head for emphasis. "The minute I started taking control of my life, Dawn started taking control of hers. Soon after, her parents took control of theirs, too."

"Funny how that works."

"No more fighting. They spend more time with Dawn and together. Not to say I don't use that load of guilt from time to time to get things for Dawn, but it's for a good cause. And after we accomplish something new, everybody feels better. Especially me."

"Will she make it to the beach, Mae?"

She frowned at Gaff. "It's not a question of 'if,' but 'when.' Dawn's made such progress the physical therapist gives her great marks every session. Then Dawn feels the work is worth it."

"And the therapist pats herself on the back."

"The therapist doesn't realize that we sometimes do twice what she suggests. Her goal is for Dawn to move from bed to chair by herself. We don't let on what our goals are. Not yet, maybe never. We just talk about it between us... and we do the work."

Gaff walked down to his rods, communing with the water and sky and those fish out there just waiting to jump into his cooler. He reeled in the lines and replaced the bait before casting again into the surf.

Mae joined him to stand near the edge of the waves. "Thanks for helping me see why my life was going in the wrong direction."

"Those who have ears to hear, let them hear."

"Do you mean that I only heard the message because I was ready to hear it?"

"That's exactly what I mean. Other people probably said the same thing to you. You didn't understand what they were saying because you weren't ready to change your life. Change takes courage, a lot of courage."

They watched the birds fishing for lunch.

Finally, Mae came out of her thoughts. "Just like I said about the Harpers. The answer was right there in front of me all along."

She paused before going on. "I've been wondering. Was my divorce preventable? If I acted different, would my husband have been nicer? Just like the job changed because I changed."

Gaff shrugged.

"I guess the real question I'm asking is whether I'm ready for a loving relationship now?"

Gaff looked to the water for an answer. "I don't know what happened in your marriage or if you could have prevented the split. I do see great changes in you, changes that make you more beautiful from the outside and more interesting."

Gaff thought he saw a blush under the tan. "There are two sides to every story. Your husband's would be different from yours. By asking the question you show how you've grown. And growing is good."

Mae persisted. "But do you think I'm ready for a new relationship, a romantic relationship with a good man?"

The Water spoke through the man. "You'll know you're ready when the relationship comes into your life. Use this alone-time to grow, to learn more about yourself and learn new skills to encourage that growth. When you're ready to use those new skills, a man will come into your life to provide the opportunity."

Mae returned to the cooler to ponder in silence next to this man who believed in the power of the Creator expressed through the water and the clouds and the wind. They sat allowing that power to change them, to mold them into the more they knew they could be.

Mae's voice was slow and low. "When I think about my marriage, I realize he wasn't the only one who was narcissistic. I was, too. When I started focusing on others in my job, my whole life changed. That change in focus would have helped my marriage."

"Good insight."

"I never felt loved when I was young. I was shuffled around from relative to relative. No one seemed to want me."

"If you don't feel loved as a child, it's hard to imagine that anyone could love you. Ever. Move past that to love yourself in a healthy way. When you do, then you'll be able accept love from others. And to give it. The first step is feeling that you deserve to be loved. I've seen it again and again."

The silence gave Mae time to think about her life, and about love.

Suddenly, the peace of the moment was broken by the cell phone ringing in Mae's pocket.

She answered it and jumped to her feet to wave toward the house. Laughing, Mae explained that it was Dawn reminding her to walk.

Her expression became quizzical. "She somehow knew that I needed this conversation, but that it's time for the walk now... Gaff, sometimes Dawn points out things I don't see. As we've grown closer during this last bit of time, she's told me things I don't understand. She sees things and hears voices. I'd think she was crazy if it didn't make so much sense. More maturity there than most girls her age. Gives me the willies sometimes."

Gaff smiled as Mae went off down the beach. Dawn has more wisdom and maturity? A connection with the Mother that she developed during her moments of pain? Gaff thought about Dawn and felt in his heart that she would walk. She would walk after lessons were learned… by her and by those around her. Maybe that's when Mae's relationship would show up.

He walked to stand in the waves washing the sand. He felt the sand shifting under his feet as it was pulled by the water. The water was comforting, but powerful. Was it comforting because it was so powerful? It had been there for always and would always be there. The words didn't just stop in his heart. They came from his lips and he didn't care who heard them. They were a prayer of thanksgiving. A thank you for healing the nurse, the parents, and the child. So be it.

# chapter 9

Wind blew from the land and the biting flies started harassing Gaff. He reached for the bug spray, but decided to net for bait instead. Kill two birds with one stone: get away from the flies and replenish his supply of bait.

It was September and the baitfish were running south to beat the cold weather. The mullet minnows that were small on their run north this spring had grown to a nice size. They would attract the larger fish Gaff was after. Some genetic clock inside told them when to migrate… and they did by the thousands.

Gaff thought a moment about going south himself this winter, but only for a moment. Kure Beach would do. For him it was a beach for all seasons.

The third time he threw out his net, he heard Bubba call to him. His friend was pulling a wagon loaded with rods, cooler, chairs, and everything he needed for night fishing.

Gaff waved with his free hand, but went right back to the job of pulling in the minnows. Empty the net into the 5-gallon bucket, coil the line properly in his hand, straighten the net and hold it half way down, hold the edge with the other hand up so it would open when he threw it. Throw it into the water toward the migrating minnows. Like a robot, he went through the movements over and over. Didn't require much thought, so his attention was far away. His attention was so far away that Bubba startled him by suddenly appearing in the water behind him.

Bubba had a large cigar in his mouth. That's what you noticed first about him. He talked around that cigar and had the habit of rolling it around in there. Gaff had never seen it lit, but he imagined that with all that exercise Bubba's lips and tongue must be muscular.

The next thing you noticed about Bubba was the hint of a laugh that was always on his round face. That laugh was ready to jiggle the belly jutting out over the place where his belt should be. A big front porch, Bubba called it. He said he got that belly from lack of exercise, sitting in the cab of a tractor for decades. After spending his life cultivating the rich soil, he sold out to developers so he could move to the beach to fish. His sparse hair was gray and tended to stick up all over his head. Sometimes it looked downright comical.

Bubba gestured back to the beach. "I set up next to your gear."

Gaff glanced in the indicated direction and nodded his approval.

"Catch much today?"

"Some."

"That means the big ones got away again. You gotta change your answers."

"How do you know I didn't? Maybe 'some' means 'a cooler full' today?"

His friend's eyes twinkled. "'Cuz I checked your cooler."

Gaff pulled in the net and walked up to empty it into the bucket.

Bubba leaned over the bucket. "Here's your 'cooler full.' That bait's worth a hundred dollars if you buy it from Sam."

Gaff covered the bucket with a towel to keep the energetic young ones from jumping out. He walked into the surf again.

Bubba swatted at a fly. "Damn biting flies."

"Net bait and they'll leave you alone." Like a machine, Gaff continued: wind the rope.

Bubba grimaced. "Net fish? That sounds like work. I'll buy the bait and spray the flies."

"I'm thinking the flies only bite if you're lazy. Work and they leave you alone." Grip the net just right.

Bubba guffawed at the joke. He raised the towel to look into Gaff's bucket again, thinking. "That would save me a heap of money at the bait shop."

Gaff wiped his brow on his sleeve. Throw the net into the school of fish.

Bubba watched. "Some of them fellers ain't gonna make it south this fall."

"Yep." Pull the net and empty the fish into the bucket. "They're headed for the freezer for a cold vacation till I use them to bring in the big one."

"With your luck it'll take more than a freezerful to bring in the big one." Bubba let out a silent whistle. "Lotta fish in that bucket. Save money and keep me in bait for a good long while."

Gaff waved toward Bubba's wagon. "Get your net and start hauling them in."

"Too much work."

Gaff chuckled. "Just think about how you're going to spend all that money you save. Makes the work go easy."

Bubba ran his fingers through his hair making it stand on end. "No need to think. Beer and boiled peanuts at the Fishing Hole Bar and Grill."

Gaff shook his head as he threw the net again. "What about buying Ethel a new sewing machine. I know she likes to sew. Saw a quilt she made. It was beautiful."

Bubba scratched his head. "My money. I work for it and I spend it. She gets what she needs to run the house."

Gaff glanced at his friend as he pulled in the net. "What does Ethel do for fun?"

He said around the cigar, "Yell at me. She's constantly on me about something. If it ain't about fixin' somethin' that's broke, it's about goin' to church. Yells at me to put in screens in the spring. In the summer, it's do the yard and paint the house. In the fall, it's put up the storm windows. I just did the mowing again. Thought that would stop when we sold the farm." Bubba shook his head in disgust.

"Didn't you like farming?"

"Never did. Only farmed 'cuz my family had the land. I wasn't fast enough getting out the door to escape the trap my dad set. Had three brothers and they all managed to go to college and get jobs in the city. As youngest and dumbest, I ended up working with Dad till he passed. By then Ethel and me had kids and the only thing I knew to do was dig and pull."

Gaff was laughing. "You didn't like it? But you worked that farm for years."

The disgust in Bubba's voice was so thick it would choke a shark. "What could I do? Bills kept coming in and I went out to the fields to grow money. My two boys helped when they got up enough in age. Ran off to college as soon as they could hitch a ride."

"Your boys have done well for themselves."

Bubba grinned. "I'd say. They was smarter'n me-- got out before I could set the trap. Ethel was on their side, too. She kept telling them to go to school and of course they end up working in the city. Probably right next to my brothers! Dang. All I wanted all my life was to live here on the beach to cut bait and fish."

"You got your wish. Here you are, fishing almost every day. Life of Riley."

"Was my good luck the highway got put in and I sold that pile of dirt for enough to support this 'life of Riley.' Until then I didn't see how I was ever gonna escape. Not ever, never." Bubba's rod was nodding to tell him that a fish was taking his bait, but would he get stuck on the hook? Yep, it was hooked and it was a good size, pulling yards of line out to deeper water.

Their conversation was interrupted while Bubba brought in the fish. Pull the rod, reel the line in. It did put up a fight. Over two feet long they guessed. Bubba put on gloves to take the hook out and put his prize into the cooler.

Gaff was disgusted. "Better than I got all day. You're here for a minute and already hooked a good one."

Bubba was grinning as he came back to his gear. "Takes good living. That's all. Good living and beating your wife once a week no matter."

Gaff almost fell over laughing. "You'd never beat Ethel, would you?"

Bubba cut his eyes around to his friend as he baited the hook, "I'd beat her in a heartbeat if I didn't think she'd beat me better. She is one strong woman, my wife. Got strong on the farm."

"Is that so."

"No need for a tractor with her around. She could pull the bushhog all by herself. And with the other hand, she could pick cotton in the next field over."

"Strong woman, your Ethel. And long arms, too." Gaff put away his net and sat down to rest.

Bubba sat in his chair. "You bet. That's the only reason I don't mess with her. She's a strong one."

"My Julia's not that strong."

"Never lived on a farm or walked ten miles to the grocery. Ten miles in the scorching sun or the blizzard."

"And did she have to bring all those heavy bags the ten miles back home?"

"Of course, she did. And sometimes carry a kid on her back."

"She is a strong woman, your wife."

"Yep. My boys can't do a thing. Got sick one time and Ethel, she talked the architect boy into coming home to help. First day, he broke the tractor. Second day, he ran back to his job in the big city. Said they couldn't do without him. My daughter was more help than either of those brothers and she's only a girl."

"Only a girl, hunh? Bet she loves hearing you say that."

"Don't say it to her face. She's as strong as her mother."

"I see. As strong as Ethel."

"I thought God gave girls to a family to trade for a herd of goats or something. Isn't that what the Bible says?"

"Don't exactly remember."

"All I got when she married was a hug around the neck and one very large bill for the marrying. Glad I only had one girl, might go bankrupt with any more."

Gaff was trying to catch his breath between spells of laughing. "Ethel deserves a prize for putting up with you all these years."

Bubba asked, "What prize would that be now? The Nobel Fleas Prize?"

"Sounds about right to me."

## chapter 10

Gaff got to his spot late the next day. There were errands to run in the morning, appointments. Wasn't on his list of favorite things to do, but it was a small price to pay for living in paradise.

For a while, he stood in front of the wagon feeling sand between his toes and salt air on his face. The sun was hot for September. He looked at the cloudless sky, the ocean, the birds. It was his favorite view, no matter what time of year. He walked to the edge of the surf to say good morning to the water and invite the fish to come for a personal visit. Asked the birds to help corral some of those pesky fish right to his hook. Today's the day to reel in that big one, he thought.

Finally, he got to work: put out chair, cooler, and towel. He was ready for a visitor. The flagpole went into the sand near his chair. The wind off the water immediately set the flag in motion. The gentle flapping was like music to him.

This is the best month on the beach because most of the tourists have cleared out. Sometimes there's a threat of tropical storm to make life interesting. They're usually diverted or peter out before getting to the island. The strand is peaceful, with enough people to make it interesting. The fish migrating south mean more on his hook for more fun, more food. He loved the beach and the creatures living here.

He walked to get his feet wet. The sand was packed harder by the receding waves. Water was getting cooler, announcing fall. Waves crashed on the sand, surrounding his feet and legs, pushing and pulling him in its flow.

Baitfish by the thousands were visible in the waves as they rose just before they broke. Minnows were jumping in a swirl of water stirred up by a predator. He'd set his gear to fish for them today. Seemed plentiful in the trough. Since the minnows were over five inches long, the predators would be a nice size.

All these things he did before fishing, a ritual become sacred over the years. The trip to the water before putting his hook into it. Like a baptism, to give thanks for his life and his successes, on the beach and otherwheres. Things were only getting better.

Back to work. As he set the rod holders he thought about the city slickers who came to the beach expecting a big catch the first time they put their hook out. There was science to fishing, but there was also art. He studied both-- fishing since he was a kid and still learning. Nature offered a lesson every day.

Gaff put bait on the hooks, through the minnow's head, and cast it out. He was offering the predators an easy catch. The tip of his rod wiggled and he brought the hook in with only a head left. After several times with the same results, Gaff put a piece of cut bait to just cover the hook and cast it into the trough. When the tip wiggled this time, he brought up a fish big enough for the dinner table.

Gaff laughed to himself and said to the fish, "You get too used to the easy dinner and you get caught."

Today would be a day spent standing by his rods because the fish were really biting. He was happy. The commotion of people coming over the walkway distracted him-- sounded like a squall coming. Boys laughing, teasing. Mother's angry voice raised over the laughter. Why come to HIS beach? He stood by the rods, watching the ocean, the birds, and the family getting settled to his right. The noise stamped them as the family of his nightmares.

Dad was quietly sitting in a chair facing the ocean. The mother grabbed Gaff's attention with her loud voice. The kids dropped everything, ready to play, and she yelled, "Don't get wet till you put on sunscreen. Take that shirt off so it stays dry. I want you to wear it home."

Gaff wondered if those shirts couldn't dry in the sun.

She slathered lotion on the first boy, about 12 years old, and immediately yelled at him to stay out of the water until the lotion dried. The kid was two feet away from her, close enough to hear a whisper. Maybe he was hard of hearing. If he wasn't, he would be. Mom probably yelled in the house, too, telling the boys to use their indoor voices! The irony made Gaff chuckle.

The procedure was repeated on the second child, who looked to be a couple of years younger than the first. Now the mom's commands were aimed at both boys, like a machine gun with a stuck trigger.

Gaff watched the water and the tip of his rod, but he heard the clamorous clan. He was fascinated. The boys threw a Frisbee between them and noise was replaced by laughter. Gaff nodded his approval, smart boys. And then the flying object came too close to mom.

"Keep that thing away from me. You're getting sand all over me. I'll have sand stuck in my sunscreen. You know how nasty that is. Can't just wipe it out of that goop." She was wiping at her arms nonetheless.

Another close call with the flying disc was followed by another order barked at the boys, "Play over there. Can't you see I'm trying to relax here?" Her voice was so loud she could have been talking to someone a mile away.

Gaff noted that the boys moved about two feet farther. He figured the boys would torment mom like this all day and she didn't see it. Fun for the boys! Noise for Gaff.

This time, the Frisbee flew over mom and dad. Dad brushed the sand from his shoulders and closed his eyes again. Mom roared commands, peppered with indictments of her sons' intelligence. She turned to her husband and gave him what for because his closed eyes indicated he was out of the game. She was looking for a teammate. He opened his eyes to look at her. He said something quietly and returned to his reverie. Gaff was impressed by his ability to ignore the storm raging around him. Years of experience in operation here.

"Mom, can we go into the water now?" It was a chorus of young male voices.

She bellowed across the three feet that separated them. "OK, lotion should be dry by now. Be careful. Don't get into that man's hooks. He shouldn't be fishing here anyway. This beach is for swimming." At this she looked purposefully at Gaff.

Oops, he didn't like this shift in the target for her anger.

Gaff groaned. This was turning into his worst nightmare. She was a woman who tried to control everything and everyone.

Didn't she realize that Kure Beach is a fishing village? If she didn't want to be close to a fisherman, she could have put her chairs farther down the beach. Or go to a different beach altogether. Gaff considered this option as he reeled in his line, replaced the bait, and cast into the trough.

Mom yelled again, "Watch out boys that man's putting his hook into the water right where you're swimming. He should move down the beach where people don't swim." She glared in Gaff's direction as she said this, itching for a fight.

The boys' response was to move more in Gaff's direction. Gaff groaned again, "Oh, boy." He could guess what was coming.

The boys started wrestling and generally acting like boys, but mom didn't like this either. "Stop that fighting. You know I don't like for you to fight." Then she stood and walked down to the surf to emphasize her point.

Gaff laughed at the control the boys had over their mother and the fact that she was absolutely oblivious to it. He had seen this before, but not developed to such a fine degree. They were experts. Well-honed skills.

The wrestling stopped for a moment, but when she moved toward her chair, it resumed with greater gusto. In response, mom moved to stand in the breaking waves to shout more and louder about the boys' activities.

She was screaming now, losing control, unconcerned that other bathers saw her display of violence. "I told you not to fight. Don't go out any farther. There aren't any lifeguards on the beach. I don't want to have to swim out to save you. I know your father wouldn't move a muscle to help."

She paused in her tirade to send a scorching look in the direction of her husband who was buried in his book. No fight there. Then she turned to face her sons and continued, "He'd let you drown. Maybe that's what I should do. Let you drown so I could have some peace."

The boys splashed more. More points for them. They were really enjoying the game now.

Gaff wondered if she would know peace if she fell over it.

She yelled, "Come back over here. You're getting too close to that damned fishing line. Those hooks have barbs at the end. It'd be a bitch to get out. It'll hurt like hell if you get stuck by one."

Gaff mused about her blood pressure, probably high and getting higher, keeping the doctors in business.

The boys moved a little farther from Gaff, but as they did, they moved to get beyond the breaking waves.

Gaff thought this was a smart move because it's easier to swim in the swells. He was engrossed in this family. More than anything he was a student of human behavior and here was an extreme example.

The move to deeper water didn't escape mom's attention and she let the boys, and the entire beach, know of her displeasure. "I told you not to go that far out. You'll be caught in a riptide. What would you do then?"

Gaff pictured them ending up in Bermuda, resulting in delay of game. Until she reeled them back in, of course.

The younger boy thought the question was a serious one and answered, "Swim across it, along the shore until you're out of it."

Gaff laughed to himself. She had only to consult a tide chart to know this was low tide. Incoming tides had a lower risk of rip currents. The water was about two feet deep on the sandbar just a yard down the beach, away from him. It was perfectly safe to play on the sandbar, and a lot easier. He fished in a gap in the sandbar. AND WHY DID SHE HAVE TO YELL ALL THE TIME?

Mom interrupted her son's recitation. "Don't act smart with me, young man. I told you to stay close to the beach. I don't want to see you being pulled out."

Gaff said to himself, "Why don't you find out more about the tides?" And reeled in his line in disgust. Only the head of the minnow was on the hook. He threw it into the water.

Gaff was walking toward his cooler for more bait, when he heard, "Why did you throw that nasty stuff into the water where my children are swimming?" and the sound was getting closer.

Gaff glanced at the husband who was turning his chair, tuning out more. Amazing skill, that. He mused about the possibility of crawling into a crab hole to avoid her.

A large angry woman stomped across the sand toward him, gesturing toward the flag. "What is that? Is it absolutely necessary to have that abomination on the beach? It's an eye-sore."

She didn't expect an answer. It was only her first move in the game. Gaff worked to understand the strategy. A few more moves and he would have it.

Should he answer or wait? Fishing had taught him patience. He didn't have to wait for long in this situation.

"I've been coming here for years and my children love to swim, but your line is a hazard for them. Why don't you move?" She gestured toward the flag. "And move that horrible flag with you." Now she was waiting for his answer. Thrust and parry.

"Been coming for years, you say?"

Her lips pinched together. Gaff was surprised that her face could get harder. "You wouldn't be from New York, would you?"

Her eyes widened with surprise. "I lived there, but it was years ago. What does that have to do with the price of tea in China?"

He smiled his most winning smile. "Thought I heard the accent, just a touch. Pride myself on recognizing these things." He was on a roll, go for it, Gaff. "You're tall. Must have been a model." The years of anger hid any beauty in her face, so this was purely a wild guess. No, it was a SWAG: a scientific wild ass guess.

Her voice softened, "I was a model, but that was before marriage and children." Her eyes seemed to lose their focus. "It was so long ago, I'm amazed that you knew."

Gaff nodded and figuratively patted himself on the back. "Where do you live now?"

"Georgia, but we come here for a month every year. My husband's only here for a week, sometimes two."

Gaff cocked his head to one side. "Don't remember seeing you."

"We usually stay on the other side of the pier. We're here for a funeral and a little extra." She gestured inland. "We're staying at the motel there."

Gaff's wave took in the whole area. "How'd you discover this little backwater fishing village?" He emphasized the word "fishing" ever so slightly, subtle. No subtlety worked here, he needed a sledge hammer.

"My mother was born in the state and my family's been coming here for generations. My grandmother fished everyday on this very beach practically till the day she died." She was warming to her subject. It was all about staking claim.

"Your grandmother fished here? On this very beach? Interesting. That's a long time, isn't it?" The emphasis on the word "fished" was a little stronger this time.

"They lived over there." She waved toward the houses across the beach road. "That's why she came to this part of the beach." She was calm now, but looking to be angry.

"Where do your sons fish?"

"On the pier mostly. Been fishing for years. Swim during the day, fish at night."

Gaff pointed to the minnows running in the slough. "You noticed the baitfish running close to shore? Your sons could net for them and save money on buying bait."

She looked toward the water and her voice rose an octave. "Net for bait? Right where they're swimming?"

Gaff nodded, trying to hide his delight. So easy to manipulate! Fun. "Yeah. Run south this time of year and the predators know to find them here. Sometimes it's a right good feeding frenzy out there in front of me." It was tough to keep from laughing.

She squinted to see, scanning the water. "Predators? What kind of predators?"

Was she looking for the triangular dorsal fin of Mr. Shark?

Gaff decided to give her what she wanted. "I caught a 14 foot shark here last week." He hesitated a minute to let that sink in. "Mostly I hook drum, blues, trout. Some as long as two, three feet. Drum is the best eating to me." He stared out at the water, giving her time to catch up.

Her voice wavered. "Sharks?" She turned to look at Gaff.

"My line got tangled up last night by a spinner shark. They grab the bait and start spinning. By the time it was all done, I had to cut 50 yards off." With his hands, he showed the size of the tangle for emphasis. He took his hat off to run his hand through his hair, and to bring her eyes to his.

Her eyes were locked on his when he said, "The sandbar's down about ten feet from where your boys are. Safer there… sharks don't swim that shallow." Then he looked toward the sandbar and her eyes followed his.

"I wondered where the sandbar was."

"Moves all the time. Have to look for it sometimes."

"Oh." In her years of coming to the beach, had she not learned this?

Gaff decided to go out on that limb. "Your boys are pretty good at getting you to yell at them."

"They can't think for themselves. They're always making mistakes. And they don't hear me unless I speak over their noise."

No, not a woman of subtlety, Gaff concluded.

"And you need to keep them in line. Your job as mother, I guess. Ever heard that ad where EF Hutton whispers and everybody listens? It's true. Lower your voice to tell a secret and everybody wants to know what you're saying. Like magic, lower your voice and they listen." He waited. Would she take the bait? She had up to this point. Would she stay on the line for him to reel her in?

She was quiet for a while, standing next to Gaff but watching the boys. Then she marched over to the beach near her children. In screaming mode. "Swim over there on the sandbar." She waved in the right direction: farther down the beach. They did and she moved her loud voice back to her chair. No fare thee well to Gaff.

He noted that she wasn't ready, not yet. He wondered how long that would take. At least her voice was farther away.

# chapter 11

The next day was cloudy and the wind was blowing from the southeast. Gusts kicked up waves on the ocean. Although not a good day for sunbathing, it was a perfect day for fishing. Gaff thought his only company would be other fishermen.

Gaff was in the middle of baiting the hook after catching the biggest fish of the week when a harsh female voice announced the arrival of the clamorous clan. They probably wanted to take advantage of every minute of their time here.

Mom probably didn't let anyone speak above a whisper, while she didn't speak below a roar. He'd have to use a bullhorn to compete with that volume. No wonder the kids made so much noise.

They were the only bathers on the beach for some distance. Gaff wondered if an alert had announced her intention to come to the beach and scared the humans away. Like a shark watch... Hopefully she wouldn't scare the fish away, too. His own irritation was building.

Today she and her family staked claim to the piece of beach in front of the sandbar. Chairs, bags and this time an umbrella in what might turn out to be gale-force winds. Gaff shook his head in disgust, fully expecting his neighbor to start screaming at the wind to calm down-- and change direction, while you're at it.

Hm-m-m. Wonder if that'd work?

After going through the sunscreen ritual of Frisbees and yelling, they moved into the swimming and screaming phase of the show. The volume elevated when the boys didn't stand in three feet of water on the sandbar. Today the water was deeper: high tide. Gaff wondered if she would order the ocean to drain so her boys could swim in the shallows.

Being the kind and helpful soul he was and hoping vainly for some peace, Gaff carried his extra tide table to his neighbor.

She was so intent on getting her sons to the right place in the water that she must not have heard his approach. When he cleared his throat to get her attention, he got more than he wanted.

She barked, "What do you want now?"

Who did she think it might be, he wondered? Someone she hated? Gaff glanced at her apologetic husband to see him shrugging before Mom turned to find out who was disturbing her.

Her greeting was in a hard voice, "Oh, it's you." She must have thought she'd been speaking to her husband or did she treat everyone like that?

Then she turned to gesture at the boys, "What is wrong with you? Aren't you smart enough to find that damned sandbar today? It wouldn't move to Virginia over night."

Obviously she thought she was being funny, but the tone of her voice absolutely dripped with venom, the nastiest Gaff had ever heard. Already, he regretted attempting this act of kindness. She was like a jelly fish that would stink anyone coming close. That seemed to be her only response.

She suddenly turned on him. Her quick movement was compounded by his being lost in thought with the effect that he jumped back, startled.

She snapped again, "What do you want?"

Now Gaff really was sorry he had entered her sphere of influence: bad energy. He held out the tide table. "Thought you might need this."

She took the paper unceremoniously. No thank you. "What is it?"

"Tide table. Tells when the tide is lowest and highest. From that you can tell whether it's going in or out."

Her expression showed total lack of comprehension. She spit out her response, "I've been coming here for years, why would I need a tide table?"

"Tide's almost to the high mark now and going down. The boys are on the sandbar, but the water's deeper there now." How could she not know this if they'd been coming for years?

"Oh." Then she turned to watch her sons. Gaff was amazed to hear her call out, "Stay there. You're OK." She turned on her heel and walked to her chair without another word.

Gaff stood there in shock for a moment and then returned to his spot. People never ceased to amaze him. Just when he thought he'd seen it all, he was surprised with something or someone totally different. Fishing took his attention for the next several minutes. Fishing and watching the people walking along the surf.

Sally and Sue walked past, looking for shells. Asked about his catch today. Showed their finds, smiling as they pointed to the shark teeth. They continued their search in the high water mark and left him to his fish. They'd see him on the return trip.

Mae passed on her walk down the beach, all smiles. She waved and called out, "Better every day. Getting better." Her smile was getting bigger, too.

Sounds on the beach to his right drew Gaff's attention to a family setting up a little way down. There was laughter of young ones and discussion between the parents. Once they chose a piece of sand, everyone dropped their loads and the work of settling in began. Everyone helped. They spread towels and put the toy bag nearby. Mom and dad opened chairs and consulted on their placement. Each put sunscreen on one of the children. Dad started a sand castle with the young ones--- to give the goop time to dry, Gaff imagined. Soon all four of them moved to the water and the children jumped in.

Gaff heard the music of a lilting female voice, "Stay in front of us, please."

He glanced at the overbearing woman to his left and then back to the couple to his right talking as they watched their children play in the water. They held hands. Suddenly, the man ran into the waves and his wife teased the children, "Uh, Oh! There's a daddy shark coming for the little fish!"

Gaff almost laughed when he saw all the shananagins going on. Dad diving under the water, coming up under a child. The child squealing as he was thrown up and into a wave. Then the other child got his share of fun. Again and again, dive under, pick up a child, and throw. Laughing and shouts of "More, Daddy, more! Do me, Daddy."

Gaff remembered his children and playing in the surf. And then there were the grandchildren. He was waiting for the great-grands now. Being a daddy was the greatest thing in the world. The absolute greatest, even surpassed being the greatest fisherman. He looked out to the clouds and let them bring happy scenes from yesterday.

He was jerked from his daydreams by a harsh voice. "Some people make too much noise. My husband's having trouble reading with all that noise."

Gaff's smile shone in his voice. "It's the sound of joy and love. I enjoy hearing it myself. It's musical compared to angry yelling."

Her next comment said it all. "I don't like that either. I come for the quiet."

Before he could stop himself, Gaff said, "You must enjoy screaming at your kids. You do a lot of it." Oops. Shouldn't have said that! He readied himself for a counterattack.

His visitor was lost in her own thoughts and grumbled, "Those tide tables won't help because we get here when we get here. I don't have much choice. The kids drag their feet and don't get chores done so we can get here earlier. My husband's no help either... always reading. Says he's on vacation."

Gaff realized she probably hadn't even heard him. At least she hadn't exploded: he'd dodged the bullet on that one. "Tables tell you what to expect when you do get here."

He glanced at the tip of his rod, hoping to find a distraction there, something to require his attention. No movement. Damn!

She was talkative today. "I don't understand why there are so many crazy people around. So many negative people."

"I wonder," he said.

"Can I sit on your cooler?"

Gaff nodded to be polite. She seemed like she was going to make a day of it. Some days you just have to sit and take it. He looked to ocean and sky for comfort.

She dropped onto the cooler with a thump. Before even making touchdown, she was off and running, no preamble. "I have a dress shop and every customer through the door has some gripe. One lady this week complained that the air conditioning is set too cold. Said I could save money by having the temperature a little warmer. I like the temperature at 68 ° because I move around a lot. The heat also gets to me because I have high blood pressure."

Gaff just nodded. There was no pause in her diatribe. There was no gap into which to insert a comment.

"She didn't care about my comfort, just her own. Then another customer left in the middle of a sale because I wouldn't take her credit card. Wasn't my fault the damned thing didn't go through. Things don't always work out the way we want them to. Then I come here for a little R and R and my husband complains because I cook three meals a day for the kids. What does he expect me to do? Let them starve?"

Gaff glanced at the chubby boys and thought to himself that starvation was a very remote possibility. They looked well-fed, bordering on fat, and very unhappy.

"Was there more to his complaint? The timing maybe. Did he have something else planned?" Gaff was trying to hold up his end of the conversation.

"He said he wanted to take them to the golf game in Carolina Beach. I wouldn't let them go till after dinner. Only took an hour. Then after I hurried to get done, he decides not to go."

"Oh." But since she seemed to be waiting for more, he added, "The fight took the fun out of it, I guess."

The thought popped into his head that the fight might have been the fun. Once over, there was no desire for the outing.

"We're always fighting. One thing or another."

"Is that the only time you talk? When you fight?" Oops... where's your diplomacy, Gaff.

She stopped, stumped by this one. But the silence only lasted a moment. Her first answer was a quick no, interrupted in the middle. It's tough to interrupt a one-syllable word in the middle, so Gaff thought he might have made it at least part way into her consciousness.

"We sort through the bills and make vacation plans, stuff like that. We fight a lot, too. He gets on my nerves."

"Been married long?" Gaff thought he should move to a different topic, safer, but wasn't sure there was such an animal with her.

"Long enough to hate each other. I used to think he hung the moon, but instead of aging like wine, he's aged like vinegar." Her smile suggested that she thought she was funny. Gaff didn't.

He was nervous because of the anger so dangerously close to the surface. Gaff cautioned himself, *Take it far away from this subject, Gaff, my boy.* So he said, "There's a lot to learn from just watching." He gestured toward the water. "You can see the schools of baitfish jump and figure out that they jump to escape a bigger fish trying to eat them. You can just hear them call to each other, I don't have to sprout wings, I only have to jump higher than you do!"

She made no sound. He glanced over to see that she was watching him in confusion. No sign of comprehension. No recognition of the humor. But at least he had broken away from any source of anger although the change of topic seemed to annoy her, too. Didn't seem like he could win with this one. She said nothing.

"You can tell where the schools of fish are and what size they are by the kinds of birds preying on them. No one pushes anyone. Each has his niche. No one takes more than they need. In fact, the whole system depends on everything 'working' together. There's a kind of mutual admiration society going on here."

He listened for some hint that she was following his logic. Nothing. The more direct route was necessary. "You have high turnover at your store?"

She pushed a stray hair out of her eyes. "That's an understatement. I have a revolving door of employees. Nobody's reliable these days. Ungrateful bums." She would have gone on, but Gaff interrupted her. He didn't want to light the fire under that boiling pool of anger.

"You know other store owners on the street?" he asked.

Her lips pressed together and turned down into a frown that was emphasized by the furrows on her forehead. She cocked her head and looked at him as though he were really stupid for asking that question. "Of course, I do. I'm a member of the local business association and go to every meeting. I make it my business to know the people with the other shops on the street. Talk to them every week, if they're there. Make a point of it."

Gaff wondered if her neighbors hid in the closet when they saw her coming. "Do they have high turnover?"

"Of course, they... Well now I think of it, Joyce has the same people she started with ten years ago. Sandra lost her first employee last week. The woman got sick. Cancer, I think."

Gaff heard the unmistakable sound of churning that some people call thinking. This was evidence that the equipment up there was rarely used. He waited, patient.

"The good people must all have jobs. I get the dregs." At this she leaned over to sift a handful of sand through her fingers.

"You've described a number of problems to me. What's the common thread in all of them?"

"What do you mean?" She stopped wiping sand from her hands to look at Gaff with head cocked to one side.

Gaff hoped she'd take the bait and leave the fishing gear. He said the next slowly to give her time to keep up. "By fixing whatever is common to these problem situations, you'd fix the problems."

Her smile told him she was following... so far. "I can see that. Yeah, that's a good idea. But they're all different problems." The frown returned.

"Look at these complaints, what's the same in every one?"

She scrunched her eyes together in an exaggerated expression that indicated thinking. Gaff warned himself to tread lightly, because she might be on the verge of a breakthrough and ...

"There's nothing but stupid, selfish people. And I can't do anything about that. That's just the way the world is." She pulled her shoulders back, proud of herself and her knowledge of the world. And righteous.

" You said Sandra and Joyce don't have these problems."

"Yes-s-s?"

"There is one common thread in all these situations-- you and your behavior. What part of the problem do you contribute?"

Her voice was sharp. "What?" He could almost hear her mind snap shut like an oyster around a bit of sand. But would the result be a lustrous pearl? He just wasn't getting the sense that she was making pearls.

Need a different channel through the shoals, he thought. "The birds show us the location of fish, but sometimes they go for the bait on our hooks because it looks like an easy meal. What would you do if a pelican dove for your bait?"

"Kill him if I could. At the very least I'd hit him with a rock or shell to let him know not to mess with me."

"You'd kill him for making a mistake even though you know that most of the time, he helps you? Shows you where to throw your hook?"

"It's a mistake?"

"Yeah, sometimes when someone bumps into you, it's just a silly blunder, a slip, not a malicious act."

She said it slowly as though it were a novel idea. "A mistake?"

"Don't you bump into people by accident?" Gaff wondered if he might be introducing her to a new concept here.

"What does that have to do with the price of tea in China?"

Gaff crossed his fingers. "Everyone makes errors. If you treat it like a mistake, they're less likely to repeat it."

"Why?"

"When you punish a mistake, the person feels vindicated in lashing out. The easiest way to do that is to repeat what just upset you. It's easy to control a person who's quick to anger. And it's especially fun if they try to control everything around them."

Her frown and the blank look in her eyes indicated total lack of comprehension.

"OK, as an example, let's look at what happened yesterday when you and your family got to the beach. Every time you said not to do something, your children did something else they knew would make you angry. By keeping you angry, they kept your attention. They won because they controlled you. To a kid even anger is better than nothing. Your husband was giving nothing and you were angry. He was reading and you were engaged with the boys."

He stopped her from making excuses. "Look at that family over there. They play as a family. Sometimes the kids occupy themselves because they know their parents will play with them again later."

She looked, but Gaff wasn't sure she was seeing. No eyes to see. On cue, the mother to their right called out, "Last one in is a rotten egg!" And the whole family ran into the surf, giggling and laughing.

This got to the loud mom and she bolted. As she stormed away toward her own chair, she shot over her shoulder. "She's younger than I am. I'll bet they have more money and she doesn't have to work. She doesn't have any reason to be upset. Her kids are nice, fun to be with."

Gaff soothed himself with the thought that she would probably give him a wide berth from now on. Still, he was sad that she was so stuck in her anger that she couldn't see how she created her own misery. He didn't even know her name, another sign that she doesn't know how to relate to others. The big ones get away sometimes.

Fish weren't biting, clouds were rolling in: thunderstorms were on the way. Gaff decided to wait the storms out in his warm, dry house rather than on the cold, wet beach. He packed his gear and stood watching the family to his right putting their things together, getting ready to go. They were still laughing. Then he pulled his wagon toward home.

Just as he got to his house, the lightning crashed and the thunder rolled. Another thought came to him: maybe he would go to the pier to watch the storm from the store there. He loved storms on the water—blue clouds, crashing waves and lightning.

He wondered about the building storm in the clamorous clan. Those kids would lash out one day. They would lash out in response to their mother's controlling behavior. Or would they beat their wives instead of their mother? Too bad more people couldn't see these connections.

# chapter 12

Gaff would rather be struck by lightning than "run errands." But since rain was vacationing on the beach, he had no excuse. His wife nabbed him as he put his stuff away in the garage. Truth to tell, there was no person on the planet he would rather spend time with than this woman he married so many years ago. But the errands… he didn't like them.

Julia went over the list: groceries, more yarn, donuts from the shop in Carolina Beach. Gaff's ears perked up at that. She knew the bait to get him! Those donuts were the best fresh-made donuts in the country — maybe on the planet. He only got them on rare occasions. She usually meted them out as reward for participating in errand day. It was a game they played. Played it for decades, even when he worked every day and could pick up a dozen on the way to work. The to-do list was probably longer than she was letting on, but he'd deal with that later. For now, he'd focus on the donuts.

He put his arm around her waist and kissed the top of her head. "How about watching the storm with me from the pier house?"

Julia gave him a peck on the cheek. "I'd love to watch the storm with my honey. We'll stop there on the way to Monkey Junction."

Rain started pouring just as they got to the pier. Gaff was thankful for their good timing. There was no better place to watch the waves, clouds, lightning, and rain than from the building on the land end of the pier. It provided a magnificent show: light and action. A real natural work of art, different every time.

Errand day wasn't so bad with the bookends of storm watching and donuts. He loved to see her happy. He loved to see her, to be with her. Too bad she always had so much planned. Too bad she didn't like fishing. She'd be the perfect mate, if she did.

When he was honest with himself, and that was every day, she was the prefect mate, fishing or no.

They got extra donuts for him to take to the beach. The grandkids came over to see them that afternoon and he gave them his treats. Got to teach them about the finer things in life, Gaff thought to himself. Worth the sacrifice. The day was spent in the middle of family, laughter, and love. A good way to spend a rainy day, or any day for that matter. The sky cleared during dinner and they could see hints of the setting sun on the clouds over the ocean. The weatherman on the local news assured them that the tropical storm would pass them by, helped by himself and his loyal viewers.

After dinner, the kids left, Julia went to play bridge, and Gaff headed to the beach for night fishing. He decided that she'd be THE PERFECT wife if she didn't play so much bridge.

His friends, the stars, were waiting for him to set up the viewing stand. They loved the attention and pushed the clouds out of the way to get it. He felt that in his heart. Because he was so appreciative of their displays, they put on shows that got more and more magnificent.

Hook baited and cast into the water, glow light activated on the tip of his rod, Gaff settled into his chair for some sky watching. His thoughts flashed to Dan and wondered how he was doing. Was Dan still biking? Was he back in California and a full member of his motorcycle club? Or was he helping battered wives and their children? So many questions.

Then he tilted his head back, searching for his favorite constellations.

The sound of a slamming car door interrupted the quiet. Gaff listened for clues to what was happening. Sounded like it was in the public parking lot across the dunes from where he was sitting. The owner was making so much noise, he probably didn't think anyone was on the beach. It sounded angry, too. Firm footsteps on the walkway across the dunes. No sound for several minutes probably meant the person was taking time for the eyes to adjust? Or for removing shoes. He heard someone walking on the beach to his left. Company? They weren't coming toward him. He watched the form move toward the water. A man in long pants, not dressed for the beach. He waded into the water without regard for his clothes. Gaff was on alert now. Trouble? He pulled the phone out of his hoodie pocket—just in case. Hit the speed dial number for rescue, ready to dial… just in case.

The silhouette against the night sky kicked the waves, punched the air, shouted into the wind. Angry, very angry. Seemingly oblivious to his surroundings.

Gaff watched, patient but ready for action. Finally, the person came out of the water. Gaff breathed deeply, relieved. The man turned toward Gaff: stood watching for a while before moving in his direction. Now, he would visit the fisherman. Without a word, he plopped down on the sand next to the chair. He was wearing good clothes and still had his boat shoes on. He sat looking toward the water. Gaff looked at the stars—to give the man some time to himself.

"Shooting star," he said.

The man's eyes followed the fisherman's pointing hand. "Never seen a shooting star. Where?"

"Gone."

"That's me, a shooting star. Burning brightly and then gone."

Gaff didn't look at his companion, but thought the voice was familiar. He didn't hear a question so he didn't answer.

The man pointed to another place in the sky. "What's that? Another shooting star?"

"Meteor, probably. We just went through a field of them, sky was filled every night. What a show. This is the tail end, I reckon."

The man asked without looking at Gaff, "Are you here every night? I came to this part of the beach because I thought it would be deserted."

"To be alone? I'm here a couple of nights a week, when the wife has something planned. You must come on my off-nights. This is my spot, the place where I always sit."

"You're married, old man?" His voice said that he hadn't considered that Gaff had any other life than this one on the beach. Probably what a lot of people thought.

"I am very much married." Then he added, "For a long time to the woman of my dreams." Gaff felt the wave of warmth flood over him. He loved Julia dearly.

Gaff could hear digging in the sand.

"Fritz McNulty. That's my name." He paused for that to sink in.

"One of those movie stars with the big houses across the river?"

A smirk in his voice. "That's me. Moved into the enclave of stars, I did. Big star, big house, big failure. I wonder if my neighbors know."

"Hm-m-m."

"I come to this part of the beach to get away from all the attention. I do from time to time, just to think. Walk the beach alone and think."

Gaff took off his hat and ran fingers through his hair.

Fritz heaved a big sigh. "From the outside, everyone thinks I'm successful, but I feel like a failure on the inside."

Gaff checked the tip of his rod for fish action.

"The photogs always catch me drinking too much. Next day, I make the cover of some rag. I do drink too much. It's the only way to drown those awful feelings. Drink to kill the pain of being such a damned failure."

Gaff made a sound to let Fritz know he was following. He thought about all the people reading those rags who would like to swap lives with Fritz. All those people who thought they would be happy if only...

"Tonight, my wife told me she's leaving. Should have seen it coming. Said she couldn't take it any more."

"How so?"

Fritz didn't answer right away. "We got married years ago when I was just starting out. She tried to break into acting, but her career was going nowhere."

"Must happen to a lot of people."

"It does, but it means more when it's happening to you. She was disappointed, but she was smart enough to see the truth of it and the blessing. We were in love. So she threw herself into helping get my career off the ground."

"Sounds like perfect timing."

"She helped me figure things out. Listened around town and brought me information that I couldn't get any other way. Women talk a lot when they have their nails done. Also in the hair stylist's chair. She learned a lot that helped me."

"My guess is that the men talked to the women to get it off their chests. Yep, good to have help like that."

"Especially in Hollywood. She also helped me learn my roles—helped me grow as an actor." He paused, probably remembering.

Gaff ran fingers through his hair again and put the cap back on his head.

"I didn't realize it then, but those were the good old days. The struggle and winning against all odds. Only dawned on me tonight, now, talking with you."

Gaff checked the tip of his rod and then returned his gaze to the night sky. "Helps to talk. Must be tough for you to find anyone to talk to."

"She was my best friend, my only close friend. Other than that, I talk to the water, to the waves." He nodded toward the water. "That's what I was doing over there."

"We have that in common. In my estimation, Mother Water gives the best advice, especially in matters of the heart."

"Mother Water?"

"We are part of her because we're mostly water and originally we came from the water. I think of her as a spirit of the earth, with wisdom earned through ages of watching us make fools of ourselves."

"Are you saying that God's in the water?"

"In everything is my guess."

"See what you mean... I do see what you mean. Well, I've been telling Mother Water my troubles for years and haven't gotten any advice at all from her."

"You have to listen for it."

"Boy could I use some help right now. My career is going down the tubes, I haven't been offered any decent parts lately. I hate the part I'm doing now. Last week, I got kicked off the set. My marriage is falling apart. I'm estranged from my children.

They want more money…always telling me I'm stingy… Truth is that my manager lost most of my money. Now, I don't have a great lot any more. Not enough to satisfy my children or support my wife's spending."

His voice lowered when he continued, "We all fight. All the time. The stress sets my nerves on edge. This is the last straw." He paused for a deep breath. "The director told me I only get one more chance, and then he'll move on to his second choice for the part. We're still early enough in the filming."

Gaff could feel the depths of Fritz's despair. "You're feeling lost, like you don't know where to go?"

"Worse, there is nowhere to go. None. Kaput. Done."

"Can't be that bad. You trust me enough to talk. If there's one person you trust, life's getting better."

"I tell you, but it's not a matter of trust. I don't trust anyone. Been tricked too many times. I can talk to you because the whole thing will be in the press tomorrow. All the sordid details of my life." A pause and then he smirked, "And book to follow, written by the poor, beaten-down ex-wife." He threw a shell toward the water. Was throwing the shell symbolic of throwing his life away, giving up hope?

"Are you interested in fixing it or just moaning and groaning?"

"What do you mean fix it? I can't do anything. It's too late."

Gaff gazed at the stars, "Is it? Is it too late to figure out how to keep your job? How to make good with that one last chance?"

"Well, yeah, that I might be able to do. But the whole world has taken sides and most of them against me. What could I do? What could I ever have done? The media kill me every time they get a chance."

"The media. And who else?"

Fritz went into a tirade, gesturing dramatically throughout the monologue. "The director, the producer, all the other actors on the set. My agent doesn't get me auditions for good roles. This one stinks. And when I go home, I get it from my wife and my kids. Even my mom has it out for me. Everyone tells me what to do, but nobody listens to my side. They can't see how bad it is for me. I don't get any respect."

"A long list. Even your mother?"

The steam was gone and Fritz was limp, shoulders slumped. "Even my mother. Just tonight she told me I'm being a jackass. And that's something coming from her. That's the strongest word she uses. She hates me. They all hate me."

Fritz added quietly, "I hate me."

Gaff blew a silent whistle. "Now that's bad. You may be right. Even your mom's against you. The worst is that you hate yourself." He sat in appreciation of the situation, looking to Mother Water for answers.

Fritz dragged his fingers through the sand before he added, "Mom doesn't really hate me. She loves me. She wants the best for me, at least that's what she says. Mom just doesn't understand what I'm up against. No one can. It's tough out there."

Gaff patted his hand on his chest. "And in here."

Fritz only nodded.

Gaff felt his loneliness, his despair. "From your point of view, everybody has turned against you."

Again, Fritz nodded, head bowed from the weight of it all.

Gaff waited for more.

A grand sigh filled the silence. "I was having an affair and my wife found out. I was really stupid. That's why she's leaving."

"Is it?"

"Well, it's probably a combination of the drop in income and the affair."

"Hm-m-m. You told her lately how pretty she is?"

Gaff watched the stars, but he could feel eyes boring into him. Fritz was probably going back over the recent past.

"No, not in a while."

"You told her how smart she is? You thank her lately for helping you all these years?"

"No-o-o."

"Tell her how much you love her?"

Silence.

"Have you figured out why you had the affair?"

Fritz didn't answer.

"Talk it over with her? The drinking and the affair were probably caused by the same thing, the same hurt. Might want to talk that over with your best friend."

"My best friend?"

"Your best friend."

"How could that change the fact that the whole stinking world has turned against me? How can that change the fact that I fell from the top of the heap to also-ran?"

"Just might feel better to share your feelings with your best friend. Get them out on the table to look at."

A snort of disgust. The words were thrown in anger like a weapon. "I don't have a best friend. Didn't you hear me? The whole world is against me, including my soon-to-be-ex-wife. I'm no longer the golden-haired boy. I've become a troll to them. That's what they always see, no matter what."

"A troll. Do you still act like the golden-haired boy?"

"What?"

"Do you still act like the golden-haired boy? Do they treat you different even when you're the wonderful person you can be?"

"I am a troll and that's the way they treat me."

"I'm trying to understand who has changed, you or them? Are you being shunned for no reason or because you changed?"

"Does that matter?"

"Humor me. If we start at the beginning I might be able to understand what's going on. Remember back to the beginning of your career. Who were you then? How did you behave?"

"What does that matter?"

"Play along with me and I'll see if I can show you. How was it when you started acting?"

"I was young and handsome. That got me noticed. Got a lot of leading roles in romances."

"Romantic leads. You've aged so you no longer get those roles."

A nod in the angry silence.

"Have you aged gracefully?"

"What?"

Gaff said slowly. "When you were young, you got parts of the handsome love interest."

Fritz nodded again.

"You're older and should be in line for roles of the older and wiser gentleman. Or the seasoned tough guy. You're an actor, but you can't act the part of the young lover any more. What about acting the part of the loving mature man instead? When you change and grow, your goals have to change. How has your attitude changed? How has your behavior changed? Have you grown?"

"Right about now I'd take anything."

"That's not the attitude to have, nor does it answer the question. You told me you have a part. When you go to work, do you have a spring in your step, proud to be there, doing your part?"

Fritz ran both hands through his hair before answering. His voice was low, slow. "Can't honestly say I do."

"How do you feel?"

"Honestly, this part is lousy—beneath me. I should be doing better at this time in my life. I think about the guys my age who get the good roles, the meaty ones with substance, and I feel like a failure."

"When you were young, you didn't go to work depressed because you weren't at the top."

"No, but when you're young, it's OK to be at the bottom. You're just starting out. Not good to end at the bottom."

"How did you earn better roles?"

"I worked hard. Went the extra mile to do my best."

"Doing your best got you better parts. Learning and growing got you better parts."

"Yeah."

"When did you stop growing? Is that when you stopped getting 'good' parts?"

Gaff was patient, giving Fritz time to think.

"I see what you mean. When I started thinking I knew all I needed to know about acting, my career stalled. You're saying to focus on getting better in these new kinds of parts to get more of them? And better ones."

"It's a thought. You're frustrated and what do you do with that feeling?"

"Maybe I haven't been so nice to people at work. Maybe I'm taking my frustration out on them… And on my family."

Gaff pointed out another meteor burning through the atmosphere until it was gone. "We're never angry for the reason we think we are."

He pointed to a pinpoint of light up there. "See that star? The only way it can make enough light for us to see it is to keep making explosions, one after the other. If the explosions stop, or get smaller, we don't see the star the same. Maybe we can't see it at all."

Fritz was gazing upward, hearing.

"That star doesn't keep making the explosions so we can see it, but because there's an internal drive to make explosions. The star doesn't know it's a star to us, it just knows it has a job. As long as it does its job, we see it and call it a star."

"Are you saying I became more interested in being a 'star' than in doing a good job in my roles?"

"Could be. That's a question to ask yourself."

"Yes. To ask myself. And if I did, then maybe I acted too much like the 'big star' instead of…"

"The important question is what you really want to do with your life. Now. What adds meaning to your life? If you had just one year to live, what would you do?"

"Good question. I'm not sure how to answer it. Not any more."

"Consider the question seriously. Once you figure out what's most important to you, you can do things that fit. Get your priorities straight and then change your actions to suit."

The two men sat watching the night sky together. The one was seeing it for the first time, really seeing it. Gaff could sense that Fritz was finding himself again. How does it happen that we can "know" who we are as young men and forget when we become "mature"? How is that?

"Sometimes success is harder to handle than failure. Too easy to get distracted by the trappings. Remember, they're just trappings, superficial. Keep your eye on what's really important to you."

Without a warning, Fritz jumped to his feet and jogged toward the walkway. He yelled back over his shoulder, "I remember what's important now and I have to tell her. I hope it's not too late."

Gaff said to himself, "It's not too late. Not quite yet. She's there waiting to hear just those words from you."

Gaff turned his eyes toward the heavens.

There's another shooting star! Amazing what the night brings right to you. Right to you.

# chapter 13

Harry was sitting on Gaff's piece of beach when Gaff finally arrived the next day. No fishing gear, no chair. He looked miserable and lonely sitting there on the sand.

Gaff pulled his wagon down on the beach, to his spot, and started setting up his gear. Today he put the flag up first. "Afternoon, Harry." Chair placed in front of the wagon and cooler beside the chair. Rod holders hammered into the sand and rods placed in them, at the ready. Gaff worked at his regular pace, patient, but Harry remained in silence.

Harry didn't say anything with words, but spoke worlds with his posture and his expression. Grief, unutterable sadness. Deep to the core sadness. Lost-in-a-well with no way out sadness. He said nothing. Gaff waited, patient. Must be Harry's wife: something bad.

Gaff put bait on the hooks and cast the lines out into the water. Finally, he sat in his chair in the same spot he'd occupied for years. Waiting for the fish. Waiting for the big one.

Harry heaved a sigh, but the words stuck in his throat. "She's going, Gaff. She's going and the kids want to put her in the hospital. I don't know what to do. They say it'd be better for her, and for me. Hard thing to have your wife die in the house you've shared. I don't know what to do."

"You ever ask her what she wants?"

"Nah."

"What do you want?"

"For her not to die."

Gaff was touched by his friend's grief. "Asking for that's like trying to hold back the tides and the waves and the clouds."

"I already miss her." Harry used his handkerchief.

"When'd all this happen?"

"Visiting nurse came to the house yesterday and told me the end's coming."

"How long?"

"Not sure, but the nurse upped her morphine. Our daughter Jayne called the other kids and Hospice. I'm here because I didn't want to be there when they arrived."

"You and Jayne getting along better?"

"Had a lot of time sitting beside Doris. We sorted through the old stuff and I told her I'm sorry for things I did before I understood. I feel better. Think she does, too."

"Isn't this what you always did? Run out when there were tough times?"

Harry's voice was so low Gaff leaned over to hear. "Guess so. Couldn't stand to hang around… when I didn't know how to fix it."

"Maybe just being there's the best thing for your children."

"Just being there?"

"Yeah, they're sad and might like to see that you are, too. Might also like a hug from their dad. Just a hug to say he loves them."

"Just a hug. But men are supposed to be strong, not cry. I'm afraid I'll break down in front of them."

"That's a lie told to scare us. It's really a sign of strength to let other people see that we have feelings and that sometimes we just don't know what to do."

"I was always told it was my job to fix things that was broke."

"Sometimes only a hug can fix what's broken. Like a broken heart that needs love to mend."

Harry nodded as he searched his pockets. He pulled out a handkerchief and wiped around his eyes. "Sounds crazy, but Doris came to me last night. Must've been a dream, but I didn't think I was sleeping."

"That doesn't matter. What did she say?"

"She ain't been able to talk for days, too sedated. I talk to her. Jayne talks to her. She sometimes moves her eyes to let us know she hears, but she can't say anything."

Gaff looked to Mother Water for guidance, for the right thing to say.

Harry blew into his handkerchief. "Last night I had trouble sleeping. Worried, you know. Thinking of all the things I didn't say. Can't say them with Jayne around." Was he listing those things in his head?

"She came to stand right there at the end of our bed. Right there, looking down at me. And she smiled… She smiled her sweet, loving smile. She stood there for a long while, not saying anything. Then she told me she loves me and that she understands everything now. She told me that I'm a good man, but that I had weaknesses I couldn't resist. Even though I gave in to temptations, she still loves me just as she had in the first years. She said it over and over that I was a good man and to forgive myself for all those mistakes. She said to live the best I could now and to be a good Daddy to the kids, because they were the most important things in my life now." Tears overflowed his eyes and streamed down his face, following the creases left by the years of life experience.

Gaff gave his friend privacy by walking down to check his lines. He reeled them in and replaced the bait. As he was casting the second one, Harry came to stand next to him. Gaff adjusted the line and replaced the rod in its holder. The two men stared out at the waves.

"She's not dead yet so couldn't be a ghost. Had to be a dream."

Gaff said softly, "It's not important whether you saw a ghost or just her spirit coming to you. Her words are what's important. Remember all of her words. Might even write them down to help you remember."

The shame in Harry's voice was palpable. "She told me she knew about the other women. She knew they didn't mean anything to me. That didn't make it any more right, but she said she knew and I didn't have to worry about telling her in front of Jayne. She let me off the hook about that. But she said that instead of making it up to her, I should make it up to the kids. She told me she could see that Jayne and I were doing better and she knew that things would be better with the others, too. That's why she was going to join her mother and …" Harry's words were covered by sobs. In a whisper that was barely audible, Harry said, "I'm so sorry. I'm so sorry that I was such a fool. Such a fool. I hurt my good wife and my kids. I didn't understand what was important. I didn't understand at all."

Gaff wanted to hug Harry, to show him how it's done, but didn't want to embarrass his friend on the beach. So he had to be satisfied with an arm around Harry's shoulder. Maybe they could talk later about how to be a "daddy." He also decided to spend the next day with Julia doing anything she wanted to do. Anything. Just so she knew how important she was to him.

Harry said in a stronger voice, "I know you were always a good dad to your children and I see you with your grandkids. Maybe I could learn some things from you?"

"If you look inside your heart, Harry, I bet Doris would help you with that, too. She did a pretty good job of rearing those children and she probably has some ideas about what you could do to continue her work."

"I bet she would. Was always telling me what I should do." Then Harry turned toward the parking lot. "The kids'll be needing me. After all, someone needs to be strong to hold the family together... and I think Doris elected me."

**chapter 14**

Must be heading into a weekend, Gaff smiled as he looked around the busy beach. The temperatures were in the high 70's, with not a cloud in the sky. The sun was strong and hot and the water was flat calm for the ocean. Perfect day for the beach and someone must have sent the memo to everyone in the state. Not very good for fishing. Or was it?

Gaff felt the warmth on his skin, cooled by the breeze from the water. A wonderful combination of heat and cool.

The clamorous clan was in their usual spot in front of the sandbar, yelling. The giggling family with the "shark daddy" was on the other side to provide Gaff with the contrast, he imagined. Always the lesson to learn, to strengthen.

His next door neighbors were there with four generations visiting, spread out like a city on the sand. They brought an open tent where mothers sat in a circle around the young children. There was a castle-building team and a gossip group. Or so it seemed. And then there were the swimmers—lots of those.

There was a group of young people beyond the clamorous clan. Six or eight of them from what Gaff could see. They had fishing gear, but the girls were in very small, Gaff would say tiny, bathing suits and pranced from chairs to water with regularity and well-practiced bounces. There was a lot of standing and talking with full-body gestures as well as hand gestures. They were happy—and fishing, in a manner of speaking. The presence of beer bottles at this time in the morning ruined the picture for Gaff. He'd seen this before.

A laughing voice came from behind as Gaff watched the young people.

"I love your Jolly Roger!" The voice was jolly and colored with an English accent.

Gaff turned to see a mature man in tee shirt and shorts. Gray hair, cut short. Pleasant features, nothing special really. He was smiling, but the smile turned into a grin when Gaff turned to face him. A truly happy man.

"This is the first time I've ever been here. Been all over the world but never to this beach in North Carolina."

"Now you have."

"And I love it. I'm staying in a hotel right on the water a little way up the coast." He looked up and down at the buildings lining the beach. "Don't see any hotels like that here."

"Nope. This is a fishing village, not a fancy resort."

"Guess I won't be staying here then. I like being able to see the ocean from a room high enough to enjoy the whole thing, but not so high that I miss the details. When I get out of the elevator in the lobby, I turn to the left to go to the restaurant and to the right to the pool. I like that kind of convenience."

"Where in England do you call home?" Gaff grinned his appreciation of this unabashed display of JOY.

"Now, probably nowhere. I have a flat in London, but I'm rarely there. Don't like cold weather, so I spend a lot of time in the south during the winter. South Africa, Egypt, Greece, really any place that catches my fancy."

"And the summer?"

"Some time in London to see my sons, but then I'm off again."

"Obviously you don't work, but you must have had a good job to set you up so well."

"Won the lottery."

"Really."

"Yep. But before that I did have a good job, one I loved. I was a master printer. Worked for the government in London. I did a good job, but the retirement wasn't all that great. Bought a lottery ticket every week. Finally, my number hit. That was about ten years ago."

"I've never met anyone who won the lottery. I've read about people who win big and declare bankruptcy within five years. You don't seem to have that trouble."

"First off, had a cousin said he could invest it for me and help me double it."

"Did he?"

"Nah. Figured if he was that good, he'd be rich and not a poor working slob like he is. Instead, I studied it and ended up buying some gold, some Euros, and just putting most of it into savings. Instead of taking the full bit of money at one time, I decided to take the yearly payments and that way I know how much I have to spend every year. And it's more, too, that way." He smiled, happy with his decision.

"So you travel all the time? Quit your job right away?"

"Not right away. Sort of felt my way through it all. You might call me cautious. Even now I take the odd job from time to time. I work as a consultant. Gives me something to do and I keep my hand in it."

"It is good to know that people appreciate your skill."

"A reason to get up in the morning other than the occasional golf match. I liked my job, I did. So I enjoy taking an assignment occasionally."

"And you don't have relatives who want to involve you in their schemes or people who want to sell you a great business idea?"

"All the time. But I have my budget and those wild schemes don't fit into that budget. I did get caught up in some of those fantasies early on, but I learned that most are pipe dreams. After I lost some money, I established rules for myself. Helps that I get it doled out a little at a time. Use that as an excuse. Works well for me."

"And you don't have a wife?"

"Had one of those along the way. A wife and three sons. I decided to keep the sons and let the mother go. She and I didn't see eye-to-eye and parted ways long ago. In fact, she thought buying those lottery tickets was wasted money."

"She doesn't say that now, I'll bet."

"Have to give her credit. She never tried to get any of it. There were other women who did. Now, I stay clear of that."

"Aren't you lonely? Don't you miss having someone to travel with?"

"I have friends. Travel with some of them. Sometimes I travel with the sons."

Gaff considered the possibility of being without his wife for long periods of time, of not seeing his children. The feelings he got were uncomfortable: he'd be unhappy without his family. For him, the travel would lose its luster quickly when he started missing them.

"You read much?" Gaff asked.

"Hunh?"

"When you're alone. Do you read books?"

"Some, but mostly I stay out seeing and doing until I'm tired enough to sleep."

Gaff considered this. Maybe the old saying was right: "Ignorance is bliss."

"I think I'd miss my family too much." Then he realized he didn't know the man's name and hadn't introduced himself. Odd.

Gaff stuck a hand out to his visitor. "Name's Gaff."

They shook. "Kevin."

"You're very friendly. Meet a lot of people on your travels?"

"I do and see them the next time round. Friends all over the planet." His grin expressed his appreciation of his good fortune.

"You keep in touch at other times?"

"Sometimes we email, but mostly I just see them the next time around. Some I see a couple times a year, others I see every couple years."

They sat for a while in silence watching the water and the birds and the sky and the people walking the beach. Quiet, a time filled with pleasure and gratitude for the gifts of nature, gifts of all sorts. No sharing: just sitting.

Gaff wondered if the travel experiences were enough to substitute for real friends, for relationships with people who loved you, rich or poor. He contemplated the beach around him. But mostly he swam in a deep appreciation for his friendships. Those relationships added texture to his life, a network of loving support. Complexity and drama sometimes, too, but that was the meat of life, wasn't it? Or should he call it the fish?

# chapter 15

Kevin was still sitting next to Gaff when they heard a man and woman arguing and then a door slamming. They were still watching the birds diving for fish as they heard a faltering gait on the boards of a walkway over the dunes. Kevin was standing next to Gaff as he reeled his hook in to change the bait and cast it out again when they heard a woman muttering. The sound was getting louder, coming closer. When they turned to retake their seats, they found a woman sitting in Gaff's chair. She was disheveled and listing slightly.

Kevin looked at Gaff, eyes wide, and said, "So long, Buddy, I'll leave you to this. Think I'll drive down the coast and explore Fort Fisher. Then maybe take the ferry to Southport. See you next time round." As he came to Gaff's chair, he nodded a greeting to the woman and moved quickly past.

Gaff sighed. He wondered what Mother Water had brought to him this time. He took a seat on the cooler.

Hm-m-m, pretty comfortable, he thought.

Her words almost slurred, "Afternoon. Mind if I borrow your chair? Forgot to bring mine down."

"Nope." Gaff looked at the tip of his rod, thought it wiggled like a fish was snagged on the hook. Wondered if he had seen her on the beach before.

"Name's Gaff." He nodded in her direction.

"Harriet." Her head wobbled from side to side.

Gaff paused a tick to see if she would continue. Nothing. Watching the water was healing. Let her watch.

Then his curiosity got him. "You renting one of the houses on the beach?"

"One over there." She waved in the direction of the houses lining the dunes. Not much help. Too general.

"Just got here?"

"Couple of hours ago. Why do you ask?"

"I know most people on the beach and you're new. That's all. Curious."

She sighed a big one. "Makes sense."

Gaff could smell booze even from his seat on the cooler.

Another sigh. "My husband wanted to come here to get away from everything. Says he needs a break. From what, I want to know? From what? We argue just as much here as we do at home. Fight, fight. Seems that's all we do. Fight. We can do that just as well at home and home is more convenient. Now he's threatening to go away on a vacation by himself. Don't know why."

Gaff didn't have anything to say so he watched the fish swimming in the trough and waited. He inspected the tip of his rod and the place where the line went into the water.

Another deep sigh and the air was so saturated with alcohol that Gaff felt tipsy.

"Whole idea was to have all the kids come to the beach for the weekend. We came early to get things ready and they arrive on Friday. I love having the whole family together. Doesn't happen that much any more. They all have their own lives."

"How many kids you have?"

"Altogether we have five. He had a boy and two girls from his first marriage and I had a boy and a girl from mine. We didn't have any together."

"This is the second marriage for both of you."

"Both of us lost spouses. His wife died of cancer and my husband was in a car wreck. We've been married for twenty years."

"That means all the children lived with you."

She nodded so that her chin almost touched her chest, or did she nod off for a few?

"How long have you been drinking like this?" Gaff blamed his wild abandon on the drunken air he was breathing.

Harriet raised her eyebrows in surprise, her head wobbled on her shoulders. "How do you know I drink at all?"

Gaff waved away the cloud she exhaled. "You've only been sitting here for a few minutes and it smells like a distillery already."

She wobbled her head and pursed her lips to express indignation. "Fishermen drink. Is it a crime for me to have a nip once in a while?"

"Harriet, you have had far more than a nip. You're soused. And it's early in the afternoon. You have a problem." Gaff excused his bluntness by thinking that drunks didn't respond well to subtlety, but he also knew he didn't have much patience with them either. He asked Mother Water to help him with that.

Another feeble attempt to straighten herself in the chair and a wobble of her head. She worked her lips as though trying to regain control of them. "I don't have a problem. I can stop any time I want."

"Is that what you fight about, you and your husband?"

Her mouth formed into a pout. "Some. He's a controlling bastard."

"Why? Because he wants you to stop drinking?"

"I can stop any time I want. Any time."

"Why don't you then?" Gaff tried to squelch the irritation he felt building. He searched within him for some little pocket of patience.

"Don't want to. I like to drink. I feel better when I've had a nip or two."

Gaff grimaced. "Or ten. How did you get started? And when?"

Harriet turned to look at the group of young people. "They're in high school, wouldn't you say?"

Gaff turned to follow her eyes and nodded. "High school's about right."

"I was probably a little younger than they are. When I was a freshman in high school I dated a senior. They all drank and I did, too."

"You drank to fit in with the older crowd?"

"He thought it was cute when I got drunk. Said I danced better." She smiled and licked her lips unevenly. "I sometimes got hot when we were dancing and didn't mind taking some clothes off, too."

She shifted in the chair and returned her eyes to the water. Her lips worked in an odd way as she remembered the days of youth and beauty. "He liked it when his friends could see what a nice figure I had. We came to the beach like those kids. A whole group of us. It was a lot of fun. Sun and swimming and the drinking added."

"So your first boyfriend encouraged you to drink. I'll bet that's not all he encouraged you to do."

The corners of Harriet's mouth drooped suddenly. "He went off to college and met someone there. Never even came back for summers. Always went to her town and worked there. Humpf. Bastard."

Gaff looked at the tip of his rod for signs of a catch. And sad thoughts raced through his mind.

"When I was in college, I tried drugs, but never really got into that."

"Liquor is a drug."

Harriet's head snapped around to look at Gaff. "What do you mean? Having a few's not like dropping acid. It's just having a few drinks. Just to loosen me up to have fun."

"I can understand imbibing at a party or at dinner or on a special occasion, but you're drunk on the beach in the middle of the afternoon."

"So?"

"When do you start drinking?"

She licked her lips again and posed them in a pout that was supposed to look attractive. "It depends."

"Give a range then."

"Sometimes a Bloody Mary for breakfast. Sometimes wine at lunch."

Gaff took a deep breath to calm. "And sometimes you start with a glass of vodka with your morning coffee."

Her head seemed so loosely stuck on her neck that Gaff was afraid it might fall off with one of her wobbles. She straightened her back and her shoulders. "Well maybe. Maybe once in a while."

"That's what your husband hates. That you're someone else all the time. Did he marry you knowing you drink this much?"

Her eyes widened in shock. "I didn't drink much when we were dating. I had children at home. I had responsibilities."

"So after you got married you really let loose and stayed soused."

Her pout got more exaggerated. "Well, no. I took care of five children. I got them off to school and then I'd have a nip to fortify me for work. I kept a pretty little flask in my desk just in case I got nervous during the day. A lot of my friends had their pills and I had my flask. What's the difference?"

"You lose your job soon after you married?"

"No, I worked for a year and then we decided that I should stay home for the kids. They needed someone home when they got in from school."

"To fix them milk and cookies."

"They all had activities after school and I carried some around while other mothers took the others. We shared the job."

"And you kept the pretty little flask in your purse just in case you got stressed out."

She looked at Gaff with a big smile. "Well, yes I did. It did come in handy. Lucky I thought to carry it with me. Driving all those kids to scouts and sports was tough. So many kids and so many things to juggle."

She looked at the ocean again and became very serious. "It was all so stressful to maintain that schedule. So stressful. A few little nips would fix it all. Fix it all." These last words she said with emphasis.

"Your husband worked and left you with the children. When he retired, he found out how much you were drinking."

She shook her head so violently that she almost fell out of the chair. "He accused me of drinking too much years ago. So I cut down when he was at home."

"But he's at home all the time now and sees it all."

"He's retired and the kids are on their own so I retired, too. He does what he wants for retirement and I do what I want."

"He plays golf and you drink."

Her head snapped around toward Gaff again. "How did you know?"

"I'm psychic, Harriet, I'm psychic... Harriet, you are an out and out alcoholic. I'd be angry with you, too, if you were my wife. What's amazing is that he's still with you."

Gaff was shocked by the waves of emotion that propelled this indictment. He worked to calm himself and to regain control to do whatever he could to help. He reached over to run his hand through the sand to reconnect with nature. He found a cigarette butt in the sand which escalated his anger, instead of diminishing it.

Harriet started to cry softly and to hoist herself out of the chair. She was so inebriated and the chair was so short, so close to the ground, that her attempt to push to a standing position resulted in her sprawling on the sand. The best she could do in her condition was to get to her hands and knees. Gaff would have thought it was comical if it weren't so pitiful. The more she floundered, the more she cried. Finally she was sitting on her heels sobbing into her hands. Gaff hoped she didn't get sand in her eyes. She rejected his offer of help and stayed where she was.

Gaff said firmly, "Sit in my chair until you can travel on your own feet."

"I want to go home. You're being horrible to me." Sobs shook her shoulders.

Gaff regretted hurting her feelings, but that contrasted with his honest nature. He turned to the ocean and said out loud. "Mother Water, I do need your help now. This woman needs help."

Harriet became indignant. "I do not need help. I am perfectly fine." She finished this with a maneuver that resulted in her sitting upright on the sand accompanied by unladylike noises. Huffing and puffing.

Gaff closed his eyes to pull in patience. "OK, Harriet, you don't need help. You intended to sit on the sand. You want sand all over your face and clothes. And it is perfectly all right that you are so out of control that you cannot walk to your house or even get back into the chair."

"I'm sitting here to gather my thoughts, that's all." She tried brushing sand off with hands that didn't seem connected to her brain.

Gaff shook his head, looking at the sand in thought. "I warn kids that this happens when you drink young. Eventually the booze controls everything. You can lose your whole life."

"Are you talking to me?" She straightened herself as though she were a strand of pearls loosely strung together. Another attempt to brush away the sand, but her hands refused to obey. They made random passes on her blouse.

"Is it too late for you? Don't you want to see your children clearly? Don't they bring you enough joy for the real you to be with them?"

"I can stop any time I want." That was her refrain, he gathered.

"Then do. Stop for this weekend with your children and grandchildren so you can enjoy being with them, truly being with them. And so they can enjoy you."

Gaff gave this time to work its way through the fog in her brain. He turned his attention to his rod: to put on new bait and cast it out again. While he was there, he considered the situation and felt the depths of helplessness. He had gone through his own time of romancing the bottle, but had never lost whole days of his life. He realized what he was missing on his own. No one had to tell him. The pendulum had moved to the other side for some time and now was resting calmly in the middle. Wine with dinner on occasion was fine, but that was it. He remembered how it felt to drown his unhappiness in the well drinks.

Gaff settled himself on the cooler just in case Harriet could make it back to the chair. He waited in the silence for the answers to come.

Harriet blurted out, "Everyone tries to tell me how to live my life. I have a right."

"Yep. You do have a right to live your life as you choose."

Harriet's head wobbled again in self-righteous agreement.

Gaff cut her off before she could respond. "But just as you can choose how to live your life, the people around you can also choose. If you choose to drown yourself in that bottle, they might decide to avoid you while you do it. Drinking that much is a form of slow suicide and no one wants to watch you kill yourself."

Her lips worked into a pout that expressed distaste. "Suicide?"

"The booze is a poison that kills your organs, including your brain."

"I feel good, not like I'm dying." She tossed her head to emphasize the thought and almost tipped over onto the sand again.

"That's part of the illusion. Drunk, you probably do things that embarrass them or insult them. That's killing their desire to be with you. Do friends avoid you?"

"My friends have things to do, too. We aren't joined at the hip."

Gaff interrupted her litany of denials. "You watch television?"

Harriet's eyes widened, startled by the change of topic. "Some."

"Ever watch those shows about the ocean?"

"Some."

"There're volcanoes and what they call vents on the ocean floor. Ever hear about that?"

"Yes... I did see a show about that. Why?"

"You remember about the vents? Noxious gases come up through those vents. The kind of gases that propel lava out of volcanoes."

"Yes? Sounds familiar."

"Some animals adapted to living in that water filled with poisonous gases. The gases taint the water—make it into acid."

"Yes?"

"Those animals live segregated from other animals because that water is poison to the 'normal' ocean animals."

"I seem to remember that. The ones living in the vents were only able to live there. They changed to suit that water. They look strange."

"Which would you rather be? One of the animals who have to stay close to the vent or an animal with more choices?"

Harriet ran her tongue over her lips, thinking. "That's easy. I want to be free to live anywhere." She bounced to punctuate her statement.

"Which animal are you like now?"

"I'm not an animal at all. I'm human. I can live anywhere I want."

"Can you?"

Harriet frowned. "Of course I can."

"The next county over is dry. Don't sell liquor there at all. Could you live there if your family moved?"

Another frown. At least she was thinking.

"I could live there."

"You're used to living where you can get a drink anytime and a lot of people drink around you. There, if you did bring in booze, you'd be the only one drinking so you'd stand out and they wouldn't like it. They'd ostracize you."

"Ostracize me?"

"Yep. You wouldn't have friends. You'd be alone while the rest of your family fit in."

Thoughts were slogging around in the soggy mass of her brain.

"You'd be like a black hole in the sky that gobbles up other stars. People would stay away. They'd be afraid you'd suck them up."

This change of direction was too much for Harriet and she held her arm straight out toward Gaff, palm out. "No, no, no. We're not talking about stars and black holes. We're talking about cute little sea creatures and their ugly neighbors who live in nasty pollution."

"Which do you want to be?"

"I'm a cute little sea creature. A seahorse, maybe." She smiled crookedly at the thought. Probably remembering the cute Harriet that started drinking decades ago, blind to the marks left by years of liquor.

"You are a seahorse when you're not drinking, but when you're drunk, you're one of the mutants."

Deep creases formed between her eyebrows. "I'm a mutant?"

"You are that. Few can live in the pollution you call home."

"I'm a mutant and not a seahorse?" She slumped, dejected.

"Difference between you and them is that you can choose to be a seahorse or a mutant. It's up to you. Sea creatures don't have any choice. They're born one way or the other."

Harriet looked at hands folded in her lap.

Gaff looked to the water, to the birds diving for fish, and then his reel sang the news of a fish on his hook. Had she really taken the bait?

## chapter 16

Shortly after Harriet managed to levitate herself back to the house, Gaff heard a door slam. Sounded like a repeat of earlier and he groaned. He wondered what had happened now and if his new acquaintance was coming back. He didn't have the courage to look. Right now, he just wanted to fish: cast the bait out and reel the fish in.

A male voice startled him from behind, "Hello, I'm Sam Teabar, Harriet's husband. I came to apologize."

"Name's Gaff. No apology necessary."

"Mind if I sit on your cooler? I won't take your chair like my wife did."

"Be my guest."

Sam Teabar settled himself on the cooler and looked out at the water. "I saw you when we got here. Noticed your flag. You fish here all the time?"

"Yep."

"Then you'll get to meet the family this weekend."

He looked out at the water, probably appreciating the beauty and the peace.

"Harriet came into the house mumbling something about being a seahorse and not a mutant. Said she was going to show you. She went to bed for a while, to sleep it off. She'll start all over when she gets up. Always does. I don't understand how she does it. Or why."

Gaff listened because that's what Sam needed.

"If I thought she was drinking this much when the kids were young, I would have left her and gotten the children away from her. We talk about it now, me and the kids. Turns out she was good for them in a perverse way. None of them drinks a drop. They don't want their children to go through what they did."

Both men watched the progress of a motorboat far away, close to the horizon. Looked small from here. It was moving, but it seemed slow at this distance. Slow, but steady. A fishing boat? Charter or private? Idle musings.

"I'm sorry Harriet was a bother. She's a drunk and I don't know what to do about it. I'm ready to give up."

"Wouldn't blame you."

"I've tried every argument."

"You can't do it for her. She's got this one."

"I understand that. Still, you can't blame a guy for trying. I still love the woman I married. If I could only find her."

More silence, healing.

"What is this about seahorses and mutants anyway?"

"Just a story I used to show her how her life is going. Be interesting to find out what she took from it."

"A story?"

"We talked about the mutants living around the vents in the ocean floor. They're animals adapted to live in the toxic stuff coming through those vents. She decided she wants to be a seahorse and live anywhere rather than a mutant living in a toxic environment, meaning the drink."

"She does, does she? I wonder what she'll do when she wakes up."

"Wonder what she'll remember."

"I'll let you know."

Sam got up to pick up a shell and returned, turning it over in his hand. He heaved a deep sigh. "My first wife was always angry and I believe the cancer was a physical manifestation of that anger. She didn't let go of some of her grudges until just before she died. I thought I'd never marry again rather than risk falling into that trap. Then I met Harriet and she was happy all the time, always smiling and enjoying life. What a contrast. It only took being around her for a little while for me to fall in love with her. So beautiful and full of fun." He shook his head as memories broke on the shores of his heart.

Gaff gave him time.

"We drank while we were dating. That's normal. A drink before dinner, wine with dinner, after dinner drink. Sometimes we had too much, but it's part of the dating, too. After we got married and moved in together, I began to see a pattern I didn't like. I drank a little at night and only on some nights, but she wanted to drink every night and a lot. I got drunk too often. When it started affecting my job performance, I cut down almost to nothing. She didn't."

"You noticed this the first year?"

Sam nodded his answer. "Harriet probably told you her husband died in a traffic accident."

Gaff nodded.

"He did, but did she tell you she was driving drunk and had two toddlers in the back seat?"

Gaff blew a silent whistle. "Heavy burden."

"Not for her. Doesn't take responsibility for any of it. She's blocked out all the details. All she remembers is the part about the car wreck."

"There must be scars somewhere."

"Not that I've found in all the years we've been married. Not unless they're really deep."

"You let her drive your children around?"

"Now there's the story. I threatened to leave her if she didn't go into treatment and so she did. She came out 'dry' for the first time in her adult life. Even said she liked the feeling."

"Stay dry?"

"For a while. Only lasted a couple of years. I'm not sure how long. We stopped drinking. Nothing in the house. Changed what we did for fun. Drank a lot of iced tea. We were happy. Laughed and enjoyed being a family"

Gaff smiled. This was something he understood.

"Then I'd come home and she'd be napping. At first it was only once in a while and then more and more. She complained of being too tired to cook. I picked up the slack or the kids would. I suggested a visit to the doctor. Nothing seemed to work. With five children, the older ones could take care of the others. They didn't tell me everything that was going on because it was 'mom's secret.' Things really fell apart when the last one left for college."

"She drank all the time?"

"I put her into a residential program, but she drank as soon as they released her. I thought that when I could be home all the time, she would change. The drinking isn't from loneliness, but because she likes to feel out of it."

Gaff didn't know what to say. He shook his head and looked out to the horizon. Why would anyone want to miss all this?

"I've had it and I've told her I'm going to travel without her from now on."

"She said something about that."

"Next, I'll just divorce the bitch. In fact, part of the agenda for this family weekend is to discuss this problem. I want the kids to know first, not be surprised."

"Good to do, but they wouldn't be surprised by now anyway."

"You're probably right."

Again, they sat in silence: each lost in his own thoughts.

Sam cut into that silence. "I don't know why I'm telling you all this. It isn't right to burden a complete stranger. Guess she brought you into it when she sat with you this afternoon."

"There must be pain hidden down there somewhere."

"Someone else'll have to find it. I'm too tired and life is too short to waste on a drunk."

# chapter 17

Sally marched down the beach towing a young man along side. He was probably around 50 and that's young to Gaff. She was in a different frame of mind than normal. Her mouth was set in a determined line and her companion was carrying fishing gear and a confused look. They walked right up to Gaff and Sally introduced the man.

"This's my cousin Bobby. He's recovering from surgery. Open heart, Gaff, and at his young age."

Gaff nodded a greeting. There was some family resemblance: the same light brown hair, the same pointed chin, the same turned up nose. There were differences, too. Bobby was growing a belly while Sally was fit from her walks on the beach. The light was missing in Bobby's face, probably due to the heart attack.

"He wants to try fishing. He's never fished before, but he needs to learn to relax. Thought fishing would be a good hobby."

Gaff had taken a number of would-be fishermen under his wing, or should he say, umbrella. Not all of them stayed on the beach, but the ones who did knew how to fish. Some even returned for the refresher course from time to time. One of his protégés won the prize for the largest king mackerel caught from the pier this season. Made Gaff proud.

This guy didn't look like he'd last long, but Gaff was an equal opportunity teacher willing to convert just about anyone. From Bobby's baseball cap and tee shirt, Gaff guessed that his new friend was into sports: the Cubs. Hmmm, Chicago. The gym shorts were pretty old. Had they been worn for workouts earlier in their lives? Maybe the belly was a side effect of the heart condition. Gaff enjoyed these observations. He'd find out later how accurate they were.

Sally patted her cousin on the shoulder. "Will you let him spend some time with you, Gaff? Just to show him a thing or two about the fine art of fishing? After all, you are the old man of the beach, the master of surf fishing."

Gaff started to protest, but she waved him off.

Bobby looked expectant, rod and reel in hand. Gaff chuckled because his new friend handled the rod as though it just might bite him.

"Where's your rod holder?"

Bobby held his gear out for Gaff's inspection. "The guy at the pier said these are good rods. The other stuff's in the car."

This was the first Bobby had spoken and Gaff was pleasantly surprised by the smile he heard.

Gaff nodded his approval. "Where'd you park?"

"In the parking lot next to Sally's place. At the next beach access." Bobby jerked his head in the general direction.

Gaff could see in an instant that Sam had done a good job setting Bobby up with good rods. He bet the other things would be right, too.

"Leave the rods in my wagon while you move the car. Be easier to bring the other things down. Won't do any good sitting in the car."

Sally grinned her delight at making the connection and walked with her cousin back down the beach.

After Bobby moved his car, Gaff examined the new purchases and listed other items to buy.

Using the side of his pliers, he hammered the rod holder into the sand a little way from his own. "You can use my things until you figure out whether this's the life for you."

Bobby's rod was set up for whiting, so his first lesson was how to use the scoop to gather sand fleas. As soon as he gathered enough bait to start with, Gaff taught him the proper way to put them on the hook. Next, came a demonstration of casting. Bobby did fine for a first-timer, for a minnow, as Gaff started calling him. Once his line was in the water, he gathered more bait.

Bobby was sitting on the cooler when Sally showed up with a chair from her place. "I was wondering how long I'd last on that cooler."

Gaff laughed. "You'd be surprised how many people have sat on that cooler for hours."

Bobby looked confused, but Gaff let it go, with only a knowing nod. Sally smiled, too. Gaff thought she was laughing as she searched for shark teeth on her walk home.

Once they were settled, Gaff pointed out important signs: how the fishing rod tip moved vigorously when there was a fish on the hook as compared to smooth back and forth movements caused by wave action. Eyes moving regularly from the water to the tips of their poles, they relaxed.

Bobby grinned, "This isn't so hard."

"You haven't caught anything yet."

The grin dimmed, but not much. "Now what?"

"Now we wait. Practice patience. I thought that's what you came to learn." He pointed to a rough spot on the water. "A school of baitfish. More, closer to shore. You can see them in the waves just before they break. We're fishing for the larger fish feeding on the minnows."

They waited in silence for a while until Bobby started fidgeting in his seat. He talked to fill the quiet. "I need to learn this relaxation thing. I'm not good at it yet."

"You fishing for patience?" Gaff joked.

"I learned stress a long time ago and it got me. So now I have to change my ways. See if relaxation does better."

Gaff knew a story was on the hook.

Bobby was quiet for a while, watching. "Have you ever felt you were a failure," he said, "with nothing to show for all the years you worked?"

"Not exactly."

"That's where I am right now. I made the wrong decisions and it ended up making me sick."

"Maybe you should start at the beginning."

"It's a long story."

Gaff looked at the waves and the clouds on the horizon. "We've got time, nothing but time."

Bobby took a deep breath. "I'm one of four boys in my family. My dad owned a lot of fast food outlets in the Raleigh area.

We all worked in the business as kids. I figured out early on that I didn't like it."

"You're a wise man for that, especially if you didn't go into the business knowing that it wasn't right for you."

"All three of my brothers joined Dad. One got an MBA in IT first so he could pick the job he wanted. Dad pressured me, but I packed my bags and left town instead of putting up with his badgering or caving in."

"Go to college?"

"Nope. No money. Dad said he wouldn't give it to me unless I signed something agreeing to work in the business. Said he wanted to get value for his 'investment.' So when I graduated high school, I packed my bags and left the state to find my fortune. Harder to do than I thought. I lived in my car for a while and did whatever jobs I could get. Spent some time working in fast food restaurants."

"That early experience helped."

"Didn't like working for someone else any better, though. Eventually, I got my own place and was making it on my own. Doing odd jobs, security in a building, janitor, construction, whatever I could find, till I finally joined the Army. Figured they would help me find my niche and provide me with training to prepare me for a job when I got out. I ended up becoming an MP. Who'd a thunk?"

"You stay in long?"

Bobby broke a stick of driftwood and threw some of it toward the water. "Got out as soon as I could. Takes a special person to be career military. It wasn't the place for me," he said. "I wanted to live in a big city so when I got discharged, I got a job on the police force in Chicago. Seemed the best fit. Especially because it wasn't fast food or manual labor."

"How'd that go?"

"Great. I loved the job. But I worked an area with a lot of crime. That means a lot of guns pointing in my direction. Stress, stress, and more stress. There was a lot of adrenaline pumping around in this body."

"I wouldn't want the job, but someone has to do it."

"Yeah, but I'm not doing it any more. Department politics, tension on the street, and a short, unhappy marriage added up to a triple serving of stress. I was doing pretty well, getting the bad guys, getting promotions, getting the divorce and then boom. A heart attack. A full monty heart attack. I got opened up for a quadruple bypass. Four blockages." At this, Bobby pulled up his shirt to show Gaff a large, knotty scar an inch wide, extending the length of his sternum. It was so new it was still angry-looking. On the way to healing, but not there yet.

Gaff blew out a silent whistle and shook his head. "No wonder you want some peace. That's some big scar."

"It was some big operation, with this reminder here for me to look at every time I take off my shirt. Turns out the blood vessels are growing back all by themselves, no need for all the cutting or pain."

Bobby turned his leg for Gaff to see the scar there. "Still, the doctor said he'd rather be safe. We didn't know before surgery that the blood vessels would grow back on their own."

He threw another piece of wood. "Frankly, I think he needed some mortgage payments for that big house he built. Anyway here I am, healing and building a new life."

"You looking for a job here, too?" He was wondering how to help this young man.

"No job necessary. This beauty mark qualified me for a monthly check. I can attend to healing for as long as that takes." He looked to the horizon, thinking of all the plans that would never be as a result of his condition. "Yep, no job necessary... One day I would like to get back into something. To feel useful, you know."

The tip of Bobby's rod was jumping to signal a bite. They got up to investigate. Each reeled in his line.

Bobby looked at the fish head remaining on Gaff's hook. "Man, these fish are smart. Bite just back from the hook."

They removed the remains and put fresh on for another try. Gaff's cast was perfect. This time, Bobby cast too far and had to pull the hook from the sandbar into the slough.

Gaff joked. "Let's hope those swimmers scare the fish right onto our hooks! Whiting are skittish and might be running deeper today because of all the human life forms in the water."

"My bait was taken by something. Doesn't that mean there're whiting out there?"

"Maybe whiting. Maybe something else that's hungry for fleas."

Bobby looked in the direction of his hook, disappointed. Gaff was amused to think that Bobby might be willing the fish onto the hook. Fishing takes patience and that was something his new student was only beginning to understand.

Once back in the chairs, Gaff glanced at Bobby. "You look like you're healing fine. Still going for follow-ups?"

Bobby squirmed, getting more comfortable. "Yeah. I'm still going to the doc's. Surgery was done in Raleigh so I have to go back there for an appointment every so often. Doc'll release me when he sees it healed to a certain point. Not clear what that is, though. I ask, but he ain't telling."

"Doctors can be like that. Bet you look forward to being released."

"Oh, yes… In the hospital and at Mom's, I read a lot of stuff I didn't have time for when I had a life. One article said that policemen have the highest probability of dying of a heart attack the day after they retire. We live with stress every day, every shift. Eats you up from the inside. Adrenaline and the other stress chemicals are toxic."

"That's a hell of a note. Work for years, crazy hours, putting your life on the line day after day to get to retirement. Then boom, you die."

"See it all the time. Man talks for decades about what he and his wife have planned for the golden years. He leaves the force and kicks the bucket before they can start living it." He sifted sand through his fingers. "I know a lot of guys work longer because they're afraid it's the retirement that kills."

"That said; you're really lucky."

Bobby turned his head to look at Gaff. Anger and frustration shot into the air with his words. "How's that? I had a damned heart attack and the award-winning surgery to fix it. How can that be lucky?"

"Didn't work so many years before retiring. You didn't die.

Probably because you're young and fit." Gaff shrugged. "Most important is you're here to build another life."

Bobby relaxed again. "You can say that again. Only that's harder than you think. After years of living on the edge, it's hard to smooth out. It's hard to stand back from the edge and let someone else take your place."

"You're on your way."

Bobby hurrumphed. "Are you kidding? I'm sitting here wondering when we get to do something. I'm sitting here wanting to move, to do. Antsy."

"You've been talking about what was. Thinking about who you were reminds you of that action filled past. Then you want it again."

"OK?"

"What do you think a fish does?"

"What a fish does?"

Gaff gestured toward the water. "If you were a fish out there, what would you think right now?"

Bobby shook his head, like he questioned this old man's sanity.

"Put yourself in their place."

"If I were a fish, I'd think about swimming in the water."

"Would you know you're in water?"

Bobby's face screwed up in thought. "I don't believe I would. Even if I didn't know it was water, I'd be aware of moving. I'd be constantly on the look-out for something to eat and anyone who'd want to eat me." Bobby's face broke out in a grin. "And at certain times of the year, I'd be looking for sex."

"I'll ignore that. Would you think about yesterday?"

"Nope. Don't imagine fish brains have much space for memories."

"They learn, but probably don't worry."

"So I would learn to behave in certain ways at certain times, to certain stimuli. Then I would note the details of the current situation and react to that?"

"Most animals seem to live in the moment."

"And as I sit here, now, that translates to watching the water, the clouds, the wind and fishing according to the information I get from them." He turned toward Gaff, pleased with himself. "And from you."

Gaff smiled. "You got most of the words. Birds give information, too."

"But what do you do with the rest of your brain all that time? Surely watching those things isn't enough to occupy your entire brain."

"Watch people some. Sometimes go into a quiet place where my brain practically stops altogether. Ever study meditation?"

"I had a lot of time while I was laid up, remember? I read about it, but never actually did it. I tried once…didn't get very far."

"Meditating is basically getting your mind to stop thinking. I read somewhere that God is in the space between the thoughts. When you focus on what's going on around you without making a mental comment or judgment, I figure that's like meditation."

Bobby was surprised that this discussion was coming from an old man fishing on the beach. "It is? I've read that it's good for your immune system and for health in general."

"You're not sleeping. Don't even have to close your eyes. You can be aware of everything, but quiet the monkey chatter in your head. And listen."

"So you don't really 'think' about what's going on, you just see it."

"Or hear it, or note it. If a feeling comes up, just say, 'anger arising' and then move your mind away from it."

"What if a memory from your life comes up?"

"Note it and send it away to return your attention to the water or the clouds."

"Damn! Might not have had the heart attack if I'd known how to meditate. Never thought I'd be interested in that new age crap."

Gaff laughed. "'New age' is pharmaceuticals and surgery to move veins from legs to heart. That's new age. Meditation's centuries old! Other things have been used for eons to keep people healthy. Nice to have a choice, isn't it? New treatments and old."

"Want to go back to talking about fish having sex? I know more about that. The doctor told me what to do and I did it. I read information he gave me, but I didn't question because I was in such stress. You think differently when you're afraid you're going to die."

"You're better now. You're healing from surgery and your heart's healing itself. Take time to learn ways of staying healthy."

# chapter 18

Friday came and so did the Teabar clan. They arrived at various times in the afternoon and evening. Gaff heard their beach door slam and feet running on wooden boards soon after he heard the commotion of cars arriving in the parking lot. They must have come straight through the house from the front door to the back and down to the beach. Did they even drop things off inside?

The beach to Gaff's right became "Teabar Territory" as one of the boys labeled it with a big sign in the sand. Laughter was the primary language in this new land. Gaff smiled at all this fun: that's the way family should be. He started listening as though to a radio program.

The men of the family set about organizing the territory: a portable gazebo for shade over here, badmitten/volleyball over there, sunbathing/lifeguarding here. Sand castle building there. A male voice tried to organize a game of Frisbee, but was drowned out by shouts for lessons in body-surfing.

The kids were warned that swimming was allowed only when a male adult was watching and willing to take charge. Stress on the last part. Gaff heard instruction about riptides followed by yelling as children threw themselves into the waves. From the sound of it there were dozens of Teabar children. Were there several adult male voices among them?

Once they were in the water, Gaff could see the Teabars as well as listening to them. Laughter and rough-housing. Life is good.

Gaff thought the fish would probably visit the other end of the beach for a while. He forgot about fishing and just enjoyed this display of family togetherness. The exuberance of youth.

Then the mothers came to the water with the younger children. Water wings and giggles. Buckets and shovels and plastic star shapes for sand play.

Soon enough, Gaff smelled grilling meat. He was just considering packing up to go home when he heard a voice coming closer.

"I brought something for you to drink." Harriet appeared beside him with a glass in her hand. "Iced tea, unless you'd like a soda."

Gaff took the plastic glass she held out to him. "Tea's fine. You've got quite a group there."

Harriet's face glowed with pride. "We seem to multiply every day. We have some 'best friends' here, too. And some step-children swell the ranks. To my mind, the more the merrier." She looked to the place the fishing line entered the water. "Sorry. All this noise must scare the fish away."

Gaff laughed. "I'd rather see laughing children than snagged fish any day. Their giggles are music to me."

"To me, too." She turned to look at the family gathering in the territory. "One more family to arrive and then we're complete."

She returned her gaze to the water and said quietly, "I'm drinking tea, too. Thought I'd try it like this for a while. I'm a seahorse today."

Gaff nodded his approval, but looked out at the waves and silently asked Mother Water to help Harriet stick to the tea. He asked for Harriet, for Sam, for the rest of the family.

Her voice was brighter. "I came to invite you to dinner. We're grilling out. Hamburgers, hot dogs, chicken breasts."

Gaff smiled his appreciation. "My wife will be expecting me, but I thank you for the invitation."

"Your wife? I guess I didn't think that you'd have a family, too. We'll be here for the weekend and the invitation is good for any time." She paused a beat and then added, "We'd love to have the both of you tonight or tomorrow night. We have so many that two more won't make any difference as far as the food is concerned. And you would add a lot to the party."

Gaff nodded, "Nice of you to ask. I'll mention it to Julia."

"Nice name, Julia." She got up and started moving to rejoin her family. Then she stopped and without turning said quietly, "Thank you for being so honest yesterday. I didn't like what you said, but it made sense when I thought about it later."

When Gaff got home, he put the wagon in the garage and the baitfish in the freezer. He cleaned the eating fish at the sink in the garage and then put them in the freezer, too, in a different place than the bait. When he opened the kitchen door, his nose informed him that Julia was fixing dinner.

She said, "We'll have to eat in the dining room. I went shopping with the girls and put all the stuff on the kitchen table. I've gotten it organized, but I didn't have time to put it away."

Gaff frowned. "Shopping again? Hope there's a money tree out back to pay for all this." He glanced at the various stuffed animals and toys on the table without interest… until something caught his eye.

"Gaff, you know it takes a long time to get ready for Christmas. I like to get a head start to make sure I get the right things for the kids and grands."

Julia's voice had a laugh in it that was intoxicating, worth any money it cost him. Christmas was her favorite holiday. But right now, his attention was drawn to the stuffed seahorse almost hidden among the things on the table.

He picked it up to inspect. "What's this for?"

Too late, he realized he should have asked "who" it was for.

She leaned around him to see. "Don't know yet, just got the urge to buy it. Cute, isn't it? I'll figure out what to do with it later." She returned to the stove.

"I know what to do with it. Mind if I give it to someone?"

"Go right ahead." She was distracted by the food that was tantalizing Gaff's nose.

He peered over her shoulder and sniffed at the contents of the pots. "Hm-m-m. You do know how to cook."

"Oh, go on." Her response had a hint of a girlish giggle.

"We've been invited for a cookout tomorrow night if you feel like taking a break from the kitchen."

"Dinner?"

"Someone I met on the beach yesterday. We can give her this, too."

"And a bottle of wine."

"No wine. Your fresh coconut cake maybe. There's an army of kids and grands. Might be fun."

"Don't you get enough of kids and grands here?"

"Never. Never enough of kids. Never enough of family."

Gaff put the seahorse aside and moved to help his wife. "I'm reporting for duty as sous-chef and server. What are your orders, ma'am?"

They laughed and finished putting dinner on the table together. They used sterling, bone china and crystal because they were in the dining room. Gaff lit candles on the table for atmosphere and poured a glass of wine for each of them. They held hands and bowed their heads before eating, to thank the Creator for all the gifts they'd been given.

The next day was Saturday and Gaff wore his best beach clothes. He cast beyond the sandbar into the deeper water. Safer for the swimmers, and the fish were probably more plentiful there. Too much commotion close in. There was plenty to watch today. Some of his family was here to swim. In fact, it seemed like most of North Carolina came to the beach for one last day before cool weather set in.

As the beach filled up, he reeled in his line and put it away. He could miss one day of fishing.

Teabar Territory was teaming with laughing wildlife. What a wonderful day.

In the afternoon, Gaff saw Harriet on the beach and went to let her know there'd be two extra mouths for dinner. They'd bring fish to grill and, with any luck, Julia's fresh coconut cake. Harriet grinned with appreciation. And Gaff returned to his fishing and his family.

Bobby joined him in the late morning and was surprised to see all the chairs and beach paraphernalia around "their" spot. He fit himself into the group and cast his hook into the deep water. One of the grandsons wanted to fish so it seemed like a party compared to the quiet of most days.

The clamorous clan came after all "the good spots" were taken and grumbled their way farther down the beach. The blessing was that their screaming rituals were too far away to interrupt the fun.

Boys intermingled and parties joined and that was good until a tiff developed between one of the Teabars and one of Gaff's.

Teabar yelled, "Hey get away so you don't knock me off my board. This is our space. Teabar Territory. Don't you see the sign on the beach?"

The answer came, "You can't just take a part of the beach. I can swim anywhere I want on this beach."

"We can, too, set up our territory. We got here last night and set it all up. It's ours."

The other voice was filled with bravado. "Can not. My granddad owns this beach. No one can take a part of it. It's his."

"He does not."

"Does, too."

It would have gone on if a wave hadn't knocked both boys off their feet and scrambling to catch their body boards.

Gaff heard this exchange out of the corner of his ear. He made a mental note for later: talk to his grands.

Toward late afternoon, the beach started emptying as everybody packed up and headed for home. Gaff and his grandsons pulled the wagon and the van beat them to the house with all the beach stuff. The grands wanted to stay with Grandma Julia, but the parents had other plans and were soon on their way to wherever. Soon after, Julia and Gaff were walking to Teabar Territory.

Harriet answered the door. Her lips formed into a suspicious pout and the glass in her hand only looked like water. She was effusive in her greeting, but guilt was mixed in with all the glad-you-cames.

Gaff was disappointed. After a quick glance at her husband, Julia gave Harriet a warm hug and traded seahorse for glass. As she did this, she said, "We brought you a little gift. Gaff thought you'd like it. Here, let me help you with that."

Julia carried the glass in one hand and put her other arm around Harriet's waist. Gaff carried the cake holder and the bag of fish. That's the way they passed through the house into kitchen where Julia emptied the drink into the sink on the way to join the party. Harriet stared at the stuffed animal, guilt welling up wet in her eyes. She took the glass of tea Julia fixed for her.

"There. Isn't that better now?"

The tone of the group was somber, but perked up when they saw the glass of tea in Harriet's hand.

Julia put the cake out on the dessert table while Gaff moved outside to grill the fish. Some of the young men were gathered around the grill to supervise there. The women guarded coconut icing from the kids, while taking a little swipe of their own. There was a lot of drooling over Julia's cake.

It was difficult to eat with that seahorse in her hand, but Harriet managed. She also managed to drink tea for the rest of the night. Her pout calmed down.

The family mood brightened.

Everyone managed to eat so much food as to risk popping right there on the beach in North Carolina. After the younger set went to bed, their parents went for a swim in the chill September air. There was a lot of laughing and squealing on the beach that night.

The older couples visited and shared some of the stories from the days of their own swims on chilly September nights.

During the walk home, Julia and Gaff held hands.

Julia shook her head. "Gaff, you are a dear, but one talk with an old fisherman on the beach is not enough to solve her problems."

Gaff squeezed her hand. "I was just hoping, Julia. I was just hoping for some small change."

"You made a small change. Her husband looked grateful for the peaceful night. He saw what was possible, too."

"What's possible from a seahorse."

"From a seahorse."

## chapter 19

Bobby and Gaff grew to know each other better as the days passed. Gaff watched as his new friend relaxed. The periods of silence grew longer and more comfortable as Bobby learned to value silent communion with nature. He was intelligent and observant and soon began to point out the signals and their interpretations. He was a natural. Who'd a thunk!

After Gaff explained his own rituals, Bobby began to develop his unique ways of celebrating the spirit of the earth, of expressing gratitude for the gifts he is given. Gaff enjoyed seeing Bobby's connection with Spirit grow and flourish as he began to understand being part of the world. Better yet, Gaff watched him learn to value his own BEING rather than always wanting to DO. The peace within him grew.

One day, the younger man said slowly, "I used to really like showing how strong and in control I was. When I was on the force, I worked out a lot and sometimes pulled a guy through his car window. Because I could. Showing off how strong I was."

"You ever knock people around just for the hell of it?"

"Nah. Didn't want to hurt anyone, just make an impression, so to speak. I could pick up a lot of the people we dealt with and I sometimes did, just to make a point."

"A point?"

"For the life of me, I can't remember what that point was... Maybe just that I was 'the man.' Immature, I know."

"You're changing."

"Oh, boy, have I changed. I would never have been caught dead fishing then. Too boring."

"You wanted activity?"

"Adrenaline at work. Adrenaline at play."

"What changed you?"

"The heart attack really got my attention and then recovering from the operation forced me to slow down and gave me time to think. Don't remember doing much of that when I was on the force. Not that I'm stupid or anything."

"And you read some, too?"

"While I was laid up? Yeah, I did. Boredom motivates you to do lots of things. And somehow the oddest reading material kept showing up in my room."

"Reading material?"

"Stuff about how you get sick and what to do to get well and stay that way."

"You mean like exercise and nutrition and meditation?"

"Yeah, like. And changing the way you think about life. All that material made me see how my lifestyle had to change if I wanted to live another 20-30 years. I made some changes right away and promised myself to make others as soon as I could."

"And that's why you came to spend time with me?"

"I didn't know I was coming to spend time with you. The water and the fishing attracted me. Now I realize I wanted something else to do. You know, another activity. Sally told me you're an interesting man who seems to live forever and maybe I could learn your secret."

"My secret."

"Fishing secrets and living secrets. She also told me you've been married for a long time, and happy. Maybe some of that'll rub off on me."

Gaff waved grandly. "I fish all the time! That's my secret."

"Seriously."

Gaff thought. "Takes two to do that dance. Both people have to do their parts. You can't have a good marriage all by yourself."

"Well then, a big part is knowing how and when to find the right partner, isn't it?"

"She sometimes finds you. You have to be ready and able to recognize her sparkle when she strolls through the door."

Bobby chuckled. "You have to have your guard down enough to let that love into your heart. My marriage was so bad that I closed off tighter than a virgin's... Sorry, that just slipped."

"What about Sally?"

Bobby looked hard at Gaff, shock on his face. "She's my cousin. I may be from North Carolina, but…"

Gaff interrupted. "She has friends. You met them?"

"Nah. She's dying to introduce me, but I told her you didn't get to that lesson yet."

"The secret, the only secret, is to love yourself so you don't need another person. And to trust the Universe to bring the right person so that you can love them with all your heart. If you don't need anyone else, you are free to give your love… and to accept it."

"How will I know when I'm ready?"

"When you meet her-- and you know it."

Bobby nodded and scanned the water for signs. After some thought, he asked, "How do I do this, Gaff? Get ready, I mean?"

"You're already working on it."

Bobby pursed his lips and nodded solemnly. His face was painted with confusion, but he'd said his piece and he'd do what he was doing and see what came next. He gave himself over to the water. Mother Water.

Several days later, Bobby was quieter than usual after they settled into the waiting. His attempts to put his thoughts into words ended in mid-sentence. Gaff waited, mind open, listening.

Finally, Bobby blurted out, "I had some pretty weird experiences in that operating room, Gaff. Really weird, and I can't stop thinking about them."

"Hm-m-m?"

"You're a smart guy and don't shoot your mouth off like some guys I know." He seemed to be thinking out loud; eyes focused on the water. "I don't know. You might think I'm nuts."

Gaff waited, watching the birds dive for food. Fish jumped -- almost into the pelicans' mouths. Signs of larger fish close to shore this morning.

Bobby looked down at his hands. "I think I saw myself on the operating table. I know this sounds crazy, but I heard what the doctors were saying. I saw what they did in my chest. Then I felt someone saying that I had work to do and I'd get healthy to do it.

Sounds really crazy when I hear it out loud, but I'd swear on my
mother's grave that it happened. I was hovering somewhere near
the ceiling watching the operation." He didn't stop to breathe
between the words, almost afraid they'd dry up and get stuck in his
throat if he did.

"Saw the doctors? You felt someone talk to you?"

Bobby nodded. "I didn't actually hear any words, but I
knew they were talking to me. I understood what they were saying.
Like telepathy."

Gaff's eyes twinkled. "A near-death experience."

Bobby cut his eyes around to look at Gaff. "A what?"

"A near death experience, an NDE. Did you see a bright
light and feel drawn to it?"

"I was too busy looking at myself on that table. And at the
doctors. I sort of felt a pull behind me, but didn't look around to
see what it was."

"Should have guessed. They had to stop your heart."

Bobby smiled. "I'm not crazy? You don't think I've lost
it?"

"No. I've read about NDE's."

Bobby's voice was low, as though he was talking to
himself. "An NDE. I think I heard my grandma's voice, but the
other voice told her it wasn't time… So I'm not crazy." His voice
got louder, "Other people had these NDEs."

Gaff nodded and looked at the place where his line entered
the water, then he looked at the tip of his rod. "Fish got my bait."
He said it simply as he went to tend the rods: reeling in the line,
putting bait on the hook, and casting it into the surf. His student
tended his lines, too.

As he cast, Gaff could hear "an NDE" from Bobby whose
lips continued to move. Nothing else was audible.

On the way to the chairs, Bobby said, "I'm glad you told
me about these things. Makes me feel better to know other people
have them. Like I'm a little less out of my head. I told the doctor
I'd heard everything he said during the operation. He said that was
impossible. Told me I was totally out. His face got all white when I
quoted him. They were joking with each other, you know. Not very

professional. Even shot some blood out of my vein at a resident. Joking. Playing with my blood."

"Did he admit that you could be hearing him?"

"Nah. Kept saying I was out. Said he'd have the anesthesiologist come in to vouch for that. Still, he didn't deny saying those things. I saw him let a student do some of the work and he didn't deny that either."

"Doesn't surprise me that he didn't get it."

Bobby frowned. "You never told me what it is."

Gaff's face screwed up in concentration. "Your body dies, your spirit comes out of your body and hangs around somewhere above it. It's out of your body, but still connected. Sometimes your spirit goes to another place, following that bright light I was asking about. Sometimes you get instructions about how to change your life or what your life purpose is. Then your body's revived and the spirit's pulled back into it."

Bobby said slowly, "My spirit. That feels right, but out of my experience. The guys on the force would hoot if they heard this story. Laugh me off the force."

"Most people say they go toward a white light. They're told they have to return to the body. Many say they want to stay there because it feels so good. Peaceful, loving. In the end, though, they come back. That's how they can tell about it."

They said nothing, each lost in his own thoughts. Both of them stared out at the water, the waves, the clouds, the birds. Did they really see nature or were they seeing something else?

Bobby broke the silence, "You said some things that I felt, but didn't tell you. Makes the whole thing more believable. Could I find something about this on the Internet?"

"I guess. Or books."

"Books."

They fell into a comfortable silence again, but Gaff could tell that Bobby wasn't seeing the world in front of his eyes, he was ruminating on their conversation and the information he hadn't shared.

Gaff was considering the speed of his student's progress and was pleased. He'd soon be ready for release into the wild. What role had Bobby been given, that part of his NDE he hadn't shared? Was Gaff doing his part to prepare the young man for that purpose? Gaff turned his attention to Mother Water and silently asked to be guided in what to teach this young man… and when… and how.

# chapter 20

Gaff couldn't sleep and rather than disturbing Julia, he quietly dressed. Then he went to the beach to watch the sunrise. He expected to be alone today because Bobby went to see the doctor in Raleigh and wouldn't come to the beach until late, if at all.

It was beautiful this morning. Rosy gold coloring the clouds on the horizon. The sun was a brilliant golden orb. It had to climb up over some clouds on the edge of the world. Those clouds looked like a bit of land in the distance. Land covered by tall trees, maybe just beyond seeing. As the sun came out from behind them, they were lined in brilliant gold, too.

And then when the sun got higher, it colored the lower part of the sky, just above those clouds, with the colors of the rainbow. Pale, but all the colors of the rainbow layered on the line of the horizon. Should have brought the camera. Or take up painting. Instead, he'd have to log a record in his memory of this glorious gift.

As he enjoyed the show, Priscilla walked up. She sat down on the cooler and blew a silent whistle. "Absolutely beautiful this morning." The first word was drawn out for emphasis, each syllable given attention.

"Oh, yes. It is beautiful. Haven't seen you in a while."

She smiled at the sun. "I've been walking at odd times. A lot of sunrises. Walked in the opposite direction sometimes, too. Went down to the south end of the island to walk just before sunset. Beautiful spectacle there, too. I came to say hello since you're alone this morning."

"Bobby's fine. You visit while he's here, too." More silent thanks for the beautiful spectacle beginning this beautiful day.

Her voice was filled with awe. "I love the dawn here and I'll miss it when I have to go home."

"Take it with you. In your heart."

"I write about it, too. You were right. I'm following my dream and feeling great about writing. And if my agent can't sell the manuscripts, that's OK. I'll put them away for my children to find. I've heard of that: parents writing their story so the children will know them better after they're gone. For me, it's good enough that I lived the joy of putting my thoughts down on the page."

"Nice to hear you're happy again. More people followed their dream and the world would be better for it."

They sat for a while. When the sun was her normal gold and the sky its everyday blue, Priscilla left to continue her walk.

Soon after Priscilla left, Mae took her place on the cooler.

Gaff wondered if Tuesday was catch-up day, the day for everyone to check in.

Mae was beaming. "Yesterday, the physical therapist told Dawn's parents that her improvement was a miracle. Says Dawn will be able to walk again, against all odds. After she left, Dawn wanted to do another set of exercises, but I didn't want to exhaust her. She's excited about life again. Maybe more than most girls her age. I'm excited about life again, too."

"Great news. You've done well. You're looking good, too."

Was it his imagination or did her smile get brighter?

"Thanks for noticing. I'm feeling better, physically and mentally. We've worked together to make great changes in my life and in Dawn's. She's partly to thank for pushing me to do more everyday. She's helped me and I've helped her."

"You helped each other, but each had to do the work for herself."

"Both of us have grown through helping someone else like this. But really you're the one who started it. You're the one showed me another way of looking at my life. Because of you, I took control and really started living again."

"It's all about attitude. Your Dawn sounds like a special person. I'd like to meet her."

"You will. When she comes down to the beach."

At this, she got up to walk down the beach with more energy in her step than Gaff could believe. Amazing how overcoming obstacles can motivate a person to do their best. Too bad more people couldn't figure that out. Want to motivate a person to get things done? Tell them they can do it and then recognize their progress at every step. Works wonders. A whole lot better than fussing because the job didn't get done yet. The clamorous clan crossed Gaff's mind. He shook his head in pity, but he didn't waste his energy thinking about what might have been.

Harry stopped by to tell Gaff that his wife had passed. "We had her cremated and the memorial will be this weekend. Gives more time for family to get here."

"Sorry to hear of her passing, Harry."

Harry smiled wanly. "She's in a better place. Hear that all the time, don't you? I understand what it means now."

"No more pain."

"No more pain… She was graceful in her going. Jayne and the boys were there and we felt closer as a family. You were right. I think she could feel the forgiveness in the kids' hearts. She left us when she could leave us together."

Gaff could feel Harry's heart open. Harry was in a better place, too.

"Spending time alone with Jayne was the start. I think she helped with the boys when they got here. Mother passed when she felt all that love surrounding her. She was waiting for that. Great send-off."

They sat in silence for a while before Harry got up to go.

Gaff said quietly, "We'll be there for you at the memorial, Harry."

Harry turned to say. "You've always been here for me, Gaff. Always."

Gaff sat watching the pelicans dive for food. His bait was gone by now, but that could wait. He needed some time with his feelings. And to talk with Mother Water. And to Harry's wife.

Later, as he tended his fishing gear, Sally walked up. "Thought Bobby'd be here."

"At the doctor's in Raleigh."

"Oh." She stood to watch as he cast into the surf.

He settled in his chair. "Sorry you missed him."

Sally stood for a while longer and then she plunked down on the cooler. "I thought he'd be otherwheres today. Wanted a chance to talk with you... Alone."

Gaff glanced at her and then out at the waves. Fishing takes patience.

Sally took her time, getting comfortable with the idea, convincing herself. "Bobby's told me how you have all these great talks. About life, you know. Says you are one wise old man."

"Hmmm." Gaff settled in to allow her time.

Sally jabbed her thumb toward the pirate flag. "You're not the bad, old pirate you want people to think you are." She chuckled nervously and fell into silence. Was she struggling with herself in that silence?

Gaff tossed some bait into the silence. "Actually, the skull and cross bones are an ancient symbol from the Crusades. Symbol of the fighting monks. They used it as a sign they were protecting people. Two leg bones crossed and a skull placed over them. It was a warning for the bandits and other bad guys to stay away. Beware, this area is under the protection of the Knights Templar."

"I didn't know this. Did it keep the areas from being attacked?" Sally was interested in this more than in pirates.

Gaff shook his head. "The Knights Templar won some and lost some. At one time, they owned and protected large areas of land. Then the Arabs would win it back. Back and forth for a while. Then the monks returned to Europe, very rich. Found something very important in Jerusalem. Don't think they ever told anyone what it was."

Sally thought about this for some time. Probably long enough for the idea of protection to sink in. Protection and safety and wisdom all together on the beach in North Carolina. Safety sitting on a fisherman's cooler.

"I was married a long time ago. We were young, and maybe just in lust, now that I think of it. We both worked and we were doing OK. I got pregnant and had a little girl. He loved that little girl as much as I did. You hear about men don't like kids. He wasn't one of those."

She was quiet, lost in her memories, and Gaff left her there.

"Everything was OK for a while. Until he lost his job. Looked and looked, but he couldn't find another one. Sometimes did odd jobs for extra money, but nothing regular. Eventually he stopped looking. I was OK with that. He was good with our daughter and because he was with her I could work more hours. I didn't mind working. I liked my job. We didn't have a lot, but we could pay our bills and put food on the table."

"Hmmm."

"I thought it was OK until he started yelling at me. Said we needed more money, that I didn't make enough. I worked long hours already, as much as I could get. When I got home I was exhausted. I guess I wasn't much fun either. Anyway, he told me that I'd have to make more. When I asked if he wanted me to turn some tricks, I thought he'd hit me. Didn't though."

"Thanks for that."

"Yeah. Thanks that he didn't hit me. I wouldn't hook for him or any man. I think he knew that, but for me to ask the question was an insult to him, I guess. We had more fights, more often and more violent."

Gaff listened, waiting for the punch line.

"Here I was, getting home exhausted and having him yell at me all night. I got so upset I couldn't sleep to get rested so I could work the next day. Got worse and worse."

Sally sought distraction in a shell hiding in the sand. She leaned over, picked it up, and brushed it clean. Took her time. Then she just stared at it as it lay in her open hand. Maybe she was picking through her memories of those unhappy years.

"Finally, I couldn't take it any more. Told him I was leaving. Packed a bag and walked. He was so mad, he told me to go, but he wouldn't let me take the kid. Said he took care of her and I didn't know anything about being a mother. I believed him. All this time I'd been working myself into the ground and didn't have anything left for her when I got home. Waiting tables is physical labor, you know. Good money, but tiring." Again, she went to visit the past.

"He was a good daddy. He loved her and I thought he must be right about me not being able to work and care for her, too. So the deal was, I could walk, but I had to leave my daughter. At the time, I thought I was making a choice between life without her and a sure slow death living with the two of them. Where my head was, there was only one choice for me."

Her sadness hung in the air like mist over crashing waves.

"We got the divorce. He got the kid and he got the judge to limit the amount of time I could spend with my daughter. Soon, she barely knew me. I was more like a distant aunt than a mother. I worked and sent them money every month."

"I'm sorry to hear that."

"It did bother me. Then I got the bright idea that he would let me see more of her if I told him I'd buy all her school clothes. The deal was she spent the summer with me and I'd spend more on her than the judge said I had to."

Gaff nodded. "Good plan. Did it work?"

"It did. By that time I was married again and quit work because my husband wanted me to stay home. He was a factory representative with a big territory. When we met, he told me how he hated to be alone all that time on the road. Since he made plenty, we didn't need my pay. I traveled with him most of the time after we got married."

"Any kids?"

"Took us some time, but we finally had a boy. He traveled with us until he got to kindergarten age. Then life changed and Paul was traveling on his own again most of the time. We went with, whenever we could and he managed to work in the local area more days a week. He still had to travel to his other accounts. Because we were so happy when we were together, the traveling was easier for him. And then there were the telephone talks, too. We really burned up the airways."

These were the easy memories leading up to now.

Sadness entered the scene. "Paul helped me fight for custody of my daughter early in our marriage. All we got was more time with her. That was better than nothing. Paul would have loved to be her father, but we settled for the visits. Paul loved her like his own."

Gaff gave Sally time.

"I don't know all that went on with my ex-husband, but my daughter blames me for her father's problems. I never asked for the details of his life because it was none of my business. I do know he never did get a good job and he fought all the time with his second wife. Same as with me. I got blamed for that, too, I guess."

"Sometimes when people don't learn from situations, they repeat the same mistakes over and over. Looks like he didn't learn much."

"Not much. I was busy making a home for Paul and our little family, but I did my best with my daughter in the time she was with us. Crammed in as much time with her in those months as I would have in a whole year."

"You did the best you could."

Sally lowered her voice. "I tried. I really tried. But she's still emotionally distant from me. No matter what I do, she won't forgive me for the decisions I made when I was in my twenties. I don't know whether I should have stayed in that miserable marriage just for her sake. No matter, because it's too late to change what happened. I don't know what to do now."

"You talk with her?"

"Just about the time I think things are going better, something happens. Couple of years ago, it seemed like she wanted to visit us more and we were talking more, having a good time when we were together. Then Paul died suddenly of a massive heart attack. I think she loved him and his death really got to her. Seemed like she blamed me for that, too."

Gaff heard her voice break and stared out at the waves more intently. Give her privacy.

"Paul, Jr. and I still miss Paul. I'm building a life now that he's out of the house at college, but I miss the relationship with my daughter. Think about it sometimes when I'm alone at night. I go over it and over it to see if I can think of how to fix it. I've tried everything I know to do. Everything."

Gaff heard the finality in her voice, the resignation. He asked for a way to help her and saw footprints in the sand. Words came to him that he passed them on to her, "Life is like walking on the beach."

Sally's face showed her confusion.

Gaff was confused himself. Ok, Gaff, where do you go from here? He waited to see more of the path. "You walk the beach this morning?" he asked Sally.

She smiled. "I did, at low tide this morning, and got some shark teeth. Good ones, too."

Gaff looked up and down the beach near the water. "Which footprints are yours?"

Sally pointed in front of her. "Those are, right there next to…" She stopped to think. Shook her head and started again. "Well, no. Those can't be mine because the water's up now." She scanned the beach. "I'm not sure which ones are mine. Not now." Confusion.

"But you could tell which ones they are. If they were still there?"

She thought, looking at all the footprints in the sand. "I don't know if I could. I walk in a zigzag line following the line of shells left on the beach by the waves. A lot of people just walk straight and don't stop for anything."

"What happens during high tide?"

Sally answered in a voice filled with questions. "The sand's washed clean. All the footprints below the tide line are washed away."

"You can tell a lot about a person by the prints he leaves in the sand." He wasn't sure where this would end. A dead end?

She entered into the fun, but still didn't see the point. "I see people running; people walking straight; people walking all around the beach."

"Whether you walk straight or always look for the hard sand, those waves eventually wipe away the traces of your path."

She laughed. "A lot of times while you're making it! Unless you walk way up close to the dunes where the water doesn't go. Safe from the water."

"And is the sand hard there?"

"That's where it's softest. Makes the walk tougher, but it's far from the water if you don't want to get wet."

"How do you find the hard sand where walking is easier?"

"That's hard to do. It changes all the time. It's easiest to just walk where you want to and keep on going through the hard sand and the soft."

"Do you worry about having your path washed away?"

"I'm concentrating on finding shells and sharks' teeth."

"Life's like walking on the beach."

Sally thought out loud, trying to make sense of it. "People walk the beach different ways. Some walk in a straight line, walking through the water sometimes and through hard and soft sand. Whatever comes their way."

"Yes." Gaff nodded.

"Other people walk in a zig-zag looking for the hard sand all the time, the easy walking. Either way, close to the water, you may get wet and, for sure, your path will be washed away."

"And how do you walk?"

She smiled in understanding. "Me, I'm looking for the shells, not for the hard sand. If I looked for the hard sand all the time, I'd miss some shells."

Gaff added, "You focus on what you're doing right now and enjoy the treasures left by the waves."

Sally said slowly, "It's a waste to think so much about the past or the future."

Gaff smiled. "It's easier to focus on the present here because the waves wash away signs of the past."

The light was on in Sally's eyes. "The only thing I can do well is live in this very moment and express the joy and love I feel in the now. When I'm too distracted by where I've been then I don't see the treasures right at my feet, right in front of me."

Bingo, Gaff thought. The sound of the reel singing.

"All I can do for the relationship with my daughter is to love her and let her know that I love being in touch with her. Whenever I think of her I can feel the love I have for her right now."

"And send your love to her like a prayer."

"It does no good to regret what happened in the past or to fear what might happen in the future."

"All wasted energy."

Sally glowed in understanding. "And that takes away from the strength I can put into being my best right now!" Her grin was back and the determination to be her best.

"It's easier to do your best when you feel empowered."

"And when I'm sad about what happened years ago and the decisions I made when I was young, I feel diminished."

Sally got to her feet. "Thanks, Gaff. Bobby's right. You're one smart old man." Her step was lighter as she walked off down the beach.

# chapter 21

Gaff heard a mixture of the bravado of adolescent boys and the giggling of adolescent girls. He scanned the beach for the source of the sounds and Bobby followed his gaze.

"Young people're back."

Bobby nodded. "They are."

"Having a good time. The sounds'll change in a couple of hours. They'll be drunk and then they'll just make noise, drunken noise. Hate to see it happen."

"Why don't you talk to them? Tell them they bother you. Tell them they're making too much noise."

"Laughter and sounds of fun don't bother me, no matter how loud. It's the booze I don't like. Hate to see them kill their bodies with the booze. Hate to see them end up like Harriet or the others who believe they can't function without the help of a little nip."

"Go on, say something to them."

"I can only help if they come to me. Works best if they sit on the cooler."

"If you don't like drinking, why don't you talk to me about it?"

"Are you coming to me for that?"

Bobby shook his head. "I don't have a problem with booze. I go out for drinks, but I drank more when I was on the force. Used to hang out with the guys after work. To relax, de-stress, I guess. Ended up getting drunk a lot, too. Probably more than I should have."

"That changed."

"Yeah. I don't know many people here and I'm on all sorts of medications. Don't drink much at all any more."

"So, one blessing of the heart problem is that you live a healthier life."

"I hadn't thought of it that way, but yes."

"You get drunk in high school?"

"Of course. Only nerds didn't drink." A smile washed over his face. "Yeah, I drank. Every weekend we'd really put 'em down. Drinking contests, beer pong and other games."

"Ever drink with a girl?"

"Old man, you're not telling me you didn't drink with your dates. One reason to ply them with liquor was to get them 'ready,' so to speak. They were a lot easier to 'convince' if they were drunk. A lot easier to convince." His memories of these times were even better, if the smile on his face was any indication.

"Thought so."

The silence gave them time to think with hearts and minds.

"Those girls wanted to have fun, but they needed the excuse. The next day they could say it was the booze that made them do it. They could still say they were 'nice' girls."

"Maybe. It was OK that they didn't decide of their own free will to have sex with you?" Gaff was looking up the beach toward the group of young people who were louder now, getting rowdy. Drunker.

"At that age, I only thought about getting my rocks off. You know how hormones drive a man when he's young. Didn't care about a relationship or even whether I really liked her. Just the sex."

Gaff let that idea percolate.

Bobby looked toward the group of young people. "They don't know what they're doing, do they?"

"Nope. Not many of us do when we're young."

Bobby brought his eyes back to the tip of his rod and to the bird fishing in the waves. "It's all based on a lack of respect for the girl, isn't it?"

"Yep."

"No one's showing respect for her, including the girl herself. She's there for a guy's pleasure. If that's the way you learn to have relationships, then the girl is the lesser, to be dominated by the big strong guy who wants to get his rocks off."

Bobby was sifting sand through his fingers as he must have been sifting these new ideas through his mind.

Gaff said, "There're rules about the size of different fish that can be kept when they're caught. The rules change all the time and are different for each kind of fish."

"A lot of fishermen keep any fish they get, regardless of the size. They don't pay any attention to the regulations."

"The real fishermen, the people out here all the time, want to protect the fish as much as they want to catch them."

"Real fishermen are conservative… so there'll be fish for years to come. So they can continue to fish, to be fishermen."

"Synergy."

Bobby's eyes scanned the waves, the birds, the beach. "It all works together, doesn't it? We have to take care of the other parts to protect our part."

"Uh hunh." Gaff could almost hear the whirring of Bobby's mental equipment.

"So if I go over there to say something to those young people about how destructive that drinking is and all the stuff that goes on because of the drinking, I'll be trying to protect the other parts of the whole."

"Yep."

"You help people all the time. You help me. Why shouldn't I go over to talk with those kids?"

"Think back to you at that age, running on hormones."

"Full of myself… I'd have laughed myself silly at the old man who doesn't know anything about my life. Trying to tell me what to do. Some nerve, you stupid old man."

"When would the vacation fisherman see the value of the rules?"

"When he puts his line out there and never gets a bite."

"When did you learn not to drink so much."

Bobby was heading toward angry. "It's different for me. I had this heart surgery and the doctor told me not to drink."

"Why did you listen?"

"I didn't want the complications from mixing my medical condition and the drugs with alcohol. My doctor read me the riot act, told me all the horrible things that would happen to me. Up to and including having my manhood fall off!" He thought more of the subject and his eyes lit up when he found the golden thread. "To avoid pain."

"Uh hunh."

Bobby smiled his recognition of the truth. "We only make changes to avoid the pain. Before we feel that pain, we do the same things over and over."

He glanced in the direction of the young people. "When they realize their lives aren't going the way they wanted, they'll make some changes. Maybe after the divorce or the illness or the lost job, they'll be open to new ideas, hoping to make their lives better. Then they'll come talk with you."

"Maybe."

Bobby looked at Gaff, maybe for the first time. "Who are you?"

"Just a fisherman."

"But you have the answers."

"I'm the old man of the beach, lived here a long time. Lived a long time. Seen a lot of the world." He let that sink in and then asked, "Are the answers from me or from within you?"

"Are they in our hearts all the time?"

Gaff smiled in his heart to think that Bobby was such a good student.

Bobby's voice was colored with awe. "You point out the places where I can see the answers, but you let me find my own. The answers come from nature, from my own heart."

Gaff searched the horizon, but there was a smile dawning on his face. "Maybe the answers are in the questions if you look close."

"Isn't there some way you could help people avoid making mistakes? Like those kids. Couldn't you help them get on the right track before they hit the painful parts?"

"Parents could teach them right from the start, but parents don't always do that. Don't always know."

"My parents tried to teach me different, but I didn't listen."

"There's your answer."

"I didn't see the future. The future didn't exist. I didn't think I'd ever get out of high school, and then I only thought about being free."

"That's part of being young."

"When I was finally free, I started thinking about being in the service so I wouldn't be as free. I was having a good time and that's what mattered. Moving from place to place on automatic pilot, you might say."

"Maybe young people have it right. Only this moment exists."

"But I got distracted by things that were important to me at the time and didn't lead anywhere in the future. No, it's not just a focus on the moment that's important."

"Or maybe the problem is the focus on satisfying our own desires to the exclusion of other goals." Gaff watched the waves and hoped his friend could see the answers.

"My parents taught me a good work ethic. When I went to work I always did my job to the best of my ability. I didn't want to work in Dad's business because I didn't want to give him credit for my success. Needed to be my own man."

Patience.

"When I got married, I tried to buy her what she needed to be happy. She just needed more than I could afford."

"What do you need to be happy?"

"Not much any more. A lot less than I thought I did. And a lot less than she did."

"What, then?"

The answer came slowly. "To catch some fish?"

"We sit here most of the day without catching fish. Are you happy?"

Bobby frowned. "I am... happier here than I was anywhere in my life or at any time."

"Why?"

"You. I'm happy to have you as a friend."

"Is that it?"

"No, there's more. I'm calm now. I feel like I'm part of something bigger than me, something special." He waved his hand toward the water.

Gaff waited.

"I belong, I'm a part, but I'm also important. I have a special part to play."

"And?" Gaff could see the answer come from deep within his friend.

"I really like myself. I like who I am, not just what I can earn or the job I do. It's not because some group of people tell me I'm OK. I just know it now. That's a change for me. I didn't see it happening, but it happened while I was sitting right here on the beach doing nothing but tending that fishing gear that sometimes brings in fish and sometimes doesn't."

Gaff repeated the question, "You need to catch fish to be happy?"

Bobby shook his head, his eyes filled with awe. "No. One way of putting it is that just being in the world makes me happy. I don't think I was ever really in the world before."

"Being in the world's good."

"There were times when I thought I should have died on that operating table. I was mad at myself because I wasted my life, because I didn't accomplish anything. I was mad at myself because I failed in marriage and don't have any children and have a bum heart and don't even have a job any more. Here I am in the prime of my life and I'm already washed up, a failure."

Gaff listened.

"Now I realize there're other things to do. Maybe more important things." He glanced at the group of young people. "If I have kids, I want to teach them the right things about treating their bodies with respect. I'd teach them to treat other people with respect, too."

"Good goal."

"I have so much to learn, so much more."

Gaff smiled. "You're doing fine."

"And my wife. She wasn't the right person for me. Only saw me as a source of money to buy the things she believed would make her happy. No matter what I got her, she wasn't happy. She's remarried now to someone making a lot more. My brother sees them out and tells me she doesn't look any happier. She talks about the stuff they buy or the trips they take. I never hear that she's happy with that man."

"That's sad."

"They have kids, too. Mom's always telling me how much trouble they get into. We're from a suburb like that. Everybody knows everything."

 Gaff liked what he was hearing.

"I want to be with someone who's happy in themselves, rich or poor. Not that I wouldn't want to give her the moon, but that's not what she would think she needs to be happy." He chuckled. "What am I saying? I'm on disability. What could I give anyone?"

"You'd be surprised."

# chapter 22

They sat together in companionable silence. Gaff meditating on the clouds and Bobby lost in his new understanding of the meaning of life.

Sally and Sue stopped by the pirate flag to chat and to display the new additions to their collection of sharks' teeth.

Sally said meaningfully, "I've been telling Sue that she should come talk with you, Gaff. She could tell you how happy she is. Might be a nice change for you."

Gaff smiled, that would be a change.

Sally laughed. "Maybe some of that happiness will rub off on me."

He laughed, too. "Looks like it already has."

The two women walked off down the beach, heads down, looking for new treasures. Their footprints followed the line of shells left by the water at high tide.

Bobby watched them as they searched, "They don't even notice the schools of fish swimming close to the shore. They don't notice the waves and the clouds. All they see are the shells."

"Oh, they see the other, too, but they focus on the shells."

Mae stopped on her return from down the beach. "Howdy. I walked so much farther today that I'm exhausted. Dawn'll be proud of me, though." At the mention of Dawn, she waved toward the yellow house. She chatted about plans for the day, for Dawn and herself. On her way toward the yellow house, she turned to call back, "Dawn's looking forward to meeting you, Gaff. We talk about that a lot."

Gaff waved his response. He noticed Bobby's smile. "What're you smiling at?"

"What a wonder you are."

Several other people came to talk about the flag. They noticed it from far down the beach and wanted to see who the pirate was. They didn't stay for long.

Maybe they'll come back. One by one, alone, when they're ready.

Bobby and Gaff tended to their fishing, replacing the bait, casting into the waves. Bobby brought in a nice-sized trout and Gaff pulled in a couple of blues, but the big one eluded them today.

Priscilla came along, lost in thought. "What a glorious day!" She said when she saw Gaff.

Gaff introduced Bobby. "My new fishing buddy."

Priscilla grinned. "Someone to talk to during the long hours on the beach."

Bobby chuckled. "I'm the one does the talking. Gaff, here, probably wishes I'd shut up sometimes."

Gaff noticed a little nervousness in Bobby's manner. As Priscilla turned to continue her walk, Gaff provided the nudge. "Bobby, why don't you stretch your legs? You need exercise now you're better."

Bobby looked at Gaff in surprise, but said to Priscilla, "Wouldn't mind a little walk, if you don't mind company."

She smiled and motioned with her hand, "Let's go before the tide comes in and we can't get to the end of the beach."

Gaff grinned to himself as the two started down the beach. Suddenly Bobby turned, "Hey, Gaff, you take care of catching my fish?"

"I'll do it!"

They were gone for a long while. When they returned, Bobby had the bright eyes of new interest. He and Priscilla stood talking at the water's edge for a few minutes and then she waved to Gaff and moved on. Bobby watched her go down the beach for a time and then took his place in the chair next to Gaff's.

Gaff looked at the waves. "Good walk?"

Bobby didn't say anything. He was lost in thought.

Gaff waited.

"Catch anything while I was gone?"

Gaff grinned. "Only the big one for this week. And on your gear!"

Bobby turned to Gaff in surprise. "Oh, man, and I missed it. Let me see."

Gaff opened the cooler wide. Bobby gave a loud whistle.

After some thought, Bobby asked excitedly, "If it was on my gear, isn't the fish mine?"

"Nope. I'll share, though."

"I guess you get all the bragging rights, too." Bobby's voice had a slight tone of dejection.

Gaff looked at the tip of his rod for the signal and then scanned the water. "All mine."

Bobby sounded pleased with himself. "I've got bigger fish to fry."

"Hmmm. Looks like."

"Priscilla says you helped her see her way. That right?"

Gaff nodded.

"You help everyone on the beach?"

Loud laughing came from the group of youngsters, sloppy drunk now and it was only afternoon. Gaff stared hard at the water. "Nope."

Bobby glanced at the young people. "They'll come to you when they're ready."

"Those who have ears to hear, let them hear."

"You say that a lot. Where does it come from?"

"Something I read. It was written a long time ago and I thought it was a good way of putting it."

"A long time ago?"

"New Testament. Gospel of Mary. Other things, too."

"Gaff, you're a strange old bird, you know? You don't look like the kind of guy to be quoting the Bible."

"Don't. Don't even read it. But I do read a lot."

Gaff heard the "zing" of Bobby's thoughts returning to his afternoon walk.

"Gaff, that Priscilla's a nice woman, don't you think?"

"A question or a statement?"

"Both, I guess."

"Yep. And that's an answer." Gaff's eyes twinkled as he looked at Bobby.

"She told me she's living her dream. Happy with what she does and who she is. That's good, isn't it?"

"Question or statement?"

"Both."

"Yep."

"She's got a good figure. Pretty, too."

Gaff nodded. He cut his eyes, a sly glance, toward Bobby who was smiling.

Slurred comments from the young crowd interrupted Bobby's reverie. Without saying anything, he rose and marched toward them. He said in a loud voice, "I didn't want you to be taken advantage of, but if you want to be a slut… you do as you like."

Gaff watched the results with great interest.

The boys laughed and said some unkind things to the girls.

Bobby turned on his heel and walked back to his chair. By the time Bobby got settled, the young crowd had erupted in a yelling fight, watered by feminine tears. All fed by the beers.

One question stood out from the background. In a shrill voice, one girl asked, "Why didn't you stand up to him?"

The other girl said, "At least you should have told him to go to hell."

The first girl taunted, "Was he too big for you, two against one?"

Gaff couldn't hear the rest of the words, but he could hear sneering laughter.

The first girl said to her friend. "They're jerks. I'm leaving."

The boys stopped laughing. One asked, "Where're you going? Let's have some fun. It'll be dark soon."

The other boy spoke louder to cover the increasing distance to the retreating girls. "Have another beer and forget it. He's just a jealous old man. He's so old, he probably can't get it up any more." Laughing and more comments that Gaff couldn't understand at this distance.

The boys looked toward Bobby, for some reaction. One of them hefted a bottle menacingly. No reaction.

The girls were talking to each other, angry voices mixed in with the sounds of steps on the walkway. They were so far away by now that the sense of their words was lost. Only the feelings traveled the distance.

Gaff looked at Bobby. He was looking at the waves, grinning. When he felt Gaff's question, he shrugged and said, "What? I just wanted to make them think? You told me the big fish are only here if their food is. If the food disappears, the big fish may have to change methods or hunting areas. I was scaring off the bait."

"Interesting tactic."

Although still angry, the boys' voices lowered again into mumbles, accompanied by the sounds of packing up. Soon, they, too, moved across the walkway. Car doors were slammed in anger. Soon after, the engine revved and tires crunched across the gravel parking lot.

Bobby grinned, "Any man worth his salt would run after the woman he loves."

Gaff teased. "And leave his fishing gear behind? A man's got to have his priorities."

"Yeah, his priorities." Bobby watched the large jolly roger flapping in the breeze. "Gaff, sometimes if the fish don't come to you, you have to go to them."

# chapter 23

Priscilla stopped to see Gaff early the next morning. She sat on the cooler. "I'm supposed to go home next week, but my plans aren't set in stone. The writing's going well. I'm really happy with what I'm doing. In fact, I'm really happy."

"Good to hear."

They sat in companionable silence. Priscilla jumped to her feet when Bobby arrived to take his place next to Gaff. They exchanged greetings and both seemed a little nervous.

Gaff found this to be humorous. He made a show of watching the waves to hide his observation of the people.

Bobby was about to bait his hook when Priscilla suddenly said, "I'll be heading down the beach now. Want to get in a good walk before I start working."

Bobby looked confused for a moment. In the end, he got the right idea. "Can I walk with you? I need to get back into shape." He patted his belly. "Want to lose this. The walk yesterday proved how far off the track I've gotten."

She smiled and they started walking in the direction of Fort Fisher. Gaff heard Bobby explain as they walked toward the water, "I didn't have this gut while I was on the force. I wasn't one of those guys who ate donuts all the time. My diet was healthy and I went to the gym every day. Every day." The rest of his words were taken away from Gaff by the wind as they moved down the beach. He did notice Bobby flex his biceps to emphasize his point.

Gaff smiled and thought to himself how as much as things change and people change, they really stay the same. That's good: the way of the world.

For the next several days, this scenario was repeated early in the morning and later in the afternoon, before Bobby set up his gear and after he packed it up. Or did he time his arrival at the beach to suit her schedule?

Every day after the walk, Bobby would try to talk about other things, but always came around to talking about Priscilla.

Gaff saw it before Bobby did, but it always happens that way. Every day, the couple were more animated as they walked down the beach. Their footprints got closer in the sand.

"Boy, was I out of shape. Each time I walk, I feel less and less tired when I get back here. Priscilla's in great shape."

"Been walking twice a day for a month." Gaff chuckled.

"She tells me about her book. She's all excited about it. Last night I read the first chapter and I really liked it. I don't usually read that kind of stuff, but even I got interested in it. She says you get three pages to get the reader's attention and she got mine on the first one."

"Last night?"

Bobby's face might have reddened under his tan. Gaff wasn't sure. "Yeah, last night. We've been spending some time together. Went to dinner last night at Freddie's. Pasta night."

Gaff waited.

"Priscilla's a nice woman. Happy in herself. I like her." He cut his eyes to look at Gaff. "I think."

Gaff tried not to smile.

They slid back into silence, watching the waves, thinking their thoughts.

The shock of the week was that their solitude was interrupted by a young girl in a very small bikini. She said nervously, tightening her cover-up around her waist, "I've been sitting up there for a while."

Bobby motioned to the bench on the walkway. "There?"

She nodded.

Gaff smiled. "Watching?"

She nodded again, this time averting her eyes. "When I saw you walking with that woman, I thought you probably weren't all that bad. You know, not some serial killer like they warn about on television."

Bobby smiled. "Sit on the cooler. It's the most popular seat on the beach."

She turned to Gaff. "And yesterday all those other people came to talk with you. Didn't seem like you could be mean or weird with all those friends." This was said as she perched gingerly on the cooler, back rigid, shifting her weight nervously from side to side.

"Been watching for a while, have you?"

She nodded shyly. "I was here with my friends a couple of days ago. I noticed your flag. It's hard to miss because it's so big. We were drinking beer and I guess we got too loud. You came over and said something."

Bobby cut his eyes around to Gaff. "I remember."

She lowered her voice. "I guess you were right." She watched intently as she picked at some invisible something on her cover-up.

The men waited for her to finish. Another lesson in patience for Bobby.

She cleared her throat and said more strongly, "My name's Jennifer."

Gaff heard an invitation for the other side of the introductions in her expectant silence. He obliged. "Gaff, and my friend here is Bobby."

She repeated, under her breath, "Gaff and Bobby." Then she continued louder, "I moved here during the summer and I'm just making friends. Adam is really cute. That's the boy I was with. I like Adam so when he started paying attention to me, I was excited about it. You know, new in the area and a cute guy seemed to like me."

She twisted her fingers in her hair nervously. "We had one other date and he went right to the heavy petting. Should have been a hint. The other day was our second date and… and, you were probably right about what they planned for later."

Bobby shrugged his shoulders. "Hey, I was a young guy once and not that long ago."

Jennifer seemed to need a minute to process this admission. "Were you really trying to help us?"

Bobby looked at Gaff again and then at Jennifer. "I was. I was, indeed."

She intertwined her fingers in her lap. "Why'd you say that terrible thing?"

"To make you think, as much as anything."

Her voice lowered again. "Did I really look like that?"

"You looked like you wanted to fit in… At any cost."

"I did?"

Bobby nodded his answer.

"Did Tracey look that way?"

"She looked like she'd done this before. She knew what was coming. Maybe she didn't like it, but she'd been there before. I mean the feeling bad-about-yourself part. High price to pay for being with a guy who didn't care enough to chase after you when you left."

Jennifer giggled nervously. "He did chase after us a little later. When we heard the car doors slamming, I ducked into a yard next to one of the houses on the beach. I told Tracey to walk on down the road so I could watch what happened next. She played along."

Gaff smiled slyly. "What'd you see?"

"They tried to talk her into the car. Asked where I was. She told them I ran home, upset. Adam said something about 'who needs her anyway.' Then they tried to talk Tracey into the car to be with both of them."

"Did she go?"

Jennifer's voice was sad, "She looked like she was thinking about it, only she knew I was watching. They joked about being the three musketeers: all for one, one for all! At the time I didn't know what they were saying, but later Tracey told me they were telling her they both wanted to get off. And since she was the only girl in sight, she was good for it."

Bobby blew a noisy breath to express his disgust.

Jennifer looked at Bobby and almost whispered, "Thanks for saving me from a battle."

"Or worse."

She looked intently at her fingers as she worked designs with them in her lap. Nervous. "Or worse."

Gaff waited for the question. He could see Bobby struggle with patience, listening.

Jennifer finally asked, "Did I blow it? Already, in a new school?"

Bobby shook his head, but Gaff deflected the question. "Nice bathing suit. Looks good on you."

Jennifer was back to her small voice. "Thanks."

"Pick it out by yourself?"

Jennifer laughed, glad for the change in topic. "Oh, no. My best friend in Atlanta helped me. It took a whole day of shopping just to find two bathing suits, one for her and one for me."

"Had fun, too."

"We did. We had fun all the time." Suddenly her voice softened. "That's why I miss her."

Gaff ignored this last. "Did it take two of you to pick out the suits?"

Jennifer sounded as though she were talking to a slow learner. "It's easier for someone else to see how something looks on you. I mean, I might think it's the right color or the right shape and really cute, but Alison could see whether it was right for my body. You know, she would look at the whole picture."

"Um hunh."

Bobby was curious about where this was going.

"I did the same for her. Sometimes, if you really like an outfit, you don't see it objectively."

"So when you have strong feelings in a matter, you may need a second opinion?"

"That's right. A second opinion."

"Did you get a second opinion about Adam? Since you're new to the area and all? I know you liked the way he looked, but did you ask anyone what kind of person he is?"

"Well, one of the girls in biology class said some mean things about him, but I thought she was just jealous. I thought that she would like to go out with him and didn't want competition from me."

"What're you going to do now?"

Jennifer thought a moment. Her voice brightened. "Next time I see her, I'll thank her for the warning. Maybe I should make friends with her rather than..." She stopped and screwed her face into a frown. "I don't know what to do because some girls are jealous and would tell me lies to confuse me or worse."

"How'd you make friends with Alison?"

Jennifer giggled. "We were in freshman gym class in Atlanta and each of us got voted 'klutz of the year' by our groups. First day! We knew we were meant to be friends."

"That's a good story."

Bobby asked, "You felt like you knew each other? Did you feel as though you were old friends getting back together after a long separation?"

Jennifer looked at Bobby with wide eyes. "That's it. That's just the way it felt. No one's ever been able to understand before."

Bobby scanned the water again, looking for signs. "It's happening more and more these days. You'll find another friend who's even better for you. Just have the belief that you will and the friend will come to you in some unexpected way."

Gaff smiled in approval at the tack this conversation was taking. "You ever have any real bad health scare?"

Jennifer screwed up her face. "Health scare?"

Gaff glanced at Jennifer. "Time you were so sick the doctors weren't sure you'd live."

Jennifer shifted her weight on the cooler. "When I was eleven, but how did you know?"

"A guess. What happened?"

"I was in the hospital for a long time. I had to have transfusions, a lot of them. The doctors couldn't figure out how I was losing all the blood, but I was. They did everything they knew to do, every test. My mom stayed with me in the hospital. I could tell she was scared. She tried to hide it, but I could tell. For some reason I wasn't."

"How'd the doctors figure it out?"

"A nurse came into the room and sat talking with Mom. She said that she had almost died as a kid and she knew I'd get well. I thought she was pretty strange and when she touched me, it felt different."

"Different? How?"

"Sort of tingly, I guess. She was gentler than the other nurses and her touch was softer. More like she actually cared what happened to me. But the main difference was that when she had her hand on me, I felt this trembling, tingly feeling in my abdomen. I didn't feel that with anyone else."

"Was she touching your belly?"

"No, she touched my arm. Didn't really do anything like take my temperature or my blood pressure or anything. She just stood there looking down at me with eyes that told me she loved me. And she had both of her hands on my arm."

"What happened then?"

"After she left, the doctor came in and poked around again, but this time only on my stomach. He went rushing out and they did some other tests right away. Later, Mom told me they found a tear in my intestines." She pulled aside her cover-up and moved her bathing suit just a little to reveal a scar on her lower abdomen. She quickly covered herself and nervously pulled the sarong around her more tightly. "I don't usually show complete strangers my scar. Especially not strange men."

Bobby silently raised his tee shirt to show his scar. "I have one, too. Different from yours, and bigger. I got it this year, but they thought I had a chance of dying, too."

Jennifer giggled nervously and made a grand gesture of looking at the horizon.

Bobby patted her arm. "We're glad you came through that ordeal."

She suddenly looked at her hands in her lap. "I wish my daddy was more like you. Then maybe Mom wouldn't divorce him and we wouldn't have to move here."

"Then you wouldn't meet us. It is as it's meant to be."

The three watched the waves for a long while before Jennifer said, "Maybe you could be my friends."

"Of course, we can. We're here on the beach most of the time and you can talk with us any time. Like Bobby said, you'll meet a girl who'll be your best friend. When you do, you remember that sometimes the old guys have good things to say. But you should always check in to see what your heart says, most of all."

"I used to be a policeman and I know there're bad people out there. You do have to be careful. You seem to have a good sense about who's good and who isn't. It comes from inside and will guide you better than any person can."

"We can help you learn to listen to it."

Jennifer looked at Gaff suddenly. "Then why didn't it tell me to avoid Adam?"

"If you had avoided Adam, you wouldn't have met us."

Three sets of eyes turned toward the ocean again. In his own way, each person was thanking Mother Water for his good fortune.

# chapter 24

It was late afternoon. The beach had almost cleared out after a day in the sun when Gaff noticed a lone man sitting in a circle of empty chairs. He was reading in the last warmth of the day. He might be waiting for the bathrooms to clear before he went into the house. Smart man.

Gaff got up to be a fisherman: reel the lines in, replace the bait, and cast them out again. Just one last cast for the day. Another few minutes in the solitude of the empty beach and then he would go home. He was so intent on that task, he was startled when the man was suddenly beside him.

His visitor laughed when Gaff jumped. "I don't usually have that effect on people. You must've been really concentrating."

"Didn't hear you coming."

"Name's Pierce."

"Mine's Gaff." He looked into the man's face and recognized it from somewhere. Familiar looking.

"Nice to meet you. I've been watching you and your flag. Lots of people come to visit. You must be a local."

"Yep."

He waved in the direction of a bright blue house. "I'm renting for the week. Great place. Right on the beach."

"First time in Kure?"

"It is and I love it. Won't be the last time."

Gaff stepped back a pace to mime inspecting Pierce's face. "You look familiar. Do I know you?"

"You do if you watch television."

"You're on TV. Don't watch much myself, but my family does. What show're you on? So I know to tell them which one to watch."

Pierce laughed. "This's exactly why I love it here. I stayed on the beach the entire day and not one person asked me for my autograph. No one wanted a photograph with me and no one asked me to help them break into television. No one even knew my name here. I find that incredible and a wonderful vacation."

"Why are you on television, if you don't want people to know you?"

"I love my job. I love acting on television. What gets to me is the constant barrage of demands. Everyone deserves some privacy. Everyone."

"A number of people come here for the privacy." Gaff's thoughts went to his other actor friend. "And yet you came over to tell me who you are."

"Not so much to tell you who I am, but to find out who you are. I've been on the beach all day and I've watched dozens of people visit you. I got curious."

"Curious?"

"About who you are."

"Just a fisherman. People on the beach are friendly. Most are curious about my catch. Some pass word from fisherman to fisherman about who's caught what. Like a human telegraph network."

"Others sit to talk for hours."

"True."

"What do they talk about for hours?"

"What would you talk about?"

"The job, the family, current events."

Gaff gestured toward the book on Pierce's chair. "Books and movies and life."

"Hm-m-m. Life."

"You talked about life, your life."

Pierce straightened his back and spread his arms dramatically."My life is great. I'm living my dream."

"So am I. Best way to do it."

Pierce seemed to be doing a memory search, for a particular subject? "I once read about a fisherman on the beach. He had a flag, too. Now I think of it, the story was set here. In fact that book gave me the idea to come here... took me a couple of years to get to it. Don't remember the details, but it was a good story. It was really about the people who talked to him."

"There are a couple of us, I guess. And I always thought I was unique."

They chatted for a while about the water and the fish and just stared out at the horizon. Their thoughts were interrupted by a call from the blue house and Pierce gathered his things to go home for the night. He'd be back tomorrow.

The afternoon sky was beginning to redden and the sun would be going down soon. Bobby left early to get ready for dinner with Priscilla. Pierce's short visit was over, but for some reason, Gaff lingered in his spot, waiting. He brought in one of his lines, but baited the other and cast it out into the surf. Maybe there was just one more fish for him to catch today.

Gaff heard the sounds of young voices coming down the beach. He thought he recognized one of them and so when they stopped before getting to him, he walked down to investigate. It was Charlie Fitzgerald, just as he thought. That made him sad.

"Charlie, what're you doing here on a week night? And drinking? Don't you have to work tomorrow?"

The girl with Charlie looked at Gaff the way she would a piece of whale dung on the beach. "What's your problem, old man? This is Charlie Fitzgerald and he has a right to be here on this beach any time he wants." The booze was beginning to affect her speech.

Gaff ignored her and said, "Charlie, you'll do what you want. I just don't understand what that is.'

"I'm fishing. Just like you, old man, I'm fishing." He put his arm around the girl to pull her closer to his side.

The girl pulled away from Charlie and stepped menacingly toward Gaff. She was drunk and getting belligerent. "Get away from us, old man. Leave us alone. Charlie Fitzgerald has a right to be here—he practically owns the whole beach. And I'm with him." As she said this last, she returned to Charlie's side and put her arm around his waist. A proprietary act, if ever there was one.

"Looks like she's staking claim, my boy." Then he moved his face closer to the girl's to say, "I know very well where and

when Charlie has a right to be. Don't fret about that, my girl…
Better watch it, Charlie here has a reputation."

She laughed so hard that she lost her balance and fell
against Charlie.

Charlie stumbled under her weight, but managed to keep
both of them upright. "Come on, Gaff. Leave us alone to fish in
peace."

"Where's your gear? Better be careful, son, she's a
belligerent drunk. Bad sign."

"I can take care of myself." Charlie pushed the girl away to
stand on her own feet and under her own power.

She was becoming less capable of balancing on those feet
the longer they talked. Gaff figured they did a shot just before
leaving the car. He knew the signs.

"You can use my tackle. Come over here and let me set you
up."

Charlie looked at his date. "All the bait I need is in the car
and she's the only fish on my line for now."

His date slurred her words. "Why're we standing here?
Let's go down to the water or… or… I need to sit down for a
while. Why is this old man still standing here? Why don't you get
rid of him?"

Charlie grabbed her as she slipped toward the ground.
"Didn't I introduce you two? Amanda, I'd like you to meet
Geoffrey Andrew Fitzgerald, the fourth. Grandpa, I'd like you to
meet Amanda."

Gaff offered his hand for the shake, but instead of shaking
hands she slipped out of Charlie's arms to land on the sand. She
was definitely passed out and from the looks of it, would be for a
while. Both men looked down at her. Gaff thought it would be
comical if it weren't so sad.

Charlie rolled his eyes. "Oops. Misjudged again. She's a
lightweight. Can't hold her booze like Michelle."

"OK. Bring her over here and we'll lay her on the beach so
we can talk. You can have your way with her another night."

They held Amanda, each under an arm, to drag her the few
steps to Gaff's spot. Gaff spread the towel while Charlie held
Amanda up. Then they laid her down as gently as they could.

They turned their eyes toward the water and rosy clouds reflecting the last hints of the red sun setting behind them.

"What do you see in her?"

"Use your imagination, Gaff. Variety is the spice of life and Michelle and Georgia are both busy tonight. I was just going to practice some new moves."

"You're not talking about dance moves, I guess. At least you're honest. Do you tell her?"

"That I'm planning to boff her? Yeah, just like that."

Gaff looked again at Amanda. "She's pretty, but there's something, something not…"

Charlie interrupted, his voice harsh. "Gaff, she's a gold-digger hoping to edge her way ahead of the two other girls in my life."

"She knows you see the other two?"

"Everybody does. It helps me get what I want. Each tries to buy her way into the number one spot. Couldn't work better. Your grandson's brilliant."

"Just brilliant." Gaff wasn't convinced.

"Gaff, you're looking at the rich playboy of Cape Fear! Impressive, isn't it? I drive a nice car, wear good clothes, and all the girls swarm around me like mosquitoes on a humid summer night."

"And what if you get stung?"

"What do you mean?"

"Charlie, suppose one of these girls gets the bright idea to get pregnant and blackmail you for the rest of your life?"

"They wouldn't do that. They know I wouldn't marry them."

Gaff looked into Charlie's eyes to assess his level of sobriety. "If they had a baby, you'd be responsible for it. Until it turned 18. The judges do that now. You wouldn't have to marry the girl. Wouldn't even get the benefit of bed-time."

Charlie thought for a moment and then shrugged. "I'll start using protection, I guess."

"Best I can hope for right now."

Charlie glanced out to the water in the light of the full moon. "It is beautiful, isn't it?"

"The most beautiful thing in the entire world. I've seen a lot of the world and I always come back to this...You know the full moon is visible in the sky during the day, but people only notice it after the sun goes down. Hidden right in front of our eyes."

Maybe the night chill was seeping in through the fog in Charlie's brain. A sad tone replaced the earlier bravado. "Gaff, I don't want to marry any of these girls. I don't even want to be with them for very long. It seems so empty now. The game's not as much fun as it used to be."

"End it."

"It's not that simple. I want to be with someone... just not these girls. I remember the stories you told about meeting Grandma. I haven't met that kind of person. Grandma's special and there aren't any more out there like her."

Gaff looked out at the moonlight shimmering on the water like liquid silver. His grandson's sadness worried him. "Is that what you're looking for, son? Julia is wonderful, but there must be a woman out there for you, too."

"I want a special person to love."

"Is that why you drink so much?" Right now he was glad that alcohol acted like a truth serum to loosen the lips.

"I drink because I have a good time when I'm drunk." A pause. "But maybe I'd drink less if I had a real relationship."

"This is one of those chicken and egg questions."

"Hunh?"

Gaff stretched his legs out on the sand in front of him. "Yeah, Charlie, the question is which comes first. Does the relationship come first or putting away the shot glass?"

"I'm not following."

Gaff made a mark in the sand. "OK, let's take it point by point. You say you want to be with a special woman. How would you describe her?"

"I've never thought about this before."

"About time, then."

You could almost hear his strokes as Charlie swam through the liquor to rationality. "First, she has to be beautiful, thin, long legs, great smile. Needs a sense of humor to live in this family. A big, healthy sense of humor.

"Third, she should be really smart. I get bored with all the talk about clothes or things they want or other people. I guess that means reading or at least watching intelligent television shows."

He paused. "I don't mean just book smart, but commonsense. She should be able to figure things out, to solve problems on her own. I wouldn't like a dumb blond or someone who just recites facts."

Gaff ticked things off on his fingers. "Beautiful, able to laugh, and able to talk about concepts, problem-solving. What next?"

"Says and does nice things, not negative. Competent and independent, but not so independent that she's a 'ball buster'."

"Sounds like you want an 'alpha' woman. There may be some other things you haven't yet thought of, but you can do that tomorrow."

"If I describe the person, I'll know when I see her. Thanks for the help, old man."

"Not so fast, son. Oh, I think you'll know her, but there's more."

"Now what?"

Gaff drew another hash mark in the sand. "The next thing is to look at yourself. Are you the alpha male such an alpha woman would be attracted to?"

"Of course, I am. I'm Charlie Fitzgerald... But, I've never looked at it like that."

"Look at the situation from her point of view. You're young and beautiful, a great conversationalist, and very intelligent."

"Long legs, too."

"Long legs are a plus. If you're an alpha woman, you can have any man on the planet. What would you want? Would you want someone who does the minimum at work because he's so sure that he'll own the business one day that he doesn't need to work to earn it? Someone treading water at work? Someone not going anywhere in life in general? Someone not interested in being bigger and better?"

Gaff saw that Charlie was listening and his eyes were getting clearer.

"Or would you want an intelligent man, working in a job that interests him and enables him to be the best he can be? Someone who's growing and moving ahead?"

Charlie shrugged. "I have the money she'd like and I'll get more."

"Not enough. Again, from her point of view. If you were an alpha woman and could have any man on the planet, would you want a man known for treating women with a gross lack of respect. Would you want a man who pits one woman against another to manipulate them? Would you want a man who doesn't know how to give of himself emotionally and thinks that money is the way to a girl's heart?"

"You know, Gaff, you are a real son of a bitch."

"Or if you could have any man on the planet, would you choose to be with a man who knew how to make you feel loved and like the princess you are?"

Was there new light behind Charlie's eyes? "So what you're saying is that if I could have any man in the world, I'd be picky... She would be as picky as I am."

Gaff nodded, fingers figuratively crossed.

"I do see what you mean. If I want a princess, I have to be a prince. If I want a true princess, I have to be a prince through and through, not just on the surface."

"Those who have ears to hear, let them hear."

"What does that mean? You say it all the time."

"Only that you understand the parts of the message you're ready to understand. And finally, you're ready to hear this part of it." He felt joy flood into his heart.

"You've been trying to tell me this for a long time, haven't you?"

"Since you were in high school and I could see you moving in the wrong direction. I love you, Charlie, and want you to be happy."

"And to be happy, I have to take control of my life and begin to take it seriously and not like some joke that'll go on forever. That's pretty much what you've been telling me all along, isn't it?"

"Missed opportunities may be gone permanently. When a day's over, it's over forever. So if you haven't made the most of that day and taken the opportunities that were presented, then they're gone."

Charlie threw some shells he found in the sand. "Is it too late, Grandpa? Is it too late to become the prince my princess would want?"

"No, Charlie. Today is an excellent day to start."

Amanda stirred. "What happened? Are we still at the beach? Oh-h, my head hurts. How much did I drink?"

Charlie and Gaff got to their feet to help her up. They helped brush the sand off her clothes.

Amanda pushed Gaff's hands away. "Who's that old man? Get him away from me."

Charlie looked at Gaff with a smile tinged with pride. "Amanda, this is one smart old coot. You would be lucky to have him on your side. In fact, he is on your side."

Amanda turned toward Gaff and what he noticed most were her bleary eyes. "Looks like an old fisherman to me. Just some dirty old fisherman. I want to go home. Charlie, take me home. I don't feel so good."

Amanda leaned against Charlie and Gaff watched as they moved toward the parking area.

He called out, "Come talk to me after work tomorrow, son."

Gaff heard Amanda whine, "Why does he keep calling you son? Dirty old man. You're Charlie Fitzgerald and he shouldn't be talking to you like that. You could buy and sell him any day of the week."

"I don't think so." And then Charlie looked back at Gaff. "I'm really glad he still talks to me. Really glad."

Charlie called over his shoulder, "Might have to work late tomorrow, but I'll be here on Friday afternoon."

Gaff raised his voice to reach them as they moved toward the walkway. "Look forward to it, son."

**chapter 25**

A middle-aged man sat on the cooler next to Gaff. "Old man, what'd you say to Charlie last night. He came into work early this morning… Early, not just early for him. He's asked intelligent questions and… and he's totally changed. Did you replace my son's brain with a mature one? I'm dumbfounded. This is the closest thing to a miracle I've ever seen."

Gaff was so pleased, he grinned. "Those with ears to hear, let them hear. George, let them hear."

"You say that all the time and you've explained what it means, but I've tried to get to Charlie and you have, too. I know that. Up to this point he's managed to slip right through the net time and time again. And last night you said something that finally got through to him. Did you have to tie him down to do it?" He shook his head in amazement.

"Just have to cast the net at the right time is all. At a time when he's anchored to the spot." Gaff thought back to Amanda passed out on the towel last night. Anchored.

Gaff looked closely at his son, taking his measure. The family resemblance was there all right: slight dimple in the chin, brown eyes set wide apart, crooked smile, full head of hair. The younger man's hair was still brown with only a little gray at the temples. The big difference was that his son was pudgy and out of shape. Gaff shook his head. George looked as though he spent most of his time inside, probably at a desk. He had a weekend tan. The gut spoke to the fact that he ate too much rich food and didn't move nearly enough. An observer would guess that he spent weekends poolside rather than in an active sport and they'd be right.

Right now, he was staring out at the ocean with his father. "Gaff, how can you sit like this for hours? Doesn't it drive you nuts to do nothing?"

"I put in my time at the office and this is my reward. Besides, I move more than you think. " He nodded toward his son meaningfully, "You'd do with a little more beach time yourself. Did you walk or drive?"

"Drove and you know it. Don't get away from the office much. Not enough time to walk here anyway."

"You need to walk more, son. I walk about five miles a day, in short segments. Not to mention the exercise of sitting and standing all day long, like deep knee bends. Come to the beach, son, and drop that expensive gym membership that you never use."

"I don't think so, old man."

Gaff saw irritation building around his son's eyes.

"Hurrumpf, I can talk to anyone in the universe and resist telling them what to do. When my own son comes to see me, I spend precious visit time telling him how to run his life." He shook his head in disgust. "And I know you don't listen... I'm just wasting hot air."

George shuffled his feet in the sand. "I have the same problem. I can't talk to my own son, but I help all sorts of people at work."

"Too close to the situation." Gaff glanced at the tip of his rod for the sign. "A little girl just told me that decisions are harder when your heart's too involved. She was right."

George nodded his agreement. "Maybe I should leave the Charlie issue for you?"

Gaff went to tend to his fishing and George followed.

"Maybe. How are you and Silvia doing?"

George sighed a big one. "Better. Seems to get easier."

"Marriage's like that. Julia and I had a few moments early on."

It was George who hurrumpfed now. "You and Mom?"

Gaff smiled. "I'm glad Charlie's finally figured out where he's going."

"The baby of the family. Do they always have a harder time of it?"

Gaff thought before he said, "Must. Franny did, but then you had your fair share of troubles, too. Most of us find our way sooner or later, I suppose."

"Charlie was talking about the possibility of going to graduate school. Did you put that idea in his head?"

"Wish I had."

"Yeah, he says he wants to do a better job than he can with what he knows now."

"Is this my grandson you're talking about? Our Charlie?"

"Told you. He's got a plan now. Start by learning everything about the business he can from us and then he wants to look at going back to school."

Gaff set his reel and the two men returned to their seats.

Gaff chuckled. "How long will that first part take? Couple of weeks?"

George laughed, too. "He wasn't clear on that, but I got the idea he thought he could go on off to school next year in search of TRUTH."

"A year, hunh? Why so long?"

"He hinted that some of the hurry was girl-related."

"Uh oh."

George put his hand on his father's shoulder. "It's not really all that bad, Dad. I gather Charlie talked with that nice girl he was dating at the end of college. Her engagement didn't work out so she's decided to get the MBA instead of the MRS."

"So Charlie thinks he'll bark up that tree again, see what falls out."

"Yep."

Gaff smiled as he pictured the girl in question. "She was nice, had a lot of assets as I remember."

"Including long legs," George added appreciatively. "But Charlie was talking all morning about setting a course for himself and wanting to build toward something."

"Scary. Too much change, too fast."

"Didn't take a call from one of those girls he sees. Told the secretary that he didn't want to be disturbed. Secretary was so shocked, she came right in to ask me if Charlie was sick or something."

Gaff laughed. "She did?"

"I told her it was the 'or something' and we'd see how long it lasted."

Gaff was tickled as much by his son's reaction as he was to the situation.

"Dad, what made the difference in Charlie? He blew you off when he was in college. Drunken weekends on the beach with any girl he met. With all the drinking he did, I was amazed he got decent grades. Only believed it because I saw the transcripts."

"I remember having some talks with you about that. And with him."

"Always wondered if he bribed the professors. For a while there, I was afraid every phone call was the school telling me they'd thrown him out! Or jailed him."

"Charlie did OK."

"Yeah, he did. The Charlie I met today was a different person. What'd you do with the old one? Put him in the cooler?" He made a move to look into the cooler beneath him.

"I think he might've grown up, George. He just might have grown up. Now he has some catching up to do for the time he wasted."

"Like I did. And you, too, I guess."

Gaff shook his head at this. "The only thing I'm making up for is not fishing enough all those years. My mis-spent youth was wasted in that business, doing something I didn't enjoy."

"I remember you saying that, but I'm in that job now."

Gaff looked into his son's eyes. "George, the difference is that you like it. I never ordered you to go into the family business. You decided that all on your own."

Gaff's intensity made George straighten his back. "That's right, you never did. You kept urging me to try other things, to do what I felt happiest doing."

Gaff got up to tend his rod again. "Neither Franny nor Geoffrey went into it. Only you. You were the only one of three children to take a fancy to that office. Tell you the truth, I was afraid I'd be stuck there till death do us part."

George followed him. "I always wondered about that. Was it because you hated the business?"

" 'Hated' is a strong word, a strong sentiment." Gaff closed his eyes against the idea. "I'd rather not think I spent my life doing something I hated." Then he baited his hook.

"You think I should encourage Charlie to find himself and a job that he loves rather than planning to replace me?"

Gaff nodded, his gaze on the horizon.

For a while the two men sat together, lost in thoughts of yesterday, today and tomorrow.

George said to no one in particular, "Charlie's cousin seems to like being in the factory. That Sheryl is smart. Never thought of a girl in the head slot, but maybe I should start thinking outside the box."

Gaff nodded, "Might be time for a paradigm shift in the Fitzgerald family. But wait to see what Charlie discovers about himself before you hire someone else in."

"You were right. I tried lots of things and found that this was the best fit. In the end, I did make that decision... I'll encourage Charlie to do the same thing and hope he's more like me than he thinks. Either he comes back to take my office or I try Sheryl in it."

The two men sat, searching the water for answers.

Finally, George turned to the older man. "Dad, you are a great father. We gave you a tough moment or two, but now I appreciate being held to task. And I appreciate your guidance now, even though I don't always let on that I do."

Words got stuck in Gaff's throat so he said nothing, almost choked. He just sat there with tears rolling down his cheeks so that George could see how a father is touched by his son's love.

George didn't try to stop the tears forming in his own eyes. "Dad, I love you. I guess I should tell Charlie how much I love him, too."

Gaff gave a thumbs up to show his agreement and then he wiped his face with the back of his hand.

They sat side by side for another long while. After his son left, Gaff stood in the waves to put his attitude of gratitude into words to Mother Water and whomever else was with Her.

"Thank you, Mother/Father God for bringing my son and grandson closer to me. I do so love them." Then he allowed his tears of gratitude to join the ocean.

No one seemed to notice the old fisherman standing in the waves looking out at the horizon. And he didn't seem to notice the singing reel signaling that a fish had taken the bait.

## chapter 26

Gaff was still standing in the waves discussing the meaning of life with Mother Water when Sally and Sue walked toward him from the walkway.

He was alerted to their arrival by Sally's trilling voice. It preceded her. "Hey, Gaff, brought you lunch. Thought you should eat a proper lunch for a change."

He wiped his face and straightened his shoulders. A deep breath helped. Waving without turning to face his new visitor, he called out, "Hey, Sally." A few more deep breaths and he'd be ready to face the world in the form of Sally and Sue, collectors of shark teeth.

By the time they stood at his side, he was ready. Just in the nick.

Sue was holding the bag of food. She looked the part of the fabulous friend there to share the good times and the bad. They were all smiles and smelled of hamburger and french fries. He felt better all ready, happy to share these good times. He loved hamburgers and the smell that announced them.

Sally held up a holder full of cups, "Lunch delivered to the beach."

Gaff laughed his appreciation. "Who could ask for more?"

They settled in his spot, he in his chair, Sally on the cooler, and Sue on a towel spread on the sand. She insisted on that. Then they opened the bags and the delicious smells wafted around them setting their salivary glands to work.

His burger poised for the first bite, Gaff said, "I never eat hamburgers even though I love them."

"I don't think I've ever seen you eat anything at all on the beach. I don't know how you keep going the way you do."

Sue nodded, her mouth too full to talk.

The sounds of chewing and sipping sodas blended into the natural sounds of the beach. Sue was a fast eater, while Gaff and Sally lingered over theirs.

Sally laughed around her straw. "Sue always eats faster than I do. I try to speed up, but it must be a constitutional impossibility for me. I always finish last."

"Important thing is to enjoy the food, fast or slow." Gaff took another bite of his sandwich. He was enjoying the treat, savoring every mouthful and every whiff.

"Sue, why don't you tell Gaff about the time your father came to you after he died??

Gaff raised his eyebrows as he looked at Sue. "Sounds interesting."

Sue looked toward the pier. Gathering her thoughts or reeling in her feelings? "Dad died when I was in my early twenties. We'd been really close and I missed him dearly after he passed."

She paused for a sip of soda. "When I was a kid he would sit on my bed every night and talk to me before I went to sleep. We had wonderful talks as I got older. He helped me figure out so many things. After he died, I used to talk with him whenever I needed his help and I could swear I felt him there. Like he was in the room, only I couldn't quite hear him or see him. Still the idea that he might be there was comforting."

Sally added, "The kind of dad every girl wants."

Sue continued. "Then I met Eddie and all my attention went into that relationship. We fell in love and finally got married. Although I didn't talk with Daddy, I knew somehow he approved of Eddie."

Gaff asked, "Eddie's still your husband?"

Sue nodded. "Then I got pregnant and something strange happened. I wasn't feeling too good and went to bed early one night. I was there alone resting, not asleep, but my eyes were closed. Suddenly, I felt someone sit on the bed just like my dad used to. I looked up thinking I'd see Eddie, but it was Daddy."

"Your dad?"

"This time I could see him, really see him. He told me that I was going to have a beautiful, blond baby boy. He smiled and I felt so happy. Then he disappeared."

Sally leaned toward the others. "He never came back. Only that one visit."

"I had a sweet little girl. So pretty and I loved taking care of her. A couple of years later, I was pregnant again. I didn't feel well and went to the doctor. He did a lot of tests and found a tumor in my head. They put me in the hospital to operate, but first they wanted my permission to abort the baby."

Sally interrupted, "Can you imagine that?"

"I was devastated. I wanted this baby and didn't want to get rid of it after carrying it for so many months. I took my time to make the decision even though they were pressuring me to sign the papers right away. The doctors came in every couple of hours to see if I signed and the nurses came even more. Sign that paper. Sign that paper."

She shook her head. "Finally, I remembered seeing Daddy on the side of my bed telling me I would have a beautiful, blond baby boy. He'd never lied to me. The first baby was a girl so this one must be a boy and Daddy told me he would be beautiful. He'd never lied and so I told them I wouldn't let my baby go. I refused to sign."

Sally commented, "Rest assured she made all the doctors mad."

"The very same day, after I made up my mind, a hospital volunteer came to see me. Brought some magazines, you know. A candy striper, you know. She held my hand and told me that I didn't have what the doctors were saying I had. She pressed a crystal into the palm of my hand and told me to keep it there until I left the hospital."

"A crystal?"

"I still have it in a special place. She went out the door just as my mother came in. Mother said she didn't see any volunteer. I saw the woman's skirts going through the door at the same time Mother walked in, but Mother didn't see anyone. Weird. I gripped that rock tight and never let it out of my hand. The next day, they did more tests and found out I just had a temporary blockage that must have broken up! No surgery and they released me that day. I held that rock for an entire week and said lots of thank you prayers."

"Great story."

"From that day on, I remembered to talk to Daddy once in a while, too. I thanked him for letting me know ahead of time and for his help when I was in the hospital. Mother didn't agree, but I believe it was proof that people don't really die. They just change to a different form and stay around to help the people they love."

"The woman who gave Sue the crystal was an angel, I'm positive of that. An angel dressed like a hospital volunteer."

Gaff looked from one to the other. "I've heard of this kind of thing before. Yes, I have."

Mae came to join the group just as Sue was finishing her story. "Saw you all over here and I thought I'd join you."

She nodded to the other women. "I see you on the beach all the time, but we haven't met. I wanted to introduce myself while you're sitting with Gaff, here. Name's Mae. Didn't want to interrupt your story. It's a good one. I heard the last part of it. Very interesting."

"I'm Sally… I love to hear that story. It makes me feel all warm inside, like we're not alone here, even when we think we are. Sort of comforting to me now that Paul, Jr. has moved out and I am living alone. Sue still has her Eddie. In my heart, I know Paul's here with me, too."

Mae asked for a repeat of the first of the story and Sue gave her the short version. All three women were absolutely glowing as she finished.

"As a nurse, I've seen some of these miracles close up. This is a good one, though. A really good one."

Sally gathered the waste into the bag. "Tell us one of the miracles you saw."

Sue nodded her agreement as she passed her cup over to her friend.

Mae started, "I don't know what the girl looked like when she got to the emergency room, but by the time she was on the unit, she was hooked up to life support. I read her chart out of curiosity. Fourteen years old." Mae's smile turned upside down.

"Pretty young thing with so much life ahead of her. Well, the story is she tried to kill herself and her father found her. Kept her alive with CPR. Lucky for her he was there. Fourteen years old and here she was with tubes sticking out of every orifice. What a shame."

Sally was bouncing in her excitement. "What happened?"

"She was stabilized, but the doctors thought she'd be a vegetable if she came out of coma. Didn't say this to the parents, of course, but we talked about it at the nurse's station. Her mother stayed with her night and day. Her father was there a lot, too."

Sally was insistent, "And?"

"Well, the fourteenth day she was in that coma, the doctors said there was absolutely no hope. None at all. One day her brother's girlfriend said her mother called a healer. She said the healer needed the family's permission before she could help."

Mae leaned over and spoke in a low voice, "I was in and out checking her vitals, you understand, or I wouldn't know all this."

Sally was about to bust a gut from excitement.

"The mother said she'd try anything to save her daughter. The girlfriend called her mom right then and there. Her mom called the healer and then called her daughter back."

"She was making the calls right there in the hospital room?"

"Right there... so the family heard everything she was saying. The healer said the girl was ready to come out of coma and told them to get everyone they knew to send positive energy, love, to her. The dad thought it was all hooey. The healer also said the patient would have no permanent physical damage--- and be a lot wiser for the experience."

Gaff said, "An NDE."

"I told some of the other nurses and they laughed. How could this woman who had never even seen their patient know more than the doctors who'd treated her for two whole weeks? Nurses on the next shift laughed, too."

"What happened?"

"Girl came out of coma the next day. Damnest thing I ever saw. The very next day, she was up and talking. Next thing I know the doctors are saying there's no physical damage. Called it the medical miracle of the year. They broke their arms patting themselves on the back, saying how good they were as doctors.

The nurses who had laughed, all wanted to talk with the miracle girl. Everyone used any and every excuse to spend time with her. It was the talk of the unit for months."

"What did the doctors say?"

"That the mother was crazy with grief and there was no healer. Wouldn't let us talk about the case, but we talked about it anyway for a long time after. Some of us went back to church because of it." She was thoughtful. "It was a miracle for the nurses, too. Some of us started praying for the patients on a regular basis."

"Did it work?"

"We thought so, but some chalked it up to superstition. Told us to take care of the patients' bodies and forget this religion stuff."

Gaff said, "Not everyone can see what's right there in front of them."

Sally echoed, "Right there in front of them."

# chapter 27

At the end of the story, Sally tugged on Mae's sleeve. "Have you seen any other miracles you can tell us about? You are a nurse and there must be stuff like this going on all the time."

"All the time."

Sue said, "Well tell us more."

Mae was thoughtful. "I can't remember a lot of them. Soon after that incident I quit the hospital to go into private duty nursing. My first patient was an older woman with dementia. Sweet woman." She drew circles in the sand for a bit, probably to remember.

Her audience gave her some space, although Gaff noticed that Sally barely endured the silence.

"She'd been a dancer on the stage back in the time of elegance in Hollywood. She showed me pictures of the famous people she worked with. It was impressive. Bob Hope and lots of people I didn't recognize. They were beautiful and elegant. What a shame to see how age destroys all that beauty. She was frail when I started working with her and soon she was telling me that her mother woke her up, calling her by the pet name she was given as a child. I thought she was just seeing things because of the dementia, you know, dismissed it as imaginary. Then something started waking me up."

Sally could hardly contain herself. "How? How did it wake you up? And you weren't even related to this woman."

"The way it worked for me is that in the middle of the night I would hear a loud rap on the table beside my bed. Loud. Jerked me right out of a sound sleep. The first time it happened, I thought that since I was awake, I might as well check on my charge. By the time I got to her room, she was having trouble breathing. I helped her sit up and she was better.

"I told her daughter about the incident. She told me she, too, had been awakened on numerous occasions. Every time, her mother was having trouble. Then my charge got really sick and I felt like there was someone else in her room. Maybe more than one. I couldn't see anyone or hear them, but I felt them. You know, like you feel someone staring at your back? I talked to her about these feelings and she told me about the people she was seeing from her past. I believed her by then.

"When she was going, I stood at the foot of her bed and got the shivers, like I was standing near someone I couldn't see. From then on, I didn't stand at the end of her bed. Never. Soon, she passed. By then, I was sure there was a lot of energetic activity in the house. I think she had a big welcoming party." Mae had a far-away look in her eyes. "She taught me a lot about living and about dying. She did."

Gaff said, "I don't believe in death really. Just the transformation from this form to something invisible to us."

"I can believe that after being with my charge when she passed."

The three women chattered for a while, asking Mae questions and speculating on the meaning of all this.

Gaff listened and heard.

Finally the chatter died down and nothing more could be said about Mae's stories, or Sue's.

Mae added, "When these things started happening around me, I didn't believe they were real. I listened to the stories and figured my friends and co-workers were pulling my leg. The nurses working on palliative care really had some stories, but until I worked on that unit, I didn't believe any of it. Now, I do. I believe because I've seen it or heard it or smelled it enough times that either I believe they happen or I check myself into the psych ward."

Gaff grinned, "Believing sounds like the better option."

"That's what I thought. So now I listen and ask questions to see the similarities and differences. The biggest difference is in the way the nurses handle the situation. They can turn something from a comforting sign into a horror story. And some of my religious friends are so set against it that they'd deny Jesus Christ Himself if he said he saw the spirit of someone who was dead."

Gaff said softly, "Mary Magdalene did. And it's in the Bible. So did His Disciples."

Three female voices in union said, "Oh. That's right, she saw Jesus after He died."

Mae wasn't through with her stories. "Dawn, my current charge, tells me about strange things that happen to her all the time now, since the accident."

Her audience perked up, eager for more, but Mae waved them off.

She did say, "We don't tell her parents because the one time we did, they about had a cat fit."

"Too bad. She would probably appreciate some support from them."

Mae turned to Gaff. "That's one reason I want for you to talk with her. I talk to her, but I thought you could help her understand what's happening. Why and where it's going, you know." She was on her feet now, ready to return to the yellow house down the beach.

"I'm looking forward to the meeting. You can tell Dawn."

Sally lamented, "You're not leaving already, are you? Tell us one more story, one more before you leave."

Mae smiled at her new friends' interest, but straightened her back and took a deep breath. "I've got important things to do." She gestured toward the yellow house. "We've got important things to do and I've taken a long enough break."

Sally whined, "You haven't been down here very long, they won't fire you if you stay a little longer."

"They don't even know I'm here. I want to go back. We have an important goal and we're getting closer every day. Like reading a good book, the closer you get to the end, the faster you want to read. Like a book I don't want to put down, I have a passion for my job, a passion that only gets stronger everyday." She nodded knowingly to Gaff and he nodded to her. Then she said as she turned to go, "Thanks, Gaff."

As she walked, she raised her hand to wave to the house, to someone watching from the window on the beach. She waved to someone traveling a difficult path to visit Gaff and his pirate flag.

Gaff asked Mother Water to help Dawn and Mae on that path because the lessons were important, and tough.

## chapter 28

Bobby got to the beach later that afternoon. His eyes were still swollen from sleep and he seemed to be swimming his way through a fog. The cup of coffee in his hand smelled good to Gaff.

"Up late last night? Looks like you really tied one on."

"Tied one on? I wish. Was up, but working. This working stuff is hard to get used to when you're out of practice."

Gaff jerked his head around to look at Bobby. "Work? Since when do you work?"

"Since last night." He rubbed his eyes and tried to shake the sleep out of his head.

"You got a job?"

"A little night security job. Thought I'd ease myself into work, bit by bit. Besides they're paying me off the books."

"Why the job?"

"Priscilla and I've been talking. I started thinking how much she loves her writing. She writes because she wants to write, not because someone stands over her with a whip."

Gaff smiled to himself, looking in the waves for signs.

"There wasn't anything in my life like that, nothing that pulls me along. Got the idea that I might like the security consulting business."

"Security consulting?"

"Yeah, I could help people like that. My experience in law enforcement gave me a lot useful information about the criminal mind. Priscilla and I figured that by working security, I'd see the situation from the inside, you know. See what companies do now for security. More useful information. Practical information from inside a real company, not from books." Bobby rubbed his eyes again.

"You and Priscilla?"

"Yeah, she's decided not to go home yet. She's going stay with Sally for a while. The rent wouldn't be much, but it would help Sally. They get along fine. Company for Sally, too."

"My, how things change."

Bobby drained his cup and weighted it down with sand. "This's your fault."

"This what?"

"Before I started talking with you, I'd have thrown this cup into the water or left it on the sand figuring it was someone else's problem when it blew down the beach. Now this is my beach and my water and I know I have to take care of it. Now I get mad when I see someone littering, even if it just blows out of his truck. They should be careful and keep the stuff tied down."

"Good change."

"It took me forty years to figure out that the whole world is like that. I used to take care of my yard, but last week I mowed the neighbor's, too. He's elderly and doesn't get to the mowing like he should. No problem for me, even with this bum ticker." He slapped his chest.

Gaff marveled at his friend's new way of thinking.

"Yep, taking care of this world is important. Each of us needs to do our part. Priscilla and I talk about her dreams of being published and I encourage her. The man I used to be would have laughed. I would have thought her dreams weren't as important as mine."

"That so?"

"She read more of her stuff to me and it's good. I could see her heart in it. And her soul, I think. She deserves her dream. She deserves to try getting to the end of it, so a lot of other people read what she writes. Maybe her goals and dreams are more important than mine." He looked as though he was charting a new sea of thoughts and feelings.

Gaff heard.

"More we've talked, more I realize that I haven't found the purpose of my life yet. Why was I put on this planet?"

"She helping you?"

"She tells me I'm really smart. I haven't read as much as she has, haven't put as much into my head as she has in hers. And still she thinks I'm smart. She accepts me as I am. That feels great." He paused. "So last night at work I started reading something off her bookshelf."

"What was it?"

"Something I heard you talk about. The Gospel of Mary."

Gaff turned to Bobby in surprise. "Really?"

"Yep. Wasn't the most exciting thing I've ever read, no cops and robbers, but it was the right place to start. Easy to read, but for a little book, it made me think a lot. I didn't finish it, short as it is. Required too much thinking. Ideas that are new to me."

Gaff checked the tip of his rod. "And?"

"You should see the books she has around her place. Stacks of books all over. It's going to take time, but I plan to work my way through those stacks."

"That's a goal. Guess Priscilla'll be here for a while then. Why would you read all that?"

"One thing is that we can talk about what's in those books. She'd like that. And I'd like her to stay for a very long time."

"Hmmmm."

"Another thing is that in the Gospel of Mary, it shows how we should respect women and what they can teach us. I understand now that Priscilla can teach me and I see something in her writing that touches my heart. I want to learn what she knows because she's happier than anyone I've ever met." He cut his eyes to glance at Gaff. "Except for you, that is."

Gaff ignored this last. "That's a good thing."

"When I asked about that, she told me she's really spiritual. Nothing to do with religion like I learned in church. Something more, something deep inside her. I want to try that, too."

Gaff looked at his rod. Was there a fish on his hook?

"I don't want to be like Peter any more. I see what I missed that way."

"What do you mean?"

"Says in the book that Peter didn't like women much. And he was more jealous of Mary because she was in tight with Yeshua. After the Crucifixion, Peter asked Mary what Jesus had taught her and her alone. When she told him, he rejected it. He rejected all she said just because she was a woman. He insisted that the Master wouldn't teach anything that important to a woman." He shook his head in wonder.

Gaff heard so much more and smiled.

"I'm afraid I used to be like that. When I look back, I think I didn't listen to a lot that women were trying to tell me. Women are smart and sometimes their knowledge comes from a different point of view. Different, not less and not more. That different way of seeing things helps understand the whole picture. Fills it out."

"Kind of like seeing the same scene from two different angles?"

"Yeah, when you put the two views together you get a more complete picture."

"Like you see in a stereoscope."

"A what?"

"A device invented a long time ago to present slightly different views of the same scene to each eye. When you looked at the two together, the image looked like it had depth."

"3-D."

"That's it. 3-D. The concept is the basis for those 3-D glasses they use in the movies."

Bobby smiled. "That's a good analogy. By learning to see the situation through another person's eyes you get a more complete idea."

"That's what we do when we look at the situation from the minnow's point of view."

"That's right. We only see the minnow jump out of the water. From our perspective, we could think he was playing leapfrog with his buddies like the dolphins do. But when we think about it from his point of view, his jumping tells us about the big fish down there eating the little ones. Tells us to put our hooks into the water there."

Gaff watched the minnows jumping.

Bobby drew in the sand. "How have I missed this? Do women always teach us the most important stuff?"

"Remember when we talked about the hormones that drive a young man?"

"I remember being driven by those hormones."

Gaff nodded. He remembered, too.

"Do all men take this long to see?"

"Some men never see. They live entire lives thinking that men own the world and that women are only here because Adam donated a rib."

Bobby sifted sand through his fingers. "You mean because women owe their lives to the rib taken from Adam, the women belong to the men?"

"In the time of Jesus, the fabric of society was based on that belief. That's what made him so different. He broke many laws of his religion to include everyone, to teach the Way of Love to everyone who would listen. Everyone, including women, was equal to Him."

"Those who have ears to hear, let them hear." Bobby looked at Gaff with pride in his new knowledge.

Gaff said, "It's in the Bible, too. That's another good book to read down the road."

Bobby frowned.

Gaff shrugged. "Or not."

# chapter 29

Priscilla was sitting on the cooler between Gaff and Bobby. The sky was putting on a great show with clouds skittering across the blue stage.

"Have you ever heard of sacred sex, Gaff?"

If he hadn't been sitting so close to the ground, Gaff might have fallen out of his chair. He grunted in the affirmative.

"Bobby and I have been talking about it. Trying to figure it out."

"Um- hunh." Where was this going? Gaff's imagination was taking flight, like the pelicans over the water.

Priscilla paused. Bobby was suspiciously quiet, eyes averted.

She continued, "In church, you hear a lot about abstaining. They make it sound like sex isn't good. Priests take a vow of celibacy when they give their lives to the service of God. I'm confused. If we all abstained, we wouldn't have any children and the species would die out. So how can sex be bad?"

Gaff looked to Mother Water for the answer. He said nothing.

"Why are we here anyway? If God didn't want us to enjoy it, why did he make it feel so good?"

Bobby piped up, "If God really didn't want Eve to eat from the tree of knowledge, He'd have put it on the back edge of the Garden of Eden instead of smack in the middle."

"And He created everything, including that nasty old snake." She let that percolate before continuing. "If He didn't mean for the snake to win Eve over, He could have prevented the conversation. I didn't know a snake could talk anyway. That Eve understood the snake puts her right up there with Harry Potter." Priscilla grinned.

Priscilla was talking faster. "If Eve hadn't given in to temptation, the human race wouldn't have learned much during it's stay on this planet."

Bobby put in his two cents. "I'm not sure we've learned that much anyway in all these centuries."

Priscilla looked hard at Bobby and then turned to glance at Gaff before she settled into looking at the water. "I believe the whole thing was planned to happen like that from the beginning. There is no 'original sin' because God put the whole show in motion. He knew what would happen from the get-go. Maybe He planned it."

Gaff made a sweeping gesture with his arms. "In one fell swoop, you have destroyed the entire foundation of the Catholic Church." He leaned forward to get a better view of Bobby. "Better watch out, this is one smart woman and they are tough to handle."

Bobby laughed.

Gaff asked Priscilla, "So is sex bad?"

"That's the question. The Church says it is."

"Unless you're having children." Another two cents from Bobby.

Priscilla nodded. "A lot of spiritual people think it is, too. One book I've read says that 'The only valid use of sex is procreation. It is not truly pleasurable in itself.' Doesn't that mean to have sex only if you want to have children?"

Bobby rolled his eyes and groaned.

Gaff smiled. "First of all, help me understand your terms, or the terms from the book. Sometimes you have to read a book to get an idea of how that author uses the vocabulary. The same word might have two different meanings to two different people."

"OK?"

"Who wrote it?"

Priscilla hesitated. "Some psychologists."

Gaff frowned. "Was this a self-help book about sex or relationships?"

Again the hesitation. "No. It offers guidance for the development of your relationship with God and how to express it by your actions in the world."

"Sounds good. Maybe I should read it."

Priscilla looked at Bobby with some unspoken message that Gaff didn't understand.

He went on with his thought. "The word 'procreation' means creating children or creating in general. If we use the first definition, the sentence supports the edicts of the Catholic Church. If you use the other one, it has a different meaning."

Priscilla looked from Gaff to Bobby and back to Gaff. "I'm not following."

Gaff noticed that Bobby squeezed his eyes shut. He went on, confused by all this undercurrent communication. "When do we create?"

Priscilla answered quickly, "All the time. Every thought is a prayer and every prayer is answered in some way."

Bobby blurted out, "Not every one is answered."

Priscilla straightened her back and answered smoothly, "It's the 'in some way' that gets us. Sometimes what we get doesn't look like the answer we imagined. Sometimes healing brings death and not absence of disease."

Gaff was impressed. "What do we create?"

She smiled. "All sorts of stuff. Happiness and unhappiness, riches and poverty. Whatever. Tons of books out there talk about this manifestation stuff."

"Hmmm." In a low voice, Bobby said, "Load of crap."

Gaff ignored the comment. "Basically, you're saying the idea is that we can lump things into two categories: good and bad. Or positive and negative or love and not love. Some say there is only love or light, and no negative."

Bobby's eyes snapped open and he turned to face Gaff. "What about hate and anger and dark? I've seen too much of that. And I don't think it was a figment of my imagination,"

Gaff shook his head. "Not your imagination. But how do you create darkness?"

Bobby answered quickly, "That's easy. Turn off the light." He looked at Priscilla to punctuate his thought.

"Is that creating dark? Or is it getting rid of the light?"

Bobby turned his eyes to the water. In a small voice he answered, "Getting rid of the light."

Gaff nodded. "So there is only light and not light, the absence of light."

Bobby was quiet. Was he looking for another path? "OK, light and no light. But there is anger."

"How do you feel when you're angry?"

"Like someone needs to be taught a lesson."

Priscilla patted him on the arm indulgently. "Really, that's a thought and not a feeling. I'd say I feel as though I've been attacked, but that's more a thought, too." She paused. "I guess anger is a reaction to feeling afraid."

Gaff was surprised at how easy this was going to be and congratulated himself on his ability to present logic.

Priscilla cut these thoughts short. "I cheat. That book is based on the idea that there are only two emotions: 'love' and 'not love.' It says that whenever we feel 'not love', we are afraid."

Gaff said, "So it boils down to love and fear as opposites?"

"And the whole book talks about how to get to the 'love' place all the time."

"Well. Then. Doesn't it say that the only thing we should be 'creating' is love?"

"Yes, but we sometimes forget and create more fear. The book suggests ways to bring us back to the right path."

"In that light, the lines you quoted would mean that since we are creating all the time, sex should only be used to create and feed love and that sex without love is just not that good." Now, the congratulations, Gaff—and thanks to Mother Water.

Gaff believed the silence meant that his companions were thinking. Priscilla had a slight smile and her features had smoothed out. Her shoulders were more relaxed. Bobby, too, looked happier. Gaff wondered how this discussion fed into their private discussions.

After some time, Priscilla nodded. "That resonates with me. It does. I believe that sex as part of a loving relationship is good because it creates more love in that relationship. Yes, that sounds good."

Bobby piped up enthusiastically, "Sounds right to me."

Gaff went to tend to his fishing and Bobby joined him. When they got settled in their seats again, Gaff said, "Let me tell you the story of a man I talked to years ago. He was on the beach with a woman. Both had stories that relate to this discussion."

Bobby said, "Tell away."

"They were friends, but they didn't seem to be in love."

"Not uncommon."

"The man was a public figure. He didn't say exactly what, just that he was in the limelight as a young man. At first, he paid attention to his job and worked hard to do it well. Then he became distracted by the women who wanted to spend time with him because he was a celebrity."

"Sounds like a lot of our actors and politicians."

"Was he a Senator?"

Gaff shrugged. "As time went on, he was more and more drawn to the young women and took advantage of what they offered. He would take up with one after another and sometimes he'd see several in a week."

"Every young man's dream."

"Every man's dream."

"What made it worse was that he was married. He was married to the girl of his dreams. She was beautiful and intelligent and a really good person. He loved her with all his heart. Told me that when they made love, he heard the angels sing."

"Living his dream."

"He didn't appreciate it while he had it. As I said, he loved his wife, but most nights he left her home with the kids to go out looking for the physical release. That's what he called it. There was no love in these encounters, only the feel-good of the physical release."

"Did those women know they were being used?"

"Must have. Everyone knew he was married."

Priscilla slammed her fist into her palm. "Some women are willing to believe that the wife isn't nice enough to hold on to her husband. They delude themselves into thinking they can pull him out of the marriage by being better."

"While some may have salved their conscience with that belief, more of them probably just wanted to be around a celebrity at any price. Maybe they felt it gave them some sort of bragging rights to sleep with a famous man."

Bobby dragged his hand through the sand. "They didn't respect themselves and he didn't either. That's what it sounds like to me."

Gaff nodded. "His associates were smarter than he was. They knew to control him by supplying him with sex, like giving drugs to an addict. He didn't figure that out, but I did from his story. Whenever he got stressed about doing something on the edge of legal, they would divert his attention to sex. He wasn't really crooked, but some of the people around him had ideas about ways to shunt money to businesses owned by friends and relatives. Borderline activities"

"Must be a Senator. Must be."

"If he hesitated, they would talk about some woman's body, and soon he would agree to anything so he could get to the sex with that woman. He was usually involved with several at the same time and so one was always available."

Priscilla reached down for a shell and threw it toward the water, "Stupid women. Stupid, stupid, stupid."

Bobby went into his mantra, "No respect for themselves. Sold themselves for a moment with some nitwit."

"He was on his own path, learning his own lessons. You have to respect that."

"Did he ever learn?"

"Can't rightly say. His wife eventually left him. Although he loved her, he was OK with that because he believed there would be an endless supply of fresh young bodies. His addiction resulted in his losing his position. I guess his job performance declined. Said something about lawsuits and indictments, too. Didn't give details. When he was no longer in the limelight, the young women weren't interested in him and he spent a lot of time alone. Finally, he got hooked up with the woman he was here with. I didn't see any love between them, just convenience. Sad, really."

"That is sad."

"He tried to get his wife back, but it was too late. Said he bared his heart to her, told her how much he loved her."

"Can he really love?"

"Hard to say. His wife wasn't convinced enough to come back. She told him she loved her Self too much to get tangled up with someone so unevolved."

"Did he understand that?"

"Not then, but maybe he's learned by now."

"The relationship between love and sex is really complicated, isn't it?"

Gaff went on, "His friend also had a story. She was a big model in New York. Did magazine covers and all sorts of jobs both here and in Europe."

"Would I know her?"

"It was years ago, so probably not. Like her friend, she was desired by every man who saw her. Dates were plentiful. Several asked her to marry them, but she was having too much fun. She enjoyed being taken wonderful places and sleeping with the rich and famous, married or single. Her goal was the good time, fun and excitement."

"Short-sighted, if you ask me."

"Invitations came for the best parties in New York and Europe. She's still proud that she knew these people, even for a little while. Thought it would go on forever. It's like that when you're young. You think you'll be young forever."

"Don't I know that."

"She cared for some, but there were so many all the time that she didn't stay with anyone for long. Never gave a relationship time to develop, and they do take time."

Priscilla looked at Bobby, but said nothing.

Gaff continued, "Then she met her dream mate. He was rich and handsome and took her to all the best places. Said she let herself love him."

Priscilla asked, "Was she capable of love? Was she mature enough?"

"Doubt it. Sounded like addiction to me, but she thought it was love. He married a rich woman from a good family instead of her. Broke her heart."

Bobby asked, "She didn't seriously think anyone would want to marry some tramp, some party girl, did she?"

"Total lack of understanding, even when I met her. Blamed the other woman for 'trapping' her boyfriend. Regardless, she was devastated, heart-broken. Meanwhile, all her money was spent on fancy clothes and trips because she thought she'd marry some rich man to pay her way."

Bobby's voice hardened. "Sounds familiar."

"When her lover left, she did a lot of drugs to avoid dealing with her depression. Drugged, she couldn't work and that finished her off financially. In the end she left New York to go back home in disgrace, a failure. Got a job as a waitress and ended up with the washed up politician."

"You said they weren't in love."

"Nope. They were avoiding loneliness."

"Did they learn anything from those experiences?"

Bobby smirked, "Sounds like they learned to blame other people for their own mistakes."

"That's about it. We talked, a little like we are today, but they weren't ready to hear."

Priscilla had a far-away look. "Maybe later they remembered what you said and understood more. It could work like that."

"Sometimes it does. Probably won't ever find out though."

Bobby repeated his mantra in a low voice. "Respect others and yourself. Act out of love. Make love and not just go for the physical release."

Priscilla looked at him and smiled. "Love yourself and others. It all boils down to love, doesn't it?"

"Just as we were saying... Love, not just sex."

Bobby grinned. "The Way of Love."

Priscilla drew a heart in the sand. "But what about sacred sex? We've only established that sex is not bad if it's an expression of love and adds to that love. What about the idea that we can achieve enlightenment through the sexual relationship?"

Gaff said quietly, thinking out loud. "Sexual energy is the most powerful energy on the planet. Seems like a good idea to use it wisely." Then he looked from Priscilla to Bobby. "There are books about how to channel that energy into joining not only with the partner, but with Spirit at the same time. I haven't read them, but maybe I should."

Bobby grinned. "Priscilla has some books on her shelf that might have something about this."

Priscilla looked at him. "This may call for another trip to the bookstore."

Bobby smiled.

All three lapsed into silence.

Gaff added. "Those two were proud of their stories of the glory days. To me every new day should be a glory day."

Bobby waved his hand to take in the entire beach. "This is a great place to do that."

## chapter 30

Several months later, Gaff stood at the water's edge engaged in his morning ritual when Mae approached. He didn't put his feet in the water now. It was too cold. In fact, he wore shoes to the beach, ratty old tennis shoes. And the shorts were replaced by warm fleece. He still took off his hoodie when the sun got warm, but mostly he wore that and a windbreaker against the stinging wind. He didn't come down every day either. No sense being too cold.

Mae's smile was brighter than he remembered. "We'd like to invite you for some coffee or tea on the terrace this morning, Gaff."

"Me, Mae, you want to invite me?"

Mae didn't hide the sly look in her eyes. "Not me. WE invite you. Dawn can't make it all the way down here yet, but she can make it onto the platform just off our walkway. So she thought it was time for us to invite you for a little treat out there. A celebration of sorts."

Gaff grinned with understanding. "Ah, a celebration. I would be delighted to join you. In fact, I'd like nothing better." He left the wagon on his spot and followed Mae to the walkway in front of the yellow house. Now he understood his urge to see the water on this particular day.

They walked toward the yellow house and he noticed the spring in Mae's step. She was anxious to reach their destination. As they stepped onto the boardwalk, they stomped the sand from their shoes, but didn't attempt to clean them.

Halfway down the walkway was a square deck area furnished with a table and chairs. An umbrella was leaning against the rail in the corner. At the table sat a young girl, grinning from ear to ear. In fact, Gaff could tell she was so pleased with herself that her heart was flying among the clouds. She was bundled up and he could see her hat on the fourth chair.

When they got to the table, and Mae walked up beside him Gaff could see her broad grin. She gestured grandly toward the table and its occupant. "This is our hostess, Gaff, Ms Dawn Delaney. She walked out here on her very own legs today. Dawn, this is Gaff, the famous old man with the pirate flag."

Gaff started to protest, but was interrupted. Dawn's sweet voice twinkled with excitement, "I am very pleased to meet you, Gaff. Mae exaggerates. Really, I walked out here on OUR legs." She smiled. "And you don't look as old as I thought you would. You're just so wise that people think you're old."

Gaff liked this young woman already.

Mae ignored this last and giggled like a young girl. "The important thing is that you walked out. There isn't room on the walkway for her chair." She waved toward the boardwalk to make her point.

Gaff saw the months of work, too. Months of determined, hard work to get to this table.

Mae waved him to his seat, "Sit, Gaff, sit. We've brought pastries from Dawn's favorite bakery."

Gaff sat at the place indicated for him and they began serving. There was coffee, with cream and sugar, for Mae and Gaff. Tea for Dawn and a huge plate of beautiful pastries. Beside it was a plate piled high with Gaff's favorite donuts! There was enough to feed a dozen people.

He crooned, "You can invite me to a party any day if you're going to serve these donuts. They're my favorite." And he put two on his plate. "One for my mouth and one for my eyes."

Dawn laughed, "You can have the whole plate for your eyes."

Gaff said around a mouthful of donut, "They taste even better when there's one in the queue."

The party of three ate and drank and laughed until they were stuffed with sweets. And their bellies hurt from the laughter. Dawn told jokes she got from the Internet until there were tears of joy in everyone's eyes.

Finally, Dawn threw her hands into the air. "That's all, folks."

Mae said, "You are truly a special person, Dawn. Gaff, she did that all on her own. Must've been one of those times I was visiting you." She turned proud eyes on her charge, her charge become friend.

Gaff felt eyes watching from the house and looked to see a woman watching from an upstairs window, dabbing tears from her eyes. Mom. He returned his attention to the table. "So we're celebrating your accomplishments today, are we?"

Dawn grinned. "That and other things. Mae has told me how wise you are. I watch you sometimes, you and your flag." She gestured toward a window on the second floor. "I have a great view of the beach from my window."

Gaff looked from the window to the beach and back. "I can see that. It's a great view. You watch the kids on the beach sometimes?"

She nodded, grinning. "I used to get sad when I watched them, but now they're a reminder of why we work so hard on my exercises. Now when I watch them, I imagine myself playing with them." She looked toward the beach. "I'll go down to the water next summer. I will." Her expression radiated determination and strength of will.

"I have no doubt that you will, Dawn. No doubt at all." And he didn't.

"Mae used to be white and fat when she came to look after me, but we worked together to get her healthier. She can do lots of things she couldn't do before."

Mae frowned and straightened in her seat. "I wouldn't say I was fat. A little overweight maybe, but not fat."

Dawn giggled. "But you aren't fat now."

Mae shook her head. "Not pasty white either."

"We worked together on that and we worked together to get me stronger. And I'm going to the water next summer. We're working together on that."

"You can come visit me then, and sit on the cooler."

Dawn smile became a glow that lit the air around her. "I'd like that. And I'll bring you donuts."

Now Gaff grinned. "I'd like that, too. A visit from a pretty girl and donuts, too."

Dawn went on. "We're celebrating something else, too. Since the accident, I've been home schooled. But yesterday, Mom told me I'd be going to school next year, sooner if I feel able. That's another thing we're celebrating."

"That's just tremendous."

She became serious. "But I'm not going until I can walk. Not in a wheelchair. A cane or braces maybe, but not a chair."

Mae nodded in agreement and then said in a sing-song voice. "That's not all."

Dawn looked at her and laughed. "Yes, there's more."

Mae waved toward the house. "There's an apartment on the ground level of this house right next to the garage. It gets rented out in the summer for very high rents, but sometimes it's empty during the cold months. They had a year-round tenant who's moving out at the end of the year. Mr. and Mrs. Delaney were so happy when we showed them Dawn's progress that they said I could live in that apartment free for as long as I want when Dawn no longer needs a full-time nurse. When she goes to school, they'll need me on a part-time basis so I can live downstairs and tend her when she gets home in the afternoon. The rest of the time, I can walk the beach or fish. I can live on the beach and have my own life."

Tears filled her eyes and she could hardly get the rest out. "I'll be a part of their family forever, they said. A real part of their family because of the miracle I worked with their sweet Dawn. They called me an Angel, Gaff. They called ME an angel!"

Gaff patted her hand, "You are an angel, Mae."

Mae shook her head. "No, you're the angel here. You're the one who helped me take charge of my life. Because of you, I didn't leave when it looked bad and I was so unhappy. Gaff, this has been the happiest time of my life and if I hadn't been curious about that flag of yours, I would have missed it all."

Tears welled up in Gaff's eyes, too. And the three sat quiet in this emotional moment.

Dawn said in a quiet voice, "I had trouble sleeping last night because I was so excited about all the good things happening. I heard Mom and Dad talking when they thought I was asleep. They came into my room and said that they owed so much to Mae

for helping me. They said Mae had helped them, too. And before
they left, they hugged."

Mae turned surprised eyes to Dawn. "You didn't tell me
this, you little snot."

Dawn turned loving eyes to Mae. "I wanted to save it for
now. It's another surprise." And she looked terribly pleased with
herself.

Gaff smiled, "What a difference a couple of months
makes."

Dawn turned suddenly to look into his eyes. "There's more.
Mae and I talk about all the strange things that happen to me. I told
her that when I was really sick and they didn't think I'd live, I saw
an angel, a real angel."

Mae nodded, encouraging.

Dawn continued, "I told Mom about the angel, but she
didn't believe me. The angel told me to hold on till Mae. I thought
she meant the month, but May passed and I didn't get better. All
those other nurses didn't help and I thought the angel was a dream,
a stupid dream. Then one night she came to me again and said the
same thing. So I thought she meant to wait a whole year and I
didn't think I could do that. Now I know she meant Mae." There
were tears in her eyes.

The adults were misty-eyed, too.

"When Mae first talked about learning how to use the
energy of the Universe to put my body back together, I thought she
was nuts. She read the books to me anyway and I think it works."

Mae said, "The fact that you're sitting at this table shows it
works. Proof enough for me. Proof of a divine order that I didn't
believe in before."

Gaff said, "We learn from everything that happens to us.
Everything, both good and bad."

He waved toward the water, "Sometimes the waves take the
sand away and sometimes they bring it back. When waves take
sand, some people call it bad for destroying the beach, but really
it's all the same. It's part of the natural pattern of things. If people
just let the water do its thing, we'd be better off. There's a natural
flow of sand around the ocean, taking it from some beaches and
moving it to a beach farther south. The natural flow is interrupted

because people built jetties out into the water to trap it. Then it isn't left to build up the other beaches farther along the way."

Dawn said quietly, "It's like some people are greedy for all the good things and won't put up with the bad and that messes it up for everyone."

"Dawn, you are a very smart young woman. Soon, you'll see lots of things that other people don't."

Mae said, "She already does. She already does. She saw that you would be here today. She sent me to get the donuts for you because she saw that you would come to the beach on this day."

# chapter 31

Gaff

When I first came to the beach, my name was Geoffrey IV. At least that's what my dad and granddad called me. Most of the family went along. Too pretentious. At school they called me G4 and that was fun. At work, they called me Fitz to distinguish me from the other Geoffreys.

Whenever I met new people on the beach, I introduced myself using the entire moniker, Geoffrey Andrew Fitzgerald, IV. Then I told them to call me Fitz. Somehow Fitz didn't stick like it did at the office. Nope, I was no longer Fitz. My new friends tried a variety of nicknames, but none of them fit. Before long, the other fishermen started calling me Gaff. Sounded about right... a fishing name based on my initials. That was OK. A new name for a new life, a new me.

When I talk about first coming down to the beach, I really mean when I started spending most of my time fishing. I moved to the beach decades ago, as soon as Julia and I could afford to build a decent sized house. We had three children and we loved them and each other and living at the beach. One requirement for our home was a room high up from which we could see the water at any time of the year. That wasn't hard when we first moved here because all the other houses were one story.

During the recent building boom, they built three story condos and houses all over the island, including just on the other side of the dunes from the sand. Now, our view is over, around, and between.

We built back from the beach, for the privacy and to avoid the effects of storms, including flooding. Let the storms take the ones with the front row seats and leave us alone. As a result, we're on high ground and still have a view and a house that's fully in tact.

I had a normal life as a child and young man, the only difference being that my family owned a lot of the land around here, as well as many of the big businesses. Since my name was on a lot of things in the area, it was tough to be "normal."

After I finished college, I wanted to go on for a graduate degree and my father insisted that it be an MBA. I had no other choice, but I didn't go quietly. No one asked me what I really wanted to do, but I told them anyway. Being the third son has its perks and one of them is learning to stand up for yourself. I was fully capable of speaking my mind.

The answer was that if I wanted to study art or philosophy or religion or psychology, I could do it on my own nickel. I was prepared to do just that. I was determined to be my own person, no matter what it cost me. And that did not include going into the business that was the backbone of our family fortune.

Then Fate conspired on my father's side: I met the woman of my dreams. Julia. She was so beautiful and her smile could lift me to the heavens. Smartest woman I ever met, both intelligence of the mind and of the heart. I loved her more than I could or can express. I wanted to be with her at any cost.

I loved her so much that we got married as fast as I could manage. The wedding took place a couple of years after I met her so it wasn't at lightning speed. But nothing back then went as fast as it does today. It took even more time to plan because both mothers wanted a big wedding.

Still, we were partners and figured out how we could work it so I could live my dream. Both of us could work to put me through school and then I could become a college professor or therapist. We knew that I wouldn't make much money, but more importantly, I would be following my heart. And that's worth some sacrifices.

Again Fate stepped in and put one huge knot in the fishing line. We got pregnant! Actually she got pregnant, but I did put my best into the effort. I knew it took two of us to get her pregnant so I did my part for the family. I agreed to work in the family business because the money would be better and I already knew the job. All the while, Julia and I talked about getting me back to school later, after we got settled with the kid and put some money back.

Boom! Again, Fate put another knot and then another one in the line. We had three children in the first five years of marriage. Just when we got to the place financially where we thought I could quit my job and implement the plan to go back to school, another baby came. We loved them and they filled our home with more joy than we thought possible, but they had their own agenda.

A natural progression: having a child every couple of years. These babies were an expression of our love for each other. By the time the third one arrived, I knew I was trapped in that family business with no hope of getting to school.

Between the job and the family. I didn't have time to take night classes. No hope of working into a field that suited my personality better. Julia still talked about the possibility of "One day…" Me, I hunkered down to do my best at having a good time in the job I had, preparing to take over the whole shooting match. Never have believed in suffering and so I found things to enjoy in the job. I forgot those dreams altogether.

I loved being married to Julia and it only got better. And I loved being a daddy. Those children brought so much joy into our lives… Don't think about those things when you're a kid.

It's hard to imagine how fast thirty-five years went. Zoom! I never was tied by any umbilical cord to that business so when my younger son seemed to enjoy it, I started planning my escape. Slowly, so slowly he didn't realize what was happening, I turned more and more of the business over to George. He got busier and I wasn't as busy—I suddenly had free time on my hands.

I spent more of that free time on the beach, with my wife and fishing. We loved being together, but over the years she developed a busy life of her own. She was happy to see that I wanted to spend so much of my time fishing. After that number of years, it was still a marriage made in heaven. I smile, no I grin about that. What a blessing.

When I first "moved to the beach," I fished most days and many nights. For years, I'd spent the time I could on the beach, but a lot of that I spent taking care of children and then grandchildren. Now, I could fish.

Julia gave me a big pirate flag as a joke. She said it was to let people know that I was fishing on time I stole away from the business. Then she said it was the way she could keep track of me from a distance. It was fun and I liked it. Thought it made a statement. Also a conversation starter.

I got to know other fishermen and the ways of the fish. I studied the clouds and the planets and the stars. I read the books I had on that to-be-read shelf in the library. Some of them waited decades for me to have time for them and now I finally did.

Most of all I got to know me, myself. And just when I thought I had it figured out, myself most of all, a woman came walking down the beach. Attracted by the jolly roger. She told me the origins of the flag and some history of the Knights Templar. She didn't come on to me even though she was alone. Being with her felt like we knew each other from some other place. Comfortable, like old friends. We just sat together for hours some days, not saying anything.

She came to sit with me many days and some nights. She told me her story just as so many others have now. I told her my story when she asked. Then she asked if she could use me as the basis for a character in a book. I was flattered, of course. Said yes.

We talked about the meaning of life and where each of us was going. We talked about God and how He influences what goes on here on earth. We talked about the meaning of Heaven and Hell. I showed her the stars and meteors burning through the atmosphere.

Finally, I admitted to her that someone long ago had predicted I would be a preacher. Never saw that for myself, but someone else did.

She interrupted my protestations and waved her hand to indicate the beach and the ocean. "Here's your church," she said. "You've been sent where you can do the most good for people who probably wouldn't visit you in a building called a church."

She laughed at this. Her laugh was wonderful. I'll never forget how it had the ability to infect everyone within hearing. To this day, just thinking of it makes me smile.

I have to admit, she laughed a lot. She really enjoyed life and renewed my joy. I was always a happy man. Always focused on the good things in my life and minimized the things I didn't like. I didn't ignore them, but I did what I could to make things better and went on from there. But she ramped my good feelings up a notch and reminded me of how to get even more out of life.

She said, "People're always saying they want to leave this place and this job so they can become 'spiritual' and do the work of Spirit. God went to a lot of effort to put you right where you are and give you just the right experiences. He trains you to help those people who need you most.

Then she laughed. "It's funny that people think they know better than Spirit where they can be of service."

She looked at me more seriously than she usually ever looked. "You are in the perfect place, with the perfect training to help the people who will be brought to you. They'll be attracted by the flag, but the nudge that causes them to talk with you will be provided by Spirit. And if you are open, Spirit will give you the right words to effect a healing for each of these people. All you have to do is accept the challenge."

She was right, you know. And through the years hundreds of people have walked right up to me on this beach, attracted to this flag. They've told me what they need and the answers come to me without effort. I always thank Mother Water and our Creator who speaks through her.

I truly appreciate the process. Works like magic, you know.

When I finally got around to reading her book some years later, I found that she had predicted my future. She wrote about now and not then, when we were talking. It was right, in divine order, that I didn't read that book until so many years later. I would not have understood the message if I had read it sooner. She knew all of it, not just the outline, but a lot of details. She described some of the people I met through the years. That book described things she could not know from our talks.

She was a holy woman, or an angel. I understand that now. I didn't then. Here I was on the beach, fishing, but something was missing. She was sent to point me in the right direction when I didn't quite know where I was going. After I made that commitment to help others, my life smoothed right out and I felt a joy and peace I never imagined. Great perk. That and the working conditions.  And all the fish I can eat.

## chapter 32

Everyone on the beach has a story. Some of the stories are incredible: glamorous and filled with magical events that make our mouths hang open. But even the most ordinary life is wonderful. All of them are meaningful, filled with lessons. Those people just wait for an ear ready to hear and a heart ready to love.

All I do is offer them that ear. I'm not perfect and I don't like everyone who sits on the cooler. I do try to listen to their stories. And I've found that everything that happened in my life, good and bad, helps me understand them. Sometimes they help me understand me.

I once fell in love with a woman who walked the beach. I watched her every day, walking down the street from her house to the walkway across the dunes. I thought about speaking to her, telling her how beautiful she was, but I never did. There were days when I was on the beach and watched her walk from the walkway toward the rocks miles down the strand. She walked all the time, and talked to people along the way. Sometimes she started the conversation and other times they started it. I loved how free she was, how she seemed to love everyone she met.

I loved her. Not the way I love Julia, but I did love her deep in my heart. I loved her and thought about her all the time. Never will understand why I didn't tell her. Not a word. In the morning she stood on the walkway to the beach, her lithe form a silhouette against the sunrise over the water. Beautiful... awe-inspiring.

She always wore a straw hat with a brim that turned up on the edge. And sunglasses most of the time. Maybe those sunglasses were a mask to allow her to watch anyone she wanted, to choose the next to receive her attention.

My woman of mystery will remain forever in my heart. Maybe because she's surrounded by mystery or maybe because she was so beautiful. Or maybe because I still hope for a chance to tell her how I feel. I don't know. I do know that I continued to look for her after she left, even years later. I hoped she would return to the beach, that I would have another chance to tell her that I love her.

From time to time I saw other women with hats and sunglasses. They, too, stood on the walkway at sunrise, watching the spectacle played out in the sky that separated night from day. The sunrises were as beautiful, but the women were never my woman of mystery. They fell short in some way, even though I tried to fit them into the spot she created in my heart.

I guess the lesson here is that when you love someone, you should tell them. Tell them as soon as you realize how you feel. Bust through that barrier of embarrassment or shyness or whatever it is, to spread your feelings out for the world to see. By expressing that love, you feed your own heart and that of the other person. You may even feed the heart of the planet... I do this now. Am I hoping that by being open with people, I can bring back my woman of mystery? I do still have her in my heart and sometimes I feel her special light illuminating the path before me. Illuminating the path with the Way of Love.

# Notes from the Author

Every word I write has a message for me. Every time I revise this story, that message becomes clearer, sinking deeper, deeper into my heart. Although the characters in this story are fictional, they express the same problems as many others. Some of them are based on a group of people I actually met. They are various stages of development. Some of them have not yet understood the value of their trials. Gaff has helped them and he has helped me. There were times during the writing when I cried because the words flew like arrows right to my heart. Open your heart and accept them, too.

I had lots of help writing this book. Thanks are due to so many people. First of all, thank you to the many people who believed in me and to the ones who did not. Each in his own way pushed me to continue to write when I might have stopped. Thanks to Jim Selway for reading drafts of other books and making honest suggestions about how they could be improved. He taught me so much from the reader's point of view. Thanks to all those editors of all those publishing houses who read and passed on my other manuscripts, they taught me through their comments. Priscilla Reagan, my agent, repeatedly assures me that I can write. My Sisters in Crime writing group taught me more about writing and about persistence. Karen Block is my talented editor and guided me to so many improvements. Becky Fangman works wonders with the Internet. My friend Robert McBeath read almost every draft of every manuscript and truly deserves a medal of honor for service above and beyond. Another friend, Drew Allgeier helped me release it into the wild with ideas about how to let people know I built a better mousetrap.

Most of all, I am grateful that Mother Water gave me the idea as I walked the beach beside her. She also brought the people on the beach to tell me the stories that gave me ideas for the details of this book. One who deserves specific mention is Cliff who is a real fisherman with a real pirate flag on a real beach. Thanks for allowing me to use the device of the flag. He is not Gaff, but he did help me understand the art and science of fishing.

I send waves of gratitude to my muse: the spirit that sat with me during the long hours at the computer (and during my long walks). She helped me string together the words to tell this story. Our goal is reach the hearts of those who have eyes to see and ears to hear. So be it.

Gaff is available to talk with anyone walking the beach in his mind. Ask him any question and let's see what Mother Water says. Is there another book from Gaff? Bring him your story and see if my muse will help me put it out there. No details, only a short synopsis. Gaff is not providing therapy, but a wisdom that comes from the heart and soul of man, guided by Mother Water, spoken through a fisherman. Go to my website, www.lorenapeter.com to see what's coming and to contribute to Gaff 2.

Made in the USA
Monee, IL
06 August 2021